SURRENDER

Jared's eyes danced as his arms tightened their grip and he held her powerless in his hands. Slowly, inexorably, she felt him draw her closer within the circle of his arms and watched bemused as his head slowly came down and his mouth claimed hers in a gentle caress.

She made no effort to struggle for she knew it was useless and decided it would be best to just remain passive in his arms. But her body betrayed her by warming to his touch. As the pressure of his mouth increased she could feel her heart rising in her throat until she felt she was choking.

Shivers of excitement coursed down Amanda's spine, and her arms, acting with a will of their own, crept up around his neck. Her mind whirled warnings around in her brain but her body dismissed them.

Other Avon Books by
Kasey Michaels

THE LURID LADY LOCKPORT
THE RAMBUNCTIOUS LADY ROYSTON
THE SAVAGE MISS SAXON
THE TENACIOUS MISS TAMERLANE

THE BELLIGERENT MISS BOYNTON

KASEY MICHAELS

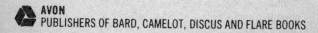

AVON
PUBLISHERS OF BARD, CAMELOT, DISCUS AND FLARE BOOKS

THE BELLIGERENT MISS BOYNTON is an original publication
of Avon Books. This work has never before appeared in book form.

AVON BOOKS
A division of
The Hearst Corporation
1790 Broadway
New York, New York 10019

First Avon Printing, February 1982

AVON TRADEMARK REG. U.S. PAT. OFF. AND IN OTHER COUNTRIES,
MARCA REGISTRADA, HECHO EN U.S.A.

Printed in the U.S.A.

WFH 10 9 8 7 6 5 4 3 2

To Holly,
who had her foot in my back all the way

Prologue

AS FAR as the *Beau Monde* was concerned, the center of the civilized world in 1811—now that Paris was lamentably in the clutches of that upstart Corsican and no longer open to them—was their own fair metropolis of London.

The first few grey, damp months of the year had already produced many newsworthy *bon mots,* all debated and discussed and dissected within the drawing rooms of the mighty few who presided over Society with wills and rules of iron.

The Prince of Wales, charming Florizel himself, had at last wheedled Parliament into passing the Regency Bill, finally gaining for himself some little bit of power, and dazzling his long-suffering creditors with his importance—while tumbling ever more deeply into their debt.

That pesky Little Corporal might now claim most of Europe as his own, but England still ruled the seas, and as long as French silks and brandy could be smuggled into the country, Society glibly ignored the hubbub across the Channel.

Of more importance to those pampered pets of Mayfair were the current *on-dits* about the eccentricities of that odd but harmless peer, Sir Lumley Skeffington, better known as Skiffy, who had taken to penning mediocre plays and—horror of horrors—painting and perfuming himself with a liberal hand before strolling about the town in satin suits of varied but equally ghastly hues.

They tittered behind their goose-skin fans as they made absurd conjectures as to the persons Lord Alvanley had in mind when he scribbled in his Club betting book: "Lord Alvanley bets Sir Joseph Coply twenty guineas that a certain person outlives another certain person." Could it be Prinney and poor mad

King George themselves his lordship had in mind? And who was to outlive whom?

As the Spring Season neared, Society's attention became more and more centered on opening night at Almack's—that London institution to which only the most lofty of their number were allowed entrance; to drink its insipid warm refreshments, play at tame card games for tamer stakes, and dance to tunes some musicians half-heartedly ground out hour after endless hour. Here the matrimonial hopes of the maiden and the aspirations of her mama could be piqued and satisfied or mercilessly dashed forever in the space of one country dance.

It was on the opening night of Almack's in that first flush of the Regency that a most deliciously titillating charade was to be played out before the avid eyes of this same exaulted Society that prized a *scandale* above all things.

Chapter One

J ARED DELANEY bowed over his partner's hand as he returned her to her hovering mama and left her to regale the turbaned dowager with a word-by-word recitation of everything the handsome, eligible Lord Storm had said during their turn on the floor.

His lips curled into a secret smile as he recalled the girl's blushes when he commented on the "fetching" neckline of her gown, as they came together during one of the movements in a boring country dance.

She had trod heavily on his foot in her agitation, but there was always the chance that she would collapse in a horrified swoon in the middle of the floor, which would be worth the pain. Anything, *anything* to relieve the crushing boredom of his enforced visit to this Marriage Mart.

Out of the corner of his eye he spied his aunt beckoning to him, clutching a Chatsworth chit done up like a Christmas pudding to her side. There wasn't much he wouldn't do for Aunt Agatha, but he'd be damned if he'd squire that antidote. Miss Charity Chatsworth was cursed with a decided cast to one eye, so that one never knew which eye to look into when she spoke—not that she had ever said anything of interest in her entire life. Not a one of the Chatsworth females was up to snuff, which was a pity for Baron Chatsworth as there were so many of them.

Ignoring his aunt's frustrated signals he made for the foyer, where perhaps he could bury himself until he could politely retire. He was a big man, nearly a full head taller than most of the men present in the room, built along the lines of the true Corinthian, with the broad shoulders and slim hips of the sportsman. His profile, reflected in a nearby gilt mirror, was a study in planes and angles, softened only by startling blue eyes that were surrounded by absurdly long, coal black lashes. Idly he inspected his reflection and gave an unaffected push to an unruly black curl that had burst the confines of his studiously casual Windswept style. He had been lingering there for some minutes when his attention was caught by a movement near the door.

First to enter the hallowed portals was a little mouse of a woman, her turban slightly askew. Hers was an understandable dishevelment, as the clock was dangerously near eleven—the hour after which not even Prinney would dare try gain entry to the Assembly.

Her charge must be unconscionably ugly to take this long at her toilette, he mused. He pushed himself away from the wall, ready to find another bolt hole out of his aunt's way, when the door opened wider and a small female shape huddled in a black velvet evening cloak moved into the room.

As she passed through the door she shook her head free of its enveloping hood, and Jared's breath hissed audibly through his teeth. She had hair as dark as night, yet shot with flashes of gold as though lit from within; hair which cascaded in enticing curls from the topknot on her head, while wispy tendrils caressed her slim white neck.

But it was her face that captured and held Jared's interest. Brows like raven's wings perched above darkly fringed, tilted eyes the color of old gold coins. A pert nose, deep rose lips, and stubborn pointed chin all fitted nicely into the small face. Two high spots of color appeared on her creamy cheeks as her eyes swept the room and lighted on Jared.

Her gaze became so imperious, one brow lifted in mock derision, that he found himself looking away in confusion. Who was this chit to openly bait him? Just then a footman relieved the girl of her cloak and the little mouse gasped as the gown beneath the rich velvet was revealed.

Strong men had been known to pale when Lord Storm used his famous quizzing glass. His grossly magnified eye raked over a gown of dark golden silk—a color no debutante would dare wear, let alone to Almack's—its simple lines accenting a small but perfect body. Tiny puff sleeves capped creamy shoulders, and then the material plunged to a deeply squared neckline that did no credit to the girl's modiste, as it was sadly puckered in places and a few rather large stitches were obvious to even the undiscerning eye.

Black velvet ribbons encircling her neck and accenting the high waistline, as well as the tiny matching bows marching along the hemline, did nothing to soften the gown's flamboyancy. She wore no jewelry other than two thin hammered-gold bracelets studded with topaz, over elbow length kid gloves. Innocence and decadence combined to rouse his lordship from his practiced ennui, and he stood amazed by the sight.

The girl returned an assessing gaze to Jared's face, obviously searching out his reaction to her appearance. Her eyes lit with pleasure at the sight of the tall handsome man with the quizzing glass stuck to his eye, his full mouth hanging open, and she favored him with a dazzling smile—disclosing small white teeth and turning her pretty face into a thing of perfect beauty. The quizzing glass fell unheeded to his waistcoat as he made haste to cross to her side. Bless Aggie, he thought, for insisting he attend Almack's first session. This promised to be much more amusing than Faro till dawn at White's.

In reality, all this drama took but a few moments, just long enough for the little gray mouse to build herself into a high flight of hysteria. She moaned, "*Oh, Miss Amanda!*" and her knees buckled under her. She would have toppled headlong to the floor except for Jared's intervention, as he easily supported the swooning female with one arm until a footman could secure a chair for her in a hidden alcove.

With a contriteness belied by her amused expression, the girl called Amanda searched in her reticule for a restorative as she knelt beside her victim's chair and ministered to the stricken woman.

"Dear, dear Mrs. Halsey, forgive me for shocking you like this. I should have let you in on my little secret so you would have been prepared."

Jared laughed out loud. "I see the wisdom of your thinking, Miss—Amanda, is it?" he broke in cheerily. "If you refer to your ensemble, informing the poor Mrs. Halsey of it prior to your arrival would have saved her this embarrassment, for she would have swooned at once and you would not be here at all."

Amanda rose to her full height, which put her at cravat level with her antagonist. "I do not recall granting you permission to address me, sir. Kindly have the decency to remove yourself while I attend to my companion. I'm sure there are ample spectacles to poke fun at scattered thick on the ground all through this Assembly." She turned back to Mrs. Halsey and then, remembering her manners, turned once more to face the stranger . . . "I must thank you for your assistance, sir," she recited grudgingly. "You have my permission to retire." Her soft voice was rather husky, and to Jared's mind, it fitted her perfectly.

He gave a deep bow, raised himself to his full height, and winked at her. "A thousand pardons, Miss Amanda," he pleaded, "but perhaps you should save your indignation for a more suitable moment." He looked beyond her to the hapless Mrs. Halsey. "It would seem your companion has further need of us, as she appears to be listing heavily to port."

Amanda whirled in time to catch the toppling Mrs. Halsey, the unlikely oath of "damn" escaping her lips as she did so— thus intriguing Jared even more.

He stood silently by as Mrs. Halsey slowly recovered, then stepped forward to bow over the elder lady's hand. "My fervent hopes for your full recovery, ma'am. Allow me to present myself: I am Jared Delaney." He raised her trembling hand to his lips. "Your servant, ma'am." As usual he had declined the use of his title, one he scorned in favor of his family name.

Nothing in her hitherto uneventful life had served to educate Mrs. Halsey in the handling of such a disaster. And to think she could have stayed in the country as companion to eighty-year-old Lady Forsythe. But no, she wanted the excitement of a London Season. Next time she'd stick to leading nursery brats or pressing flowers in books for octogenarians. For now she did the only thing she could do: She threw herself on his lordship's mercy, looking up at the notorious rake with a fearful plea for help in her eyes. "Lord—Lord Storm?" she asked incredulously.

"One and the same, dear lady. But do promise not to let that influence you one way or the other, and grant the favor of making me known to your charming charge here. It seems she will not speak to me until we are properly introduced—and rightly so I might add."

"Of, of course, yes, to be sure. . ." Mrs. Halsey blustered, and with much stammering and hesitation the introductions were made.

"Boynton?" Jared questioned the belligerent-looking girl. "And are you by chance any relation to the late Sir Roger Boynton, the gentleman horse breeder?"

"He was my father," Amanda shot at him, with a look that told him to speak well of her father or not at all.

12

So much for his idea that the girl was an actress foisted on the Patronesses by some young bucks as a wager. She seemed, if outrageous, at least legitimate.

"I greatly admired your father's horseflesh, and in fact have several of his bloodline in my stables at Storm Haven," he informed her solemnly, noticing that he had struck a chord. The girl was decidedly interested.

"You knew my father?" she breathed, the hardness leaving her eyes.

"Most assuredly, Miss Boynton, though I was no more than twenty when he died. England lost a fine man in your father: he was a good soldier in his prime, and a gifted horse breeder."

The chit was more than half won and Jared knew it. He turned to Mrs. Halsey and requested her to allow him the pleasure of Miss Boynton's hand in the next set. His tone brooked no denial, and the flustered Mrs. Halsey quickly agreed—for even she knew better than to nay-say wealthy Lord Storm. Besides, she needed a few moments alone to think up a suitable story to tell Amanda's stepfather, her employer, Peregrine Denton.

Unfortunately, the musicians took that particular moment to strike up a waltz. "I beg your pardon, Miss Boynton," Lord Storm said, "but you may not waltz until you have been approved by the Patronesses. A bore, but a necessary one, I assure you. Have you this permission?"

"Of course," Amanda lied calmly.

Mentally Mrs. Halsey packed her shabby portmanteau and resigned herself to Lady Forsythe and her three pug dogs. She was near to swooning again. "Miss Amanda, you know you have no such permission. You will be banished in disgrace. Think of your stepfather: how desperately frantic he was to secure you a voucher; how angry he will be!"

"That pleasant thought is uppermost in my mind, Mrs. Halsey," Amanda countered sweetly, and held her hand out to Jared. "Are you game, my lord, or shall silly *ton* edicts force you to abandon the cause at the first fence?"

In answer, he offered his arm, and she laid her small gloved hand on his sleeve. Together they headed toward the dance floor. In warning, he shook his head in the direction of the approaching irate Countess of Jersey—Almack's leading and most feared Patroness, whose face had turned an unbecoming red at the sight of Amanda's gown. Lord Storm didn't know what audacious rig his companion was running, but whatever it was he was more than slightly interested. "I would not miss this for the world, Miss Boynton. We shall both be served up for breakfast all over Mayfair tomorrow, you know."

As they joined the other dancers, Amanda and Jared patently ignored the gasps and turned heads all around them. Jared could feel the tension in her young body but her smile was brave. The girl had spirit—pluck to the backbone, by God!

They danced in silence for a few moments, and then Jared said quietly, "We are causing quite a stir, Miss Boynton."

"I am cognizant of that fact, my lord."

"Your gown is as enchanting as it is inappropriate, Miss Boynton."

"You flatter me, Lord Storm. Inappropriate was the most I aimed for."

He tried again. "You will be denied access to these portals from this night forward, and be shunned by all but the most daring of the *ton,* Miss Boynton."

"Huzzah, Lord Storm."

Jared cast an eye toward the rank of dowagers. "Don't look over there just now, but your companion has swooned yet again, Miss Boynton."

"A pity, but unavoidable, my Lord Storm."

He cocked an eyebrow and looked down into her face. "You seem to have planned your disgrace with great care, my little golden vixen."

Amanda addressed his cravat. "Have a care, or I shall further embarrass myself by slapping that silly grin from your face, *my lord.* This dance was your idea."

Jared threw back his head and laughed aloud. "You delight me, Miss Boynton, and for that I would suffer gladly your punishment. You are definitely your father's daughter: He had the same flair for the ridiculous and the same fiery temper."

"I thank you for the compliment, my lord, for I can only consider it as such. But I must apologize for involving a friend of my father's in this scheme. I had not planned on anyone being brave enough to partner me. The gown was to be sufficient outrage."

"You can do nothing to my reputation that has not already been done by myself, Miss Amanda. I call you Miss Amanda because I must have seen you at your father's home when you were a child. Do you mind?"

She shrugged her delightful shoulders. "It matters not, since after tonight you will not see me at all."

The dance ended before he could reply, and he guided her through the staring throng to a secluded couch half-hidden by a hideous towering plant. He seated himself beside her, his face serious as he asked the obvious: "Why have you done this to yourself? I detect an anger beneath your banter that tells me you are in some distress."

Amanda scanned the room to see that all eyes were on them. She had not planned to remain past a few minutes and wished fervently that the man beside her would disappear. "It is not your concern, Lord Storm," she answered curtly. "Please escort me back to Mrs. Halsey so that I can remove her before she goes into another taking. My purpose for coming here has been served."

She made to rise, but Jared pulled her back down beside him. She admonished him through gritted teeth. "Unhand me, my lord, before I do you a mischief! I wish to retire."

"Don't try to rattle me off in that high-nosed tone, madam," he gritted back. "I demand an explanation of your actions, since it appears I have lent an at least minor part in standing the *haut ton* on its ear. Not that I mind, may I add," he finished, with a wicked grin that set his sky-blue eyes twinkling.

Amanda settled herself reluctantly. "I do not have time for this, you know. But since I do not put it past you to restrain me physically, I have appeared here tonight in this outrageous gown in order to thwart my stepfather."

"And who might this unfortunate man be?"

"Peregrine Denton, the most odious snake on this earth."

"Ah, Denton," his lordship sighed. "My condolences, m'dear. I would not care to have him numbered among my relation."

Amanda lapsed into silence for a few moments, obviously reliving something distasteful to her. "He says he will sell Tempest. I'll see him in Jericho first!" she muttered under her breath. But Jared heard her.

"Tempest? What, pray, is a Tempest?"

She raised her head and golden eyes met blue. "My horse. The last of the bloodline my father established left at Fox Chase, and the only thing in this world—except for Nanny and Harrow—that I truly love. He banished Nanny and treats poor Harrow abominably, but he shall not sell Tempest!"

Jared dismissed the unknown Nanny and beleaguered Harrow, feeling they were unnecessary to the plot of this interesting story, and instead pursued the matter of the horse. "Perhaps I am intolerably obtuse, but what does this horse—er, Tempest—have to do with your somewhat bizarre appearance here tonight?"

Amanda turned on him in a fury. "It has everything to do with it, you simpleton! Oh, all you London dandies are alike. Why am I wasting precious time here with you?"

Jared grinned, thus infuriating the young girl even more. "I am cut to the quick, madam. I am not a London dandy. Nor am I a Pink or a Tulip of Fashion. I, madam, am a Corinthian."

"I fail to see the difference, my lord, but I can tell you are about to enlighten me."

In answer, Jared raised his quizzing glass and passed his gaze along the room. "Ah, there is one excruciating example of a Tulip of Fashion. Kindly direct your eyes to the right, Miss Amanda. Do you see the young blade talking to that horror in all those flounces? Yes, now observe his padded lilac satin coat, and that monstrosity he calls a neckcloth. Note also his pink brocade waistcoat and the ten—no, it is twelve—fobs hanging about his chest. Then, too, take in his deep rose breeches and burgundy high heeled shoes . . ."

Amanda suppressed a giggle.

"Now, madam, if you would please direct your eyes to my attire. A plain blue satin coat and matching breeches, the best Weston has to offer. A striking but subdued waistcoat. An intricate yet unexceptional cravat . . ."

"Stop! Stop!" Amanda raised her hand in laughing protest. "You have my apologies. I could never call you a dandy. Excuse my ignorance. But, please, you must escort me back to my companion. I have not much time."

"You speak again of the time. I confess you intrigue me. Again, I refuse to let you go until you tell me about this obsession with the hour."

"It seems I have no choice, for if I refuse you will keep me here until all my plans are ruined. So, if you must know, I am running away from my stepfather."

Jared cocked an eyebrow. "Running away? All right, I will accept that answer. He is an intolerable bore, although bolting to Almack's makes no more sense than anything else you have said tonight. I insist, what does this have to do with your rigout?"

"I altered this gown while Mrs. Halsey was resting," she said in exasperation at his dull wits. "It has done the trick quite well, I think. You see, my stepfather demands that I marry well, thus affording him a fat marriage settlement and a wealthy son-in-law to pay his way for the rest of his life. I refused, and he threatened to sell Tempest unless I obeyed him. I made myself a spectacle tonight to make certain no one will offer for me, and to embarrass my stepfather so that he cannot show his face in town for the rest of the Season. If he *can* be embarrassed, which I doubt highly. Now, if you will let me pass, I will return to my stepfather's house and gather my belongings for flight to Fox Chase. There," she concluded, "I shall saddle Tempest and disappear into oblivion." She sighed deeply in satisfaction at her Machiavellian plot and made to rise. "Now that your curiosity is assuaged, may I leave?"

She sat down again quickly at Jared's next words. "Of all the cork-headed schemes I have heard, that carries off the palm! It is too late to do anything about your foolishness in appearing here tonight, but perhaps it is not too late to salvage something from the wreckage. Go home and throw yourself on your stepfather's mercy and he may take you to Fox Chase to live down your shame. Your appearance tonight will be a nine-days' wonder, and by next season you can make your debut with no fear of reprisal."

Amanda was incensed. "You dolt! Have you heard nothing I have said? My stepfather wishes to *sell* me into a marriage I neither want nor need."

Jared shrugged his shoulders. "So? It is no different with the hundred or so young misses you see here tonight. You have an added attraction in that you are an exceedingly fine-looking specimen. You would have your choice of the young bucks, even your lack of fortune would not dissuade them."

"Oh, you are despicable! When I marry it will be for love, as it was for my parents. It will not be on orders from my stepfather."

"So what is to keep you from falling in love during the Season? Besides, you may find—as I have—that love is a highly over-rated emotion."

"Obviously you have never been witness to a great love, as I have, and in any event, I would not subject anyone I loved to the avarice of my stepfather. How could you suppose such a thing?" she exclaimed with some heat.

Jared raised his hands in mock fear. "I submit, I submit, please do not attack me further! But, if you are sincere in your plans—and I am sure you are—just how do you plan to escape your stepfather's clutches? I doubt you would make good time in the carriage with the die-away Mrs. Halsey by your side."

"Do not be ridiculous, at least not more than you can help. I travel alone."

"Ah, it becomes clearer. You are going to travel on the public coach."

"I intend to hire a chaise and drive myself," Amanda admitted, not without some pride.

"In truth?" Jared leered at her. "And where do you propose to find such a conveyance in the middle of the night?"

"I shall walk until I find one," she answered, with the reasonableness of a female fresh from the country.

"And what about the footpads?" he questioned, a hint of mischief in his eyes.

"Footpads?"

"Yes, you simpleton, footpads. Thieves, robbers, no-goods who would slit your pretty throat for a penny. And a young female alone on the streets? Oh, you would wish all they would do is murder you. This is not the country where you know everyone and everyone knows you. This is London, where even strong men take care to travel in groups after dark."

Her face fell. "Oh, I see. Footpads."

He leaned over and patted her gloved hand. "But cheer up, my dear. Perhaps you will be picked up by the Watch before the footpads spy you out. I hear our local gaols are one experience to be missed, however."

"Oh, shut up! I will not listen to you! My way is clear; I leave London tonight. I should never have confided in you! You took unfair advantage of me by speaking nicely about my father."

She turned from him and took a few quick steps in her companion's direction, then turned again and flashed him her bewitching smile. "Thank you so much for the waltz, Lord Storm. It will be something to tell my grandchildren." With an imperious toss of her head she was gone.

Jared watched until she and her companion had taken their leave of the Assembly, Amanda walking proudly ahead of the trailing Mrs. Halsey and acting as if her sojourn at Almack's was a bore not worth enduring. He then approached his aunt and had her gathered into her carriage before she could so much as utter a word.

She made up for this lack throughout the journey back to Jared's town house in Half Moon Street, however, much to Jared's amusement.

"Who on earth was that atrocious female, Jared? Sally Jersey was livid with rage and was just preparing to ask her to leave." She punctuated her next words by rapping her ivory-stick fan on his forearm. "And you, too, young man, when the chit had the belated good sense to remove herself. Sally is furious with you for standing up with her. Why did you do such an outrageous thing?" She shook her grey head in dismay. "Why, oh, why did I force you to come with me tonight? I should have known you could find mischief anywhere, even Almack's."

Lady Agatha Chezwick was famous for her monologues and it seemed this one would be no exception. Jared took his cue when she finally had to stop for breath and broke in quietly, "Her name is Amanda Boynton, Sir Roger Boynton's daughter, from Fox Chase."

Lady Chezwick sniffed. "Her name does not signify." She drew herself up on the velvet squabs of the coach, her small body rigid with righteous anger. "She offended the entire Social World tonight and you—you *helped* her. I felt ready to sink when you stood up with her. And then to sit and chatter away together like old friends, why, Honoria thought she must be a relative of ours. Are you dead to all shame, Jared?"

"Curse the woman. Honoria Appleton was always a snoop and a gossip. Pay her no mind, Aunt, I implore you. And do not blame me for conversing with the girl. She amused me."

"Amused you? *Amused you!* If you need diversion so badly, go to Drury Lane. I hear they are putting on a splendid farce this week. But to make a mockery of Almack's? How could you?"

"It was really quite simple, Aunt. I begged her companion for an introduction, asked the girl to stand up with me in the next set, and *voilá,* the deed was done," he supplied cheerfully.

"Do not try my patience, Nephew," his aunt returned, punishing her nephew's arm with one more reprimanding blow that was sufficiently forceful to break two sticks of her fan. She looked at the thing, sniffed, and tossed it to the floor. "What are you going to do now? Please tell me you are not going to see that shameless creature again. Or are you under the hatches and need an early inheritance from your loving aunt, who will be sent to an early grave by any such scheme?"

A slow smile lit Lord Storm's face, making his eyes twinkle in the darkness of the coach. "See her, Aunt? Why, I am going to do a great deal more than see her. I am going to marry the brat."

For the second time that evening, Lord Storm was forced to administer aid to a fainting female.

Chapter Two

IT WAS almost four o'clock in the morning before the sounds from her stepfather's room became the nasal snores of his deep, drink-induced slumber. Amanda had been perched on the edge of her bed for what felt like hours, and she was stiff and sore from her self-inforced stillness. She had tried stretching out across the bed, but found the position too comfortable and had to continually shake herself awake. It would not do to fall asleep.

But now the waiting was over and she could safely leave the house. With stealthy movements, she gathered up her cloak into which she had placed a single change of clothes and picked up her shoes, tucking them under her arm. On quiet, stockinged feet she tiptoed down the narrow back staircase to the kitchens and let herself out into the mews. She leaned against the door for some moments regaining her breath, for it seemed she had not breathed since leaving her room. Her heart had been pounding so heavily she was sure her stepfather could hear it, but the worst was almost over.

One step onto the dew-wet stones reminded her of the shoes still under her arm, and she balanced herself on one foot in the darkness to put on the first shoe. Her skirts were cumbersome and her balance precarious, so she was grateful for the steadying hand under her elbow.

Hand? She whirled around to face her attacker, for what else could it be? One shoe poised above her head as a weapon, she confronted the devilish grin of Jared Delaney.

"You took your bloody sweet time, madam. I had about given you up."

"What are you doing here?" Amanda gasped.

"Softly, my little runaway, softly, or you'll have the whole house down on us."

Amanda cast a frightened look toward the darkened windows and repeated her question in a fierce whisper.

"Isn't that strange?" drawled Jared calmly. "I have noticed that phenomenon more than once but assumed you above it. Why do people always persist in repeating something when you tell them they were too loud in saying it in the first place? No matter. I shall answer your question—all your questions—forthwith. But first I suggest we remove ourselves from the premises. I have two horses waiting beyond the stables, for I assume you ride. Come, brat, before we are found out. I have a decided aversion to viewing Peregrine in his nightcap."

Without looking to see if she was indeed following him, he turned and made for the stables—a hopping Amanda close behind, still trying to put on her other shoe.

In the few short moments it took to reach the horses Amanda had reached the end of her patience. "I repeat, although I know it fatigues you to listen a third time: What *are* you doing here?"

Jared made an elaborate bow. "Since I heard of your plight and your infantile plans, I felt it a duty to an old friend to offer my services to his daughter. I am *here*, as you have so needlessly pointed out, to escort you to Fox Chase and wherever your final destination demands. Am I not gallant, Miss Amanda?"

Amanda threw down her bundle in disgust. "If that isn't beyond anything stupid! What right have you to interfere? And don't prattle on about my father. You no more care about him than you care about me."

"Oh! Unkind! How you malign me in my sincerity." Jared put his hand to his heart as if he were in mortal pain.

Amanda waved her arms in exasperation. "I have no time to stand here and bandy words with you. I accept your offer of a mount, but only as far as the nearest stable yard where I can hire a chaise. There I will be more than happy to see the back of you. Now, help me up onto that curst sidesaddle I see on the mare's back."

Jared shook his head in an expression of sorrow. "All my life I have been surrounded by ingratitude. It seems you are no exception. Very well then," he said, "up you go."

Amanda landed on the mare's back after an ungentlemanly shove, the ridiculous chip hat she had refused to leave behind knocked askew by the force of her landing. "Blackguard," she hissed, just as Jared's hand came down on the rump of her mount, and she was off through the gate—clinging to the mare's mane while striving vainly to get her hands on the reins. Luckily the horse was a docile creature, and settled herself almost at once into a leisurely walk that promised to be her pace throughout the journey to the stable yard.

Jared, astride a mount vastly superior to Amanda's, came abreast of her as the horses' hooves first made contact with the cobbled street.

"I had considered tying rags around their hooves to muffle the sound of their shoes on the stones, but it seemed too much like something out of a Penny Dreadful, don't you agree?"

Amanda turned on him in a fury. "You're enjoying this, aren't you? To you this is just a lark, something with which to regale your low friends at one of those horrid clubs you overgrown boys seem to need in order to survive."

"Well, m'dear, you must admit escorting unattached females in moonlight flight from domineering stepfathers is not an everyday experience. Yes, I admit it, I am enjoying myself enormously."

Amanda decided it was fruitless to argue with a man who refused to be serious. "Where can I hire a chaise? Is it far from here?"

Jared reined in his horse and sat as if pondering her question. He made an elaborate business out of tapping his head in thought and casting his eyes in all directions as if looking for outside guidance, while murmuring under his breath for several minutes as Amanda's temper was pushed past its limits. With a muttered exclamation, she dug her heel into the mare's flank and started off down the lane.

"Amanda, you addlepated female, wait for me! You cannot go off alone!" Jared called, and spurred his horse forward. But in his haste, Amanda's bundled clothes, which he had deigned to carry, fell to the ground and he was forced to dismount to collect the scattered belongings. By the time he remounted and rode on, Amanda had turned down a side street and Jared lost sight of her.

"Mad as Bedlam," he muttered to himself, "that's what she is. And that's what *I* am for allowing her to lead me along like a tame bear trailing behind her. Damme if I won't just leave her to her fate!"

Just then he heard a female scream and turned his horse down

23

the dark alley from whence he thought the sound issued. In the distance he could see Amanda, deliberately rearing her horse as if to trample the two rag-covered figures pressing in at the mare's flanks. Brandishing his whip he sped his horse into the fray loudly calling, "Help ho! Footpads! Forward, men, we've got them now!".

Two pairs of startled eyes saw the mad horseman bearing down on them and, abruptly letting go of Amanda's horse, scurried quickly off into the darkness.

By the time Jared drew abreast of Amanda she had regained her poise enough to demand: "Where were you, you idiot? I thought I would have to beat them off myself."

Jared, who had been expecting tears and hysterics, threw back his head and laughed uproariously. "That's my girl, nothing missish about you, is there?"

"I am *not,* as you say, your girl. I thank you for your timely rescue, but don't expect me to fall on your neck in gratitude. I would not be on this road if not for you. Now, if you don't mind, I should like to proceed to the nearest posting inn."

"Fancy you should mention that, madam, for before you rode off I had decided that it would be better if we proceeded all the way to Fox Chase on horseback."

"And *I* thought, my lord, that I had already made it clear I do not require your services."

Jared cast his eyes about him at the dark alley that reeked of garbage and filth. "Do you then know where you are?"

"I can manage."

"As you managed a few moments ago?"

"Oh, do be quiet! I must think."

Jared took one foot from the stirrup and crossed it in front of him on the saddle. "Think, is it? Very well, my dear, but please make haste in your ponderings. I am sure our two friends have long since vanished, but there may be others lurking in the area and I do not wish to number them among my acquaintance. May I also remind you that if you hire a chaise it will be leaving a remarkably clear trail for your stepfather to follow." He flashed her an impudent smile. "Or did you, I sincerely pray not, leave him a note?".

"Naturally I left him a note." Jared's groan was cut off by her indignant explanation. "I don't wish Mrs. Halsey to take the blame for my actions. I told him what occurred at Almack's tonight, making no mention of your name, may I add, and then informed him I had taken passage on a ship crossing the Channel at Dover. That should send him off completely in the wrong direction." Jared's snort of amusement impelled her to ask, "What is so hilarious in that?"

"Nothing. Nothing. But I am willing to wager a monkey that even Denton won't fall for that clanker. No one, my little scholar, flees to the Continent in the midst of war, not even such a nodcock as you."

"That was a sinister remark, sir. Besides, I strive never to do the expected if it can be helped," Amanda said, and then her sense of humor rose and she laughed with him. "You are right. That is the last thing I would do, even if I had the fare, which I don't."

A sound from a doorway reached Jared's ears and he sobered immediately. "Come, brat, it is time we removed ourselves from this den of thieves. Follow me as best you can. We are off to Fox Chase!" Allowing no time for her to answer, he turned his mount and started back down the alley at a canter.

Amanda hesitated for a moment, and then a dirty face appeared in that same nearby doorway and split in a toothless grin as he spied her. Amanda needed no further persuasion. "Wait for me!" she called as she barreled after Jared.

They rode in silence for what seemed to Amanda an interminable stretch of time, finally clearing the congested city and heading into the country. Dawn was breaking when Jared stopped at an inn.

Turning to her he commanded, "Listen carefully. You are my sister and we are on our way to our aunt's house. We require breakfast in a private dining room, and separate accomodations in which to freshen ourselves. After we have eaten you can retire for a few hours sleep and we'll be on our way. With luck, we will reach Fox Chase by nightfall."

Amanda nodded dumbly. She was far too tired to resist. The tension of the past hours and her lack of sleep were fast taking the fight out of her. She allowed herself to be escorted to her chamber.

A quick wash refreshed her enough to do justice to a country breakfast of eggs and thick slices of ham. Jared too tucked in ravenously, downing his meal with relish and following it with a mug of ale. When finished, he rose and made to leave the room.

"Where are you going, my lord?" Amanda questioned.

"For someone who was in such a panic to be rid of me you are oddly curious. I am off to blow a cloud, if you must know, and keep an eye out for your stepfather, though I doubt he is even aware yet that you are gone," he replied. "Why don't you go have a rest for a few hours? I'll call for you when I think we should leave."

It was only when Amanda arose from an hour's nap that she realized Lord Storm had completely taken over the venture and was giving *her* orders. How dare he! She was more than capable of taking care of herself. Well, she *had* been thankful of his intervention back there in the alley. Then she remembered that if she had not been trying to get away from him, she would probably never have turned down that particular street, and her anger rose again.

She would have to be rid of him! She paced the floor of the bedroom for some minutes, deep in thought, until she suddenly halted and an evil smile curled around her mouth. She crossed the room and rang for the maid.

Within moments a young girl appeared and Amanda quickly put her plan before the thrilled servant.

"That man downstairs is abducting me from my parents so as to compromise me into marriage. You must help me, Betsy. You did say that was your name, didn't you?"

"Yes, mum, that Oi did. Oi knew there wuz somethin' smokey about hiz lordship. An' you not even in a ridin' 'abit. Abduction, is it? Well, Oi could see you wuz a lady from the moment Oi clapped eyes on you. How can Oi help you, m'lady?"

Amanda stifled a giggle and proceeded to outline her plan. The girl was proving ridiculously easy. Within minutes Betsy was leading her down the back staircase and across the yard to the stables. The horses had not been unsaddled, so Amanda wasted no time there—although she did stop by Jared's mount for a few moments. Betsy gave her a boost up onto the sidesaddle and blushed her thanks as Amanda pressed a coin into her hand. Then, with a loud whoop, Amanda urged her mare through the stable doors and out across the yard, brushing past a startled Jared.

"You can pick up your mare at Fox Chase, my lord! Farewell!" she called over her shoulder, and disappeared down the road.

Jared cursed under his breath and whirled to run to the stables. Just as he was preparing to mount he was confronted by the burly innkeeper, and a young girl who kept screeching, "There he is, there's the bounder what tried to lope off with the pretty miss. Stop him, Da, box his ears!"

Jared eyed the approaching mountain and quickly took refuge behind his horse. "Hold on there, innkeeper. I don't know what your daughter was told, but that girl is my sister. She ran away from school with some young fop and I was bringing her home. Now you've let her escape."

He could see the doubt creep into the innkeeper's eyes and pressed his advantage. "Now, innkeeper, do I look the sort of man who must steal a woman?" He smiled broadly as the innkeeper ran his eyes over the immaculately dressed man in front of him.

"No-o-o," he concluded uneasily.

"Of course not. Amanda was always a mischievous hoyden. I quite understand your daughter falling under her spell, but I assure you it was nothing of the sort. But please, if I wait much longer she will have escaped again and you will be responsible for her possible ruin."

Betsy took that moment to intervene. "Don't believe him, Da. Oi know m'lady wuz tellin' the truth! Besides, he wuz goin' to lope off without payin' us our due."

The innkeeper's hands bunched into great fists once again, and Jared hastily pulled out some coins and offered them. Satisfied at last, the big man stood back to allow Jared to lead his horse into the yard. He swung himself into the saddle and spurred his mount forward into an immediate gallop. Before he had traveled more than a few yards the saddle slipped to one side, the stallion reared, and Jared was suddenly seated on the muddy ground.

His breath was knocked out of him for a few moments, and as he shook his head to clear it he saw Betsy's plump feet planted in front of him.

"Oh, that wuz a good trick her ladyship pulled on you, that it wuz. A right fine one, the ladyship is," she chortled—and Jared raised his eyes to see the gold bar pin that had so lately been on Amanda's dress being lovingly fingered as it rested against Betsy's ample bosom.

The ostler had trouble rounding up the frightened stallion and

27

it was several minutes before Jared was again ready to leave.

"Read her out proper, my lord, when you find her," the innkeeper advised.

"Read her out? I'll throttle the brat!" he called over his shoulder, convincing the innkeeper that the girl was indeed his sister, and Jared was gone. But the girl had a good hour's start on him.

Amanda pushed her horse for about an hour and then settled down to a more leisurely pace, thoroughly enjoying being on horseback again. Thoughts of the insufferable Lord Storm being held prisoner by an irate innkeeper brandishing a pitchfork, or lying in a puddle after being dumped by his horse, kept a smile on her lips.

She was in familiar territory now and could soon take to the fields where not even Jared Delaney would know how to follow. She would reach Fox Chase long before him, and once on Tempest's back he could not possibly catch her—even if he knew which direction she had taken. He would be just in time to pick up his mare from Harrow and return to London. Occasionally she felt a qualm of conscience about her hapless rescuer, but it served him right for interfering. Honestly, she thought, I have never before met a man who infuriates me to this degree!

She rode on, her eyes searching for her planned turnoff from both the road and possible pursuit, and she was just about ready to set off cross country when she saw a small shape huddled by the side of the road. She slowly eased her horse past, and the sound of muffled sobs came to her ears. She rode on a little further and then muttered "damn" under her breath and turned back.

Dismounting, she approached the small body and saw that it was a child, a child so dirty she could not make out its sex. She knelt down by its side.

"What is the matter, little one?" she questioned softly.

The small figure jumped up and made to run away, but Amanda reached out and grabbed one thin arm. "Ho, now, I'm not going to harm you. Are you lost? What is your name? Are you hurt?"

The grimy face turned and peered into her eyes. Obviously something there convinced the child the lady meant no harm, and it collapsed once more at her feet.

"Tom's me name," he said, "and I not be hurt." A grubby chin went up in defiance. "It's runnin' away I be."

Amanda sat back on her haunches and gave him a conspiratorial smile. "Ah, well then, it seems we have something in common, young Tom, for I, too, am running away. What are you running away from?"

"Jake."

"Is he your master?" Amanda inquired.

Tom nodded his head vehemently, and then his story came out in short, disjointed sentences. It seemed Jake had taken young Tom from the foundling home and used him to beg in the villages. There were about ten others like Tom working for Jake, but only Tom had been brave enough to defy him. Jake beat him when he refused to beg; Tom just couldn't take it anymore and so ran off. He had been on the road for about three days—he wasn't sure—and he hadn't eaten for at least two of them.

By now he was crying again in earnest. Amanda reached out instinctively and gathered him into her arms, unmindful of the resultant dirt on her already travel-stained garments.

"How old are you, Tom?" she whispered.

"I dunno, ma'am," he replied, "but I thinks I be twelve."

Twelve! Amanda was appalled. He was so little, he seemed no more than seven or eight. She weighed her need for haste with her conscience and her conscience won. She could not leave Tom to fend for himself. She would mount him in front of her and take him to Harrow. After that her plans were vague, as her plans usually were. Amanda operated on a grand scale, leaving details for lesser minds—like Jared Delaney's.

Delaney! She had forgotten all about him. She looked down the road behind her and, sure enough, she could see dust rising in the distance.

"Now I'm in the basket for sure! Up, Tom. We must be off." But Tom had fallen asleep in her arms and, though slight, he was too heavy for Amanda. She sighed and resigned herself to her fate.

It was not too many minutes before Jared reined in before the seated Amanda, his eyes wide in astonishment at the sight of the now wide-awake bundle in her arms.

When he had regained his composure he dismounted and walked full around the seated pair, two sets of frightened eyes

29

following his every movement. When he finally spoke, his voice was calm and somewhat amused. "You do have a penchant for consorting with the most outlandish creatures, imp."

Tom could feel his rescuer's arms tighten about him, and he jumped up to defend the beautiful lady from this nasty man who had frightened her.

"Yer shove off and leave me loidy be, Guv'nor! Her be a fine loidy and me frien' and 'less yer want a pop on the noggin' yer'll take yerself away."

Jared threw up his hands in surrender. "Well, well, Amanda. Once again you have a champion. First I must contend with an irate innkeeper and his simpleton daughter, and now you have this young gallant to fight your battles. I must admit I am impressed." He turned his attention to the boy. "Have no fear, lad, I'll not hurt your lady. We're old friends." He winked at Amanda. "Isn't that *right,* my dear?"

Amanda's eyes went from Tom to Jared and back again. It would accomplish nothing to upset Tom further, for the child looked about to drop. "It's true, Tom, Lord Storm is indeed my friend—and your friend, too." She glared at Jared fiercely. "In fact, Lord Storm is going to let you ride up in front of him all the way to my home, where my groom, Harrow, will fill your belly with some good food and find you a bed for the night." She smiled broadly at Jared. "Isn't *that* right, my lord?"

Jared eyed the boy and could see the fear on his face. He shrugged his shoulders, then leaned down and hoisted the boy into his arms. "Right you are, madam. Up you go, lad. Now sit here on Devil until I help Miss Boynton mount. I'll be up behind you in a moment."

As he offered his hand to Amanda he whispered between gritted teeth, "If you felt in such dire need of a chaperon, Amanda, I think the chit at the inn would have been a better choice. She was a regular dragon in your defense."

Amanda giggled as she adjusted her skirts around her ankles and back over the horse's rump. "How you do run on, my lord. I find Tom an exceptionally fine chaperon. But do be careful: I think the boy feels some allegiance to me. You might be wise not to be your usual insulting self in front of him. He may just make good his threat to—er—'pop yer on yer noggin'."

Jared's mouth opened and closed several times as if he was going to say something, but he finally settled for an abrupt "Hrruumph" and crossed to fling himself up behind the dirty urchin who sat patting the stallion's neck and muttering unintelligible praises into his cocked ear.

Amanda led the way down the road, with Jared's black horse dancing along under the slight extra weight. By midafternoon the trio arrived at Fox Chase.

They drew the horses up at the crest of the hill and gazed down at the view before them in the small valley. Jared, astounded at the rundown look of the manor and stables and the general neglected air of the surrounding fields, turned to Amanda with a question in his eyes.

Her voice was bitter as she swept an arm across the scene. "Behold what Peregrine Denton has done to the finest estate in the district. Now do you question my running away from him and all he represents?"

Jared shifted the sleeping Tom into a more comfortable position and urged his mount forward. "I am sorry, Amanda. I didn't know."

"No," she countered. "Nobody knew. And nobody wanted to know. All my father's friends melted away when he died and left Mama and me to the mercies of someone like Denton. He promised my mother he'd look after us if they married, and then proceeded to drain every cent he could out of the land and the house. You should take a tour of my home while you are here, my lord, and see how he stripped away anything he could sell in the markets. Even," her voice broke, "even my parent's portraits."

Jared suddenly felt very ashamed about the plans he had for this young girl. But the special license he had badgered from his friend Cunningham before going to meet Amanda was still in his pocket, and a wealthy husband such as he could do a lot to ease the burden she had been carrying these years.

"How long did you live there alone with Denton?" It bothered him more than he cared to admit that Amanda had lived under a roof with Denton with only servants for protection.

"Three years," Amanda answered. "After Mama died Nanny stayed awhile, but my stepfather finally sent her away. She lives in Sussex now with her sister, and I will join her there once I get Tempest." Her head jerked up as she realized what she had revealed. Curse her blabbering tongue!

Jared chose to ignore her disclosed plans since he had no thought of allowing her to pursue them, and motioned for her to precede him down the hill to Fox Chase.

As they neared the stables Amanda called out, "Harrow! Harrow, you old reprobate, where are you? It's Miss Mandy come home again."

She reined in and jumped down from the mare, skirts lifted high as she dashed toward the bent-over figure of an old man shuffling toward her with arms outstretched in greeting. She flung herself into his arms and gushed, "Oh, Harrow! How glad I am to see you!"

"It's glad I am to be seeing you, Missy, glad and happy. But what are you doing here and," he looked over her shoulder to the horse now coming into the yard, "who are these folks you have with you?"

Amanda disengaged herself and turned a dazzling smile toward Jared. "Harrow, I introduce to you my rescuer, Lord Storm, and my new friend, Tom. Lord Storm accompanied me here from London and Tom, well, Tom we met on the way." She turned toward Harrow with a plea in her voice. "Tom is very hungry, Harrow, and so am I. Do you have something cooking on your fire?"

"Aye, lass, as you knew I would. All of you, come inside and I'll dish it out."

Jared held out his hand to Tom, who took it warily, and they followed the old man through to a room at the back of the once-fine stables—following an appetizing aroma that wafted from that general area.

Amanda did not follow. Instead she ran over to the fence and gave a low whistle. Out in the meadow a proud head lifted and gave an answering whinny. The spring sun glinted on the chestnut coat of the huge stallion as he raced to the fence, his tawny mane and tail flying in the breeze.

Amanda climbed to the top of the fence and pressed her face close to the horse's neck, hugging him while the stallion nuzzled her shoulder. "Oh, Tempest, my dear, lovable friend, how I have missed you."

Jared watched bemused from the shadows of the stable as the small girl motioned to the huge red horse, and the stallion moved alongside the fence so his mistress could slide her leg over onto his back. Grasping his mane in her hand, she slid the rest of her body sideways until she was mounted astride. And then, in a flash, the two were off, pelting across the meadow as one perfect unit—freedom of line and spirit apparent in their fluid movement, Amanda's full skirt and unbound hair trailing in the wind.

Jared stood transfixed until they were out of sight, the magnificent stallion and the beautiful young girl.

"I knew she couldna ate 'til she rode on Tempest," Harrow chuckled. He had come up beside Jared quietly and the sudden voice startled him. "Do not fret, my lord. My girl knows what she's about. That horse wouldna harm her none."

"I never saw anything like that before in my life! She was astride him bareback. That slip of a girl!" Jared shook his head in amazement.

The cackle came again. "Miss Mandy's been riding since afore she could walk; her Da taught her, you know." Suddenly he was serious. "I fed the boy and he'll be eating yours and Miss Mandy's if I let him alone in there. But, before you be goin' in, can I ask you a question, my lord? What's my Missy doing here? She was apposed to be havin' a fine do-up in London."

Jared turned to the man and explained softly, "Denton threatened to sell Tempest if Amanda refused to marry the man of his choice so she ran away. I see now her great attachment to the beast. Anyway, she plans to ride off on Tempest to live with her old nurse."

"But she cannot! Mr. Denton will find her sure, and then there'll be the devil to pay." Harrow was silent for a moment and then asked, "What affair be this of yours, if I may be so bold, my lord?"

"I—er—*met* Miss Amanda at Almack's and she told me of her plans. I knew her father and couldn't let her do such a hare-brained thing, so, not being able to talk her out of it, I came with her."

"No one talks Miss Mandy out of somethin' she's made her mind up to do, my lord, so don't let that worry you none. But you say you knew his lordship. I guess I didn't quite catch your name, sir."

"Jared Delaney, Harrow. Or, by my title, Lord Storm. I have several of the Fox Chase bloodline in my stables, though the strain is diluted now. Best horses I ever owned."

Recognition dawned in Harrow's eyes. "Ah, aye, now I place you, my lord. It's been some years, though. I thank you for bringin' my girl home to me. But what are we to do now?"

Jared cast his eyes toward the meadow but there were no signs of Amanda returning. He placed a companionable arm around the old groom's shoulders and began, "Now, Harrow, that is just what I wanted to take up with you, over that stew you mentioned."

When hunger finally forced Amanda to return to the stables she saw Jared sitting in Harrow's modest room, his legs propped up on the table and a mug in his hand. Tom was fast asleep in the corner, dirty as ever, and Harrow was just ladling out more stew.

Although secretly amazed the debonair Lord Storm would condescend to spending his evening in the stables, she ignored him as she crossed to the old groom and planted a light kiss on his cheek. "Is that for me, dear Harrow? I'm famished."

"That it is, lass, that it is. Sit yourself down and tuck into this while I go rub down Tempest. I wager you ran him to a standstill."

"Harrow! As if I would ever do such a thing! I walked him all the way back to the stables, and well you know it." She playfully made a face at her old friend's departing back and then dutifully attacked her meal.

Jared watched in silence until she was finished, then swung his legs down and sat up. "All right, imp, now that you've eaten I think we had best get down to cases. Where do we go from here?"

Amanda put her fork down carefully and stared at Jared. "*We* are not going anywhere, my lord. *I* am going to Nanny. *You* may go to perdition for all I care."

"What of young Tom over there?"

Amanda's eyes went to the small figure lying on Harrow's narrow bed. She answered in a small voice, "I don't know."

Jared pursued his advantage. "And what of Harrow? When your stepfather discovers his part in this escapade of yours he will turn him off. Have you stopped to think of that, or of anything but your own selfish desires, madam?"

Amanda was depressed. She knew she had planned badly, but the need to hurt her stepfather and rescue Tempest had made her act hastily. Delaney was right, of course. Her stepfather would sack Harrow and the old man would be cast off to roam the countryside. That would leave no place for Tom either. Pushing her mind even further she could well imagine her stepfather tracking her to Nanny's door. Oh, she was so tired—too utterly exhausted to think.

"All right," she sighed, "you have made your point. I have made a horrid jumble of everything." She put her head in her hands, the picture of dejection.

Jared was more than ready to offer his suggestions for the solution of her problems. "I would be willing to have Harrow at Storm Haven. If your father trusted him, that is all the reason I need to employ him. I would even be willing to have him bring Tom along. He seems to like Devil, and Harrow could train him for some small duties around the stables."

Amanda's head flew up like a shot. "You would do this for me? After all the trouble I have caused? Oh, thank you, my lord, thank you!" A slow flush crept up her cheeks as she saw the gleam in Jared's eye. "Why are you being so amenable?"

Jared got up and paced the small room, looking as if his head would brush the rafters at any moment. "I am insulted. Once again, after I offer my aid in all sincerity, you question my motives." He swiveled and faced her, grinning like the proverbial cat who's just caught up the canary. "But in this instance you are quite correct. I do have a condition you must agree to before I offer your friends a home."

Amanda was too exhausted to argue. "State it," she sighed, leaning back in her chair and looking up into his face.

"You will allow me to accompany you to your nurse."

"Agreed."

"Do not agree too hastily, Amanda. I am not finished. You will allow me to accompany you—yes, eventually—but first you will journey with me . . . to my home at Storm Haven. I fancy your company for a few weeks in the country."

Amanda sprang up in a high temper, the chair crashing unheeded to the floor. "How dare you!" she exclaimed, and dealt him a resounding slap across the face.

Jared raised his hand to ease his stinging cheek. "That was unfortunate, Amanda. I had thought you above such things."

"And I thought you above nothing! You have to be foxed if you think Harrow will let you take me off to your estate willy-nilly."

"Harrow will not know, for you would not jeopardize his future secure life at Storm Haven by telling him. If, however, you are so foolish as to confide in him I will rescind my offer to him and the boy and still carry you off—biting, screaming, or kicking. I have made up my mind to tame you, you little tiger-cat, and tame you I will. You owe me for that incident at the inn."

Amanda backed slowly toward the door, her face a study in anguish. "You monster!" she cried, and turned and fled into the night—almost colliding with Harrow, who shook his head sadly as she went past.

"You were a mite hard on the child, my lord, if I may say so. I was a-standin' outside and couldna help but ta hear you," he said as he entered the room and sat down in front of the fireplace.

"The girl needs a lesson, thinking she can travel all over England unescorted. Besides, I'll never get her to travel with me to Storm Haven any other way. I showed you the special license, Harrow, and I mean what I say when I tell you I will marry Miss Amanda. But do you really think *she* would believe me, and if she did, that she would consent?"

Harrow shook his head sadly. "No, my lord, not my Missy. But she will come about when she sees you mean to keep her safe from her stepfather."

Jared took a long drink of ale from the mug by his side. "I hope you are right, Harrow. Where has she gone?"

"If I know Miss Mandy she's up in her room by now, rainin' down curses on your head. I spoke pretty plain in front of her all these years, my lord, and she picked up some unladylike sayings, I fear. Later she will sleep well enough, she be that tired, and we'll all be able to set out in the morning. I can take the young fella up with me on the horse Miss Mandy was riding. My few belongings will take little room."

Jared rose and walked toward the door. "Good enough, my friend, but I'll sleep near Tempest just to be sure. It won't be the first time I've bedded down in a stable." He gave Harrow a jaunty salute and left the room.

Out in the stable yard he raised his eyes to the house and could see a light in one of the bedrooms. He waited until it went out, then returned to the stable where he made himself a bed out of the straw and blanket Harrow had put out for him, and laid down in his clothes. If Simmons, his valet, could see him now he would hand in his notice. Jared chuckled to himself and almost immediately fell into a deep sleep.

He awoke to the sound of Tom singing a bawdy ditty in a

voice that threatened to break on every high note, and there were several in the song. "Stop that curst caterwauling, you young scamp, or I'll duck your head in the trough," he called out.

The boy turned and ran to Jared's side. "Yer be up then, Guv'nor. The old one is cookin' for me, but yer to take yerself up to the house."

"Very good, Tom. Fetch my belongings from over there on the back of my saddle, will you now, and I'll be off."

Jared let himself into the house and walked purposefully to the kitchens, ignoring the shabby furniture and the lighter patches on the wallpaper where pictures had once hung. Bending over the dirty kitchen table was a slovenly looking female—Denton's village woman, Harrow had told him.

"Look lively there, wench. I require hot water and some towels upstairs in the master's room in ten minutes. In thirty minutes I want to see a good breakfast for two set up in the morning room." When the woman made no attempt to move he took a threatening step toward her which resulted in the woman dipping into a hasty curtsey while whining her agreement.

He passed Amanda on the stairs. She looked fresher this morning for her rest, although the worn habit she wore was obviously too small for her.

"Good morning, my dear," he smiled.

Amanda raised her chin and gave a dignified sniff. "Go to the devil," she announced coolly and passed him without looking back.

Jared laughed and proceeded up the steps to seek out Denton's room. As he had suspected, it was by far the most comfortable room in the house. He quickly laid out his razor and the clean shirt he had brought with him, then stripped to the waist and bellowed for the wench to bring him hot water.

A short time later he faced Amanda again, this time over the breakfast table. They ate the tasteless meal in silence, until finally Amanda could stand it no more.

"What do you want of me, my lord? Why are you doing this?" she pleaded.

"Please, do not whine at me Amanda. It is out of character. It would be more in keeping with your disposition if you hurled that plate at me."

She went to pick up her dish—he exasperated her so!—but at his laugh she stopped. "You think you have me bested, don't you? You dangle Harrow and Tom over my head and think I shall fall into your arms like a ripe plum. I'll see you in Hades first!"

Jared leaned back in his chair and applauded her briefly. "Ah, that is more like it! For a moment there I thought you were beaten. I confess I like you better this way, my dear. It is much more stimulating."

"I am happy to be able to entertain you, my lord, but perhaps you would do better to hire a jester. I promise to be a poor companion."

"I shall trust my instincts, Amanda, and they tell me that it will be a long time before you could possibly bore me."

"Are you dead to all sense of shame? Do you really think you can keep a lady of gentle birth as your mistress without a public outcry?"

"I'd as lief you let me worry about my reputation. It is yours, or the lack of it, that would worry me if I were you. Do you really think anything that you may do, including living with me at Storm Haven, would surprise the delicate ladies whom you so distressed just two nights ago at Almack's?"

Amanda shut her eyes and pressed her lips together, her breath exhaling sharply through her nose while her chin threatened to collide with her chest. He was right, curse him. After making such a cake of herself at the Assembly with him, no one would even lift an eyebrow if she became Lord Storm's mistress. She was beaten and she knew it.

"Very well, my lord. You obviously hold all the cards. When do we leave?"

Jared pulled out his watch and consulted it. "Harrow and young Tom left about an hour ago. We shall be ready to depart whenever you decide."

Amanda's clenched fist came down on the table top. "Why did you send them on ahead? I do not choose to ride with you alone."

"And I do not choose to travel across England with a groom and an urchin. We travel alone, Amanda. As you have stated, I hold all the cards. By my reckoning, if we start out immediately we shall arrive at Storm Haven by tomorrow night. We shall pass your friends on the road, so you can be assured I am keeping my side of the bargain. I gave Harrow funds to stay at an inn for the two nights it will take them to reach Storm Haven on that mare they are riding."

He rose from the table and stretched his limbs. "Do you have any further questions, or shall we leave now? Your stepfather's wench is pressed up against the door and has heard every word I've said. With Denton not too far behind us, I'm sure, and her to tell him our general direction, I think a little haste on our part would seem prudent."

"I may wish to remain and greet my stepfather."

"Really?" He moved toward the door and opened it for Amanda to pass through in front of him. With a shrug of her shoulders she did so, sticking her tongue out at him as she passed—a childish gesture, but one she couldn't resist. He answered with a playful pat on her lower regions, which set her off at a run for the stables.

As the two horses reached the rise from which Jared had first caught sight of Fox Chase, he reined in so that Amanda could have a last look at her family home.

She leaned over and stroked Tempest's neck. "We'll be back someday, my beauty, I promise you. And we will set it all to rights."

Jared turned to her and thought he saw a tear in the corner of her eye. Strange, in spite of all she had been through these past days he had never before seen her cry.

As they turned the horses away Jared looked back over his shoulder at Fox Chase. There was a thin white line around his compressed mouth, and he too made a vow.

Chapter Three

AN EARLY spring had come to the countryside that year. Flowering trees and shrubs dotted the roadside as they rode along, although Amanda was unaware of either the view or the fine weather. She rode behind Jared, declining speech and seemingly content to bore a hole in his back with her eyes.

They had passed Harrow and the boy some three hours before, and her old friend had been maddeningly unconcerned that his mistress was in the company of the terrible Lord Storm. No, Harrow had waved merrily as they passed and wished them a pleasant journey.

Amanda had never felt so alone in her life. Even when her mother died she had Nanny and Harrow to comfort her. Now everyone was gone and she was deep in the clutches of a man bent on violating her. Her heart pounded wildly in her chest at the thought of those great hands on her body. She still was not quite clear on exactly what men and women did together in bed, but she remembered her parents kissing and holding each other and had once discovered one of the kitchen maids in a rather heated embrace with one of the grooms behind the stables—her skirts hiked high and the groom's hand on her bare leg.

Jared would not touch her! She would kill him first, or failing that, kill herself. She raised her hand to her breast for the hundredth time to be reassured by the cold feel of her stepfather's stiletto, secreted in her riding habit. If no one else would aid her she would be more than able to defend herself.

Oh, why had she not stayed in London? Nothing her stepfather could do to her would have been worse than the fate awaiting her at Storm Haven. At least Denton had planned for her to marry. After Jared was done with her she would be soiled forever. She narrowed her eyes as she stared at Jared's wide back, imagining the hilt of her knife sticking out between his shoulder-blades. The man was getting into her soul: She was even thinking of him by his first name!

Jared could feel the heat of Amanda's anger through the cloth of his riding coat. He looked over his shoulder at her and drawled, "Are you plotting my demise, Amanda?"

She refused to answer and urged Tempest into a canter. She slipped by him, not slowing down until she was well in front. If it were not for Harrow and Tom she would show him their heels in a hurry!

Jared chuckled and shook his head. He had not enjoyed himself so much in years. With every passing moment he was more and more convinced that he wanted to wed—and bed—Amanda Boynton. After so many years of women like Blanche Wade and her ilk, Amanda's innocence and candor were like a breath of fresh air after months spent underground.

He had never before seriously considered marrying, contrary to his aunt's fondest hopes, and was secretly surprised at himself for desiring to make such a young slip of a girl Lady Storm. Yet, somehow, no other arrangement seemed right. It had nothing to do with loyalty to the long dead Roger Boynton: Jared Delaney took what he wanted when he wanted it.

No, it was because of a niggling suspicion at the back of his mind that to touch Amanda without first wedding her would be despoiling a beautiful, indomitable creature.

Oh, yes, he wanted to tame her. He wanted those golden eyes looking up at him in passion and surrender. But not at the expense of her great pride. He would tame her as he had tamed Devil, teach her who was master without breaking her spirit.

How apt! Comparing Amanda with a spirited horse. Ah, and how he, Jared, would ride! He laughed silently at his own witticism.

Amanda reined in ahead of him and waited until he drew along side her before she asked, "Do we stop for luncheon, my lord? I admit to feeling a bit peckish." She hated to have to address him at all, but her stomach had been grumbling for the last few miles and could no longer be denied.

"If you can promise me no repeat of yesterday's folly I will consider stopping at the Three Feathers, which is just a little bit further along the road. I have no desire to face another irate innkeeper."

Amanda had the decency to blush. "You have the word of a Boynton, my lord."

They ate a filling—though silent—meal at the Three Feathers, Jared letting Amanda out of his sight for only as long as it took her to freshen herself. His ever-present surveillance rankled after she had given him her word not to try anything rash, and once more anger simmered close to the surface.

As they were preparing to set out once again, Amanda saw an opportunity to even the score when Jared asked if he could go up on Tempest for a mile or two.

She stopped her refusal just in time and smiled her agreement. Jared crossed to mount the red stallion but looked around just in time to catch Amanda smiling at him, her hands clasped demurely behind her back, while her golden eyes held sparks of mischief.

Now what did the chit have up her sleeve? He shrugged his shoulders at his suspicions. Hadn't she behaved circumspectly all through luncheon? He slid one booted foot into the stirrup and swung himself up into the saddle, for Amanda had chosen to defy convention by riding astride and he was amused enough to allow it. What was one more solecism after they had broken so many rules these past days?

Tempest felt the unaccustomed weight on his back and turned his head to Jared in an attempt to identify his unwelcome passenger. The horse stood quietly under him and Jared smiled over at Amanda in satisfaction. She smiled back sweetly.

Then something strange happened. Tempest knelt down on his front legs! Jared pulled on the reins to urge the horse up, but the stallion countered by collapsing his hind quarters. Jared just had time to jump clear before Tempest rolled over onto his back and gave what Jared swore to be a horse laugh.

Jared sat on his haunches in the dirt, his elbows resting on his knees while Amanda and, it seemed to Jared, half the customers at the inn stood in whoops around him. The ostler clutched his sides in mirth and the innkeeper wiped his streaming eyes with the edge of his apron.

Jared looked at Amanda, now demurely quiet again with Tempest beside her nuzzling her neck. Miserable brat, he thought. She taught the beast to do that.

He got up as unhurriedly as he could and brushed himself off. He then crossed to Devil and mounted him, calling behind him,

"Your mule does party tricks tolerably well, madam, but can he move past a trot?"

As he suspected, the last traces of her smile were wiped from her face and she called to a groom to help her mount. "Tempest could best your plowhorse on three legs if he chose. We challenge you to a race!" she shouted with unladylike glee.

The crowd in the stable yard roared its approval but their pleasure was to be short lived. Jared rode over to Amanda and whispered in her ear, "Haven't you made a big enough spectacle of the two of us, Amanda? I suggest we move on and let these people get back about their business."

"Oh, how poor spirited of you," Amanda countered, but she saw the wisdom of his words. They certainly were the center of all attention, and the innkeeper would be sure to remember them if her stepfather should pass this way. A rescue from Jared that included Denton was like no rescue at all.

"All right, I agree, my lord, but only if you will do me the honor of allowing me to have you eat your words about Tempest once we reach the open country."

"We shall see who eats her words, Amanda. But I concur. A test is called for."

They rode out of the inn yard amid the muttered protests of the disappointed customers, who were already laying their blunt on the outcome of the race. Jared would not have been too pleased to find that Amanda was already the decided favorite at five-to-one odds.

They rode on for a few miles until they reached a large open field not yet sown. Jared swiveled in his saddle and addressed Amanda. "I believe a gallop from here to that far fence should be a sufficient test of our animals. Do you agree?"

Amanda did, and at the count of three they were off. Devil took the lead and held it for some time, but when Jared cast a look over his shoulder he could see the triumphant grin on Amanda's face. She was obviously holding Tempest back! As they neared the fence the stallion passed as if Jared's horse was standing still and Amanda never slackened pace as horse and rider easily cleared the high barrier.

She rode on a few yards, then reined in to catch the look on Jared's face. Oh, no, he was going to try to jump the fence! The fool, she worried frantically, no horse but Tempest could do such a thing. She watched in horror as Devil approached the jump, and her heart went into her throat as the black horse gathered his legs for the leap. It appeared he had made it, but then one hind leg caught the top rail and horse and rider somersaulted over the fence to land in the soft grass at her feet.

She slid off Tempest and ran to Jared's side. Devil was already up and standing dazedly a few feet away; a quick glance told her he would not run off. She dropped to her knees beside Jared's still form and held her breath as she looked for any signs of life.

He lay so still that for a moment she thought he had broken his neck. She pressed her ear to his chest and could hear his heart still beating, causing her to give a soft exclamation of relief.

Hurriedly she ran her hands over his body to feel for any breaks but found no sign of injury. Then her fingers encountered a rapidly rising bump on the back of his head. Slowly she raised his head and positioned it on her lap, stroking his black hair back from his forehead as she softly called his name. "Jared, Jared, please don't die. Oh, you stupid, headstrong man, how could you try such a thing? Please, please wake up!"

She rested her cheek against his forehead and rocked his head back and forth in her lap, continuing her crooning until at last Jared showed some signs of life.

Amanda quickly lowered his head to the grass and got up, so that the first thing Jared saw on regaining consciousness was the tapping foot of Miss Amanda Boynton. Slowly he raised his eyes to her face and was rewarded for this pain by the cutting remark, "Not only do we now know which is the better horse, my lord, but we have a fair idea of just who is the superior rider."

Jared was nonplussed for a moment, but then he saw the humor of the situation. "Made a cake of myself, didn't I? I bow to your superiority, Amanda. *Ow!*" He put a hand to his throbbing head as he tried to rise but was still able to see Amanda's quickly offered—and just as quickly retracted—hand. "I don't think I can make it to my horse alone, Amanda. Would you be so good as to let me lean on you?"

"I'd as soon see you crawl, my lord, but I was taught always to help dumb animals. Very well, put your weight on me."

Other than the discomfort caused by the lump on his head Jared was already almost fully recovered. He had felt the fall coming and aimed his body for the soft clover. In truth, besides having the wind knocked out of him—a repeated occurrence since meeting Amanda—he was only slightly injured by the bang on his very hard head.

Yet now he moaned loudly and rested an arm across

Amanda's shoulders, feeling the soft curve of her breast against his side as they walked slowly to his horse. Once there he clutched at his saddle and looked as if he would indeed faint. Amanda grabbed both his arms in her hands and shook him slightly.

"Don't swoon, Jared! Help me get you up on your horse and I can lead him to the closest farmhouse for help."

Suddenly Jared seemed to experience a complete recovery. He slid his arms around Amanda's waist and stared deeply into her worried eyes. "I did not give you permission to address me by my first name, wench."

"Jared, this is no time for foolishness. You could be badly hurt and I've treated you abominably."

"Yes," he agreed solemnly, "you have." His deep blue eyes were twinkling as they looked into her worried amber ones, and slowly she stiffened under his gaze.

"You are bamming me! You are perfectly sound! Cad!"

Jared's eyes danced as his arms tightened their grip and he held her powerless in his hands. Slowly, inexorably, she felt him draw her closer within the circle of his arms and she watched bemused as his head slowly came down and his mouth claimed hers in a gentle caress.

She kept her eyes open wide for a few moments, staring at Jared's long lashes as they cast shadows on his cheeks. She made no effort to struggle, for she knew it was useless, and decided it would be best just to remain passive in his arms. But her body betrayed her by warming to his touch. As the pressure of his mouth increased, she could feel her heart rising in her throat until she felt she was choking.

Her lips opened in a gasp and Jared quickly took advantage of it to plumb the depths of her mouth with his tongue. Shivers of excitement coursed down Amanda's spine and her arms, acting with a will of their own, crept up around his neck. Her mind whirled warnings around in her brain but her body dismissed them. The amber eyes fluttered closed.

Suddenly Jared released her, and she would have fallen except for his supporting hand. She had felt him tremble under her hands and looked at him to see if he was as affected by their kiss as she had been.

He smiled down at her, but the smile didn't quite reach his eyes. His face was pale and his voice shook a little as he quipped, "You have worked quite a cure on me, Amanda. I swear I haven't felt this well in months. Have you any more miracle remedies?"

"O-o-oh, you monster!" she cried, and raised a hand to deal him a vicious slap. But his hand shot out and caught at her wrist, squeezing it between his long fingers.

"Tch, tch, my sweet, would you beat on an injured man?" Her attack had put him back on his mettle. He cast any uneasy thoughts to the back of his mind, to be pondered later, and entered into the spirit of the fight. "Much more abuse at your hands and I shall go into a decline. I have been so far unhorsed no less than three times, threatened by footpads and country bumpkins, and endured unspeakable creature discomforts— all because of you. I warn you, Amanda, think twice before you attack me again—for in future I fully intend to retaliate."

She shook her wrist free and stepped back a few paces, her face a study in fury. "You devil! Dare to touch me and I will rip out your guts and throw them to the crows, I'll . . ."

"Ah, Harrow told me of your picturesque turns of speech, Amanda. I must say my knees are knocking together. However, we have many miles to cover before we reach the inn where I wish to stop for the night—so I think we can dispense with these transports, don't you?"

Amanda's chin went up as she retorted, "If you didn't insist on carrying me off willy-nilly to your estate you could make much better time, my lord."

"Carry you off? But what folly is this, my dear? I assure you, you are free to leave me at any time. I do not force you to accompany me."

"Oh, really? And what about Harrow, and—and Tom?" she parried.

"Ah, so you have belatedly remembered your friends, Amanda? Does your memory also include Peregrine Denton and his plans for you?"

"His plans were no worse than yours, *Lord Storm*," she said derisively.

Jared cocked an eyebrow. "Indeed?"

Amanda continued to glare into his eyes for a few moments, and then her gaze shifted as she was forced to admit—at least to herself—that she would rather be with Jared than anyone of her stepfather's choice. She hated Jared, but for the first time in over three years she felt really alive!

She sighed and strode purposefully toward her horse, who

stood by idly chewing on some tender new grass. "You are wasting time, my lord. As you say, it grows late and we have many miles to cover. If you think you can manage your animal I suggest we move on." She mounted Tempest unaided and started to ride off.

Jared looked after her for a few moments. He was not sure of his own feelings during that impulsive embrace, and he was even more unsure of Amanda's. For a few seconds she had melted in his arms—and he was sure he had felt the first stirrings of passion on her lips.

It was confusing to him. All his life women had pursued him for either his fortune or his looks, or both, but this girl rejected him totally. He had to have her! Only after he had bedded her could he get himself free of this torment.

He swung into the saddle and turned Devil to follow in Amanda's wake.

It was after dark before the horses rode into the small village Jared had chosen to stop at for the night. Amanda felt tired and dirty and extremely put-upon, and she slumped in her saddle as they progressed toward the posting inn on the other end of the village.

She was too fatigued to take notice of the rather large amount of traffic on the small street. Nor did she see the several well-dressed men loitering outside the inn until two of them broke away from the group and came up to Jared.

"Stap me, Bo, if it ain't Jared! Jared, you old devil, we had about given you up. We stopped in Half Moon Street and were told you wasn't home. I told Bo you wouldn't forget a mill like this one and you'd show up by and by, so we got you a room anyway. You owe me for that, Jared." Before Jared could make a reply the man turned to his companion with a grin. "How about our friend, ay, Bo? Not only does he show up, but he brings his own love-bird to warm his nest."

Amanda's eyes flew to Jared's face and she opened her mouth to speak—but no words would come. How dare he bring her along to a filthy boxing match! Then she saw he was looking quite as astonished as she and decided to wait it out. She wanted to hear what he had to say in his defense.

"The devil take it!" he hissed under his breath, and quickly slid from his horse and approached the two men. Amanda watched as their grins faded and, as Jared talked and gestured, their eyes slid more than once to the slim girl who remained seated on the big horse. Finally the man who had spoken crossed to her and helped her down.

"A thousand pardons, Miss Boynton, for my earlier indiscretion. I will rip out my tongue at your command! Jared has explained that you lost a wheel off your carriage some miles back and were lucky enough to have my friend come along to bring you into the village before you were benighted on the road. How fortunate your uncle's horse was tied to the carriage." He cast his eyes about him. "Where is your uncle, by the way?"

"Er—he—um—Un—Uncle Roscoe chose to stay with the carriage, sir, and I came along with Lord Storm, Mr.—er, excuse me, but I don't know how to address you." Amanda's mind was racing furiously as she tried to figure out Jared's plans. Obviously he was not going to admit the truth, but who was he protecting with this Banbury Tale, her or himself?

The tall slender man lifted Amanda's hand and bowed over it. "Again I find myself apologizing, Miss Boynton. I am the Honorable Kevin Rawlings, long time friend and compatriot of your escort, and your servant, ma'am."

By this time the other two men had come up to them and a young, rather husky man with an unruly shock of red hair and innumerable freckles covering his flushed cheeks took his turn bowing over Amanda's hand.

"Chevington, ma'am . . . pleasure . . . servant, and all that," he murmured under his breath, and then the majority of him disappeared behind Jared's back.

"You have just had the pleasure of being greeted by the Honorable Mr. Buford Chevington, Amanda," Jared told her with a grin.

Mr. Rawlings gave Jared a quick look when he used Miss Boynton's first name so familiarly. There was something smokey here, and unless he missed his guess a fine tale laid behind the arrival of the beautiful black-haired girl. Wasn't there some hum about Jared and a black-haired wench at Almack's? "Yes, indeed, Miss Boynton, you are privileged more than you know. Our Bo rarely speaks to females at all," he informed Amanda as she bent her head to peer around Jared for another look at the funny little man.

"Oh," she said, "then I am truly honored, Mr. Chevington, and I return your greeting." Her engaging smile coaxed Mr.

Chevington out of hiding and he addressed Jared in his usual clipped speech.

"Cold out here, Jared. Past my dinner, too. Bad *ton* leaving a lady in the street. People staring and all that."

"You are quite right, Bo," Jared agreed, and held out his arm for Amanda who took it gratefully. "Kevin, I assume you have gotten us a private dining room where Miss Boynton can dine after she freshens herself?"

Before Mr. Rawlings could answer Amanda spoke up, "I prefer to dine in my room, my lord, if it is convenient." She felt a warning pressure on her arm but chose to ignore it. "And since my abigail stayed behind in the coach I shall require a chambermaid to help me with my bath." Her eyes danced in her head as she averted Jared's furious look.

Jared knew when he was beaten and gave in gracefully. As he watched Amanda climb the stairs—a chambermaid behind her carrying her small hat box, which was all the luggage she could attach to Tempest's saddle before they left Fox Chase—his friend Kevin appeared at his side.

"Shouldn't you be sending someone back down the road to pick up the uncle?"

Jared hesitated a second and then hastily agreed, but Kevin had known Jared too long to be taken in by such a sorry story. "There is no uncle, is there, Jared? No abigail either. And, furthermore, no coach. Tell me, have I imagined it all, or is there really a Miss Boynton?"

"Oh, there is a Miss Boynton all right, and you've just seen her. As for the rest, ah, Kevin, thereby hangs a tale!" He put his arm around his friend's shoulder and turned him toward the barroom. "Let's get Bo and split a few bottles, shall we? This is not a story I wish to tell twice."

"Before you start, Jared, tell me one thing. Did you remember we planned to meet here for the mill tomorrow?"

"Kevin, since I met Amanda it's lucky if I remember if I'm on my head or on my heels. All I could recall was the location of this inn. Excuse me my candor, but the *last* two people I expected to encounter on this journey were you and Bo."

Bo joined the pair as they retired to their reserved dining room, Jared calling out greetings to many acquaintances but not stopping to exchange pleasantries.

"Boynton—Boynton." Kevin tapped his lips with one well-manicured finger as he searched his memory after they had ordered their meal. "Could that be the Boynton who slipped his moorings about ten years back? The horse breeder?"

"One and the same, Kevin, though it was eight years to be precise and Amanda is his only offspring," Jared corrected.

"Good man, Boynton," Bo interjected. "For shame, Jared. Dirty business, running off with the daughter."

Jared took a long sip from his wine glass and raised his hand for silence. "I can see I must start at the beginning and tell all before one of my fine friends calls me out for seducing a young lady of quality."

Bo turned an astonished face toward Kevin. "Would we, Kevin? It's Jared, you know. He's m' friend."

"Relax, Bo," Kevin assured him. "I would never raise a hand to Jared. He is my friend too, and besides," he winked at Jared, "he's a much better shot than either you or I."

So Jared called for another bottle and began his tale, only to be interrupted by such sympathetic observations as:

"Ho! ho! Very good, 'pon my word! Very good, indeed!"

"Made a cake of yourself in that one, friend."

"By George, I wish I had seen that!"

"Good girl! Lots of spunk, and a devilish fine-looking woman to boot!"

But the best remarks were heard at the end of Jared's recitation, when Kevin jumped up and fairly shouted, "*Bracketed!* You must be joking!"

Bo was much more subdued in his reaction to the news that the elusive Lord Storm was seriously entertaining the wedded state. "Only proper. Pity the girl, though. Dashed loose-screw you are, Jared. Always thought so, myself."

Jared remained calm and drawled, "Thank you both, my good friends, for those stirring felicitations. But I have quite made up my mind. We marry tomorrow night when we reach Storm Haven."

Now Kevin was really incensed. "Such haste, Romeo, is unseemly."

"Oh, really, Kevin? Perhaps you think I should wait until we can have Denton give away the bride at St. George. Please, spare both Amanda and myself such a travesty."

"Quite so, Kevin," Bo interrupted. "Wouldn't want Denton either. Don't like the man above half."

The three friends talked and argued until late, and Jared left them only when he had extracted their promise not to reveal the full extent of his plans to Amanda.

"Rather mean of you, Jared! Letting the girl hang in suspense, thinking herself to be ravished at any moment. It doesn't seem the proper way to treat a wife," Kevin observed.

Jared put a tentative hand to his black-and-blue rump, a result of his numerous spills. "Let me be the judge of that, Kevin. Now I must say good night. It's been a long day."

"Where are you sleeping? Miss Boynton is in your chamber."

"I'll sleep in with one of you if you'll have me. But first I must go and say good night to my intended. I have a feeling she is expecting me, and I never disappoint a female."

After he left the room his two friends exchanged glances.

"Jared Delaney getting himself riveted. I don't believe it." Kevin shook his head back and forth in confusion. "Why?"

"Besotted," came the answer.

"Jared? In love? Bo, you're dead as a house." Kevin leaned forward to pour himself another glass. "Besotted! That's a good one!" Then his eyes turned to the door through which Jared had passed a few moments ago. He frowned in speculation and was quiet for a long time.

Although nearly dropping with fatigue, Amanda was still fully-dressed in an old muslin gown she had brought with her from Fox Chase. She was, at that moment, in her room awaiting the inevitable.

After a refreshing bath and a heartening meal she had felt better prepared to face Jared, but this waiting was becoming unendurable. She felt for the stiletto hidden in a pocket in her dress, and crossed to the mirror. Her reflection showed a young girl with wide, fear-dulled eyes. She had let her long black hair hang down her back to dry it, and in the outdated dress she saw she looked painfully young. Maybe he would take pity on her and let her go.

Her mind turned again to the two men she had met on her arrival. Would it be possible to turn to them for assistance? Somehow she doubted it. They were all three of them probably downstairs right now casting lots as to which one would invade her chamber tonight. She felt her lip quiver and gave herself a shake. It would not do to give in to her fears.

There was nothing for it but to submit to Jared's threats. After he had his way with her she would be free to leave. At least Harrow and Tom would be assured of a good home. She didn't know why she trusted Jared to make good his promise, but she did. There was only her future to be considered now. She had once thought of becoming a governess, but she knew that road would now be forever closed to her.

Perhaps she could cut off her hair and pretend she was a boy! Then she could become a famous jockey and ride Tempest in all the big races! She was certainly small enough. She gave herself a mental kick. It was time and enough she stopped living in a fantasy world.

Why, oh, why couldn't she have stayed in London and submitted to her stepfather's demands? Was marriage that bad, after all? Yes! To anyone her stepfather would choose, yes, it was. Her plan to disappear was really not all that ill-conceived. Her only mistake was to want the satisfaction of her stepfather's disgrace. If she hadn't worn that odious gown none of this would have happened. She could have gone meekly to Almack's and then slipped quietly off into the night, having never met Jared Delaney.

That brought her up short and she almost knocked over a small stool. Never to have known Jared? Her mind went back over the events of the past few days. He had really been rather gallant in offering to take her to Fox Chase. It was only her own foolishness that had pushed him into behaving like a bully.

And what about Harrow and Tom? Not many men would put a dirty orphan up in front of them and ride across country joking with the lad and making him feel at his ease. His treatment of Harrow had been even kinder—Harrow was the best head groom in the country, but he was obviously past his prime. He could have left her old friend to his fate and ridden off, following Amanda when she left Fox Chase and then kidnapping her anyway.

Yes, he was really behaving quite well, considering the shabby tricks she had played on him. And he *had* tried to protect her name with that story he gave his friends earlier. Last but not least, he was a very pretty man to look upon.

Oh, she was in a quandary. Part of her hated Jared and the other part of her looked to him in awe.

Her mind went back to that kiss in the meadow, and her skin tingled. She had never been kissed before and didn't know if hers was the normal reaction; she only knew that it had been by and large a pleasant experience. Yet he hadn't tried to kiss her again. Maybe he didn't like it! Strangely, that thought depressed her.

She started pacing again. Why didn't he come and get it over with! She whirled as she heard the latch turning and was immediately thankful she had asked the chambermaid for the key. Now that he was finally here she decided she didn't really want to see him at all.

She walked slowly over to the door and called, "Who is it?"

"It isn't Father Christmas, if that's what you thought. Open this door, Amanda, before we have the house down on us. I want to talk."

"Go away, my lord. I have nothing to say to you."

"Well I have plenty to say to you, you little hell-cat, and if you don't want the entire inn to hear it you'd better let me in and be quick about it!"

Grudgingly she opened the door, then took position behind a rather large chair. "Say what you must and get out. I am weary."

Jared looked around the large, comfortable chamber, then walked closer to the blazing fireplace. "A very nice room, it is, Amanda, that I have given up for you. The bed looks quite appealing too. Do you think we both will fit?"

Amanda's hand closed over the hilt of her knife in the pocket of her gown. She glared at him.

"No? How tedious. My hopes are quite cut up," he said when she didn't answer.

Amanda ignored him and returned, "You wished speech with me, my lord."

Jared lowered himself into a chair and said, "Very well then, if you want to be serious. I think we must discuss our plans for the morning. I have convinced Kevin and Bo that you are who I say you are, and since they will be leaving for the mill quite early we shouldn't be seeing them anyway. I propose we wake fairly early ourselves and breakfast somewhere along the road. This inn is far too full with men of my acquaintance for my liking."

Amanda grinned at him. "Are you afraid one of those so gallant gentlemen downstairs will come to my rescue?"

Jared shook his head. "Indeed, no. On the contrary, I am afraid they will try to steal a march on me with someone they consider fair game. Well-bred ladies do not stay in towns where a mill is to be held."

Amanda felt her face grow hot. "Oh."

"Yes, oh. Now, to keep us both from embarrassment I suggest you do as I say."

"Yes, Jared."

"Ah, 'Jared' again. I must admit I like that better than 'my lord' or 'Lord Storm.' Does this mean we are friends?" He stood up and came over to where she stood. "Bo snores, and I would much prefer the company of a softer bed partner."

"You are impudent, my lord." Amanda skittered out from behind the chair and made as if to flee the room, but Jared's arm shot out and caught her neatly.

"And you are an incorrigible nuisance. Do you really think I would try anything rash here, where your screams—or perhaps cries of pleasure—could be heard by all and sundry? I am jesting with you, my infant. I assure you I can live without your charms for one more night."

Amanda spun and dealt him a resounding slap on the cheek. Jared's face took on a hardened look, and he advanced toward the furious girl. "I told you I would retaliate if you ever raised your hand to me again, brat. Now it's across my knee with you."

Amanda danced out of his reach and fumbled in her gown for the stiletto. She closed her hand around the hilt and drew it out. "Stand back, my lord, or I shall cut out your liver and fry it for breakfast!"

Jared stopped in his tracks and looked at the slim blade glinting in the firelight. "You never cease to amaze me, Amanda. First you threaten to tear out my guts and toss them to the crows. Now you have designs on my liver. You really should strive to be more consistent, though I daresay I prefer neither possibility." The smile left his eyes as he slowly advanced toward her. "Now stop this foolishness and give me the knife. You might injure someone."

"Never! Stay back or I'll turn the blade on myself."

Jared ran a hand through his hair. Perhaps the joke had gone far enough. "Of all the dim-witted, stupid females I have ever met, you are the most . . ."

"Cork-brained? Feeble-minded?" she offered coldly. "Cabbage-headed? Do you have no end to the charming descriptions you keep hurling at my head?"

"So that's it. You take offense at my speech." He made a deep bow, ignoring the threatening blade. "Please accept my humble apologies for insulting your vanity." He straightened, and a grin played on his face. "Any dolt could see that you have behaved with only the highest of intelligence throughout the past days, climaxing your brilliance by brandishing a toy knife at one of the best swordsmen in England." He looked past her to the doorway. "Isn't that right, Kevin? Tell Amanda how small her chances are of using that blade on either my person or her own before I could disarm her."

Amanda whirled to face the intruder and ask his aid, but before her mind could take in the fact that she and Jared were alone in the room Jared had moved quickly to her and wrenched the stiletto from her hand.

"Oh, hang you!" she cried, rubbing her sore wrist. "You tricked me!"

Jared crossed to the window and, opening it, tossed the stiletto into the darkness below. "It wasn't hard, Amanda. You are really quite gullible." He turned and advanced toward her again. "Now, about that punishment . . ."

Before she could run, he picked her up and deposited her unceremoniously on the mattress. She looked up at him with frightened eyes, but he did not join her on the coverlet. Instead he pushed her over onto her stomach and gave her several resounding smacks on her bottom. Try as she would she could not get away, and tears of frustration ran down her cheeks.

When he had finished he sat down heavily next to her and put a hand on her hair. "I'm sorry for that, Amanda, but you deserved it."

The events of the past days had taken their toll and Amanda dissolved into muffled sobs, her head pressed down into the pillow. Jared watched as her slim shoulders shook with grief, her long hair spread about her like a fan, and he put his arms around her and drew her up against his chest.

"Don't cry, infant, I really am sorry." When she showed no signs of stopping he added, "I'll let you cut up my liver if you like."

Her head pulled away from his shoulder and she gulped, "Don't try to be nice to me now. I understand you better when you are being horrid."

"Nice? Oh, that is good!" Jared laughed. "I can do nothing to please you, can I, Amanda? If I am mean you attack me, and if I am nice you doubt my motives. Ah, brat, how can I make you happy?"

"By letting me go."

Jared's eyes darkened. "Anything but that, sweet child. I am not sure why, but for some reason that solution appeals to me not at all."

Amanda felt a queer relief at his words and relaxed slightly in his arms. Jared felt her capitulation and slowly covered her trembling mouth with his own. He felt her stiffen for a moment, but as he slid her mouth open with his fingertip she gave a soft moan and wrapped her arms around his neck.

Suddenly Jared drew back. Amanda was confused and embarrassed by the strange look in his eyes. She hastily rolled to the far side of the bed and curled herself into a tight little ball. Jared sprang from the bed and looked about nervously. "Not here, dear Amanda. Not here and not now. Forgive me."

Before she could utter a word he was gone. She turned her face into the pillow and wept, whether in relief or frustration she wasn't sure.

Amanda endured the questioning looks of the chambermaid the next morning when the girl discovered that her female guest had slept in her clothes on top of the covers. In truth, the servant had expected two heads on the pillows when she tiptoed in with two cups of hot chocolate—she was that sure the fine gentleman would share the little lady's bed.

Amanda had no choice but to don her travel-stained riding habit once more, and she was terribly upset at the thought of Jared seeing her looking as she did. There were faint violet smudges under her eyes, and even pinching her cheeks until tears came to her eyes did nothing to add color to her face.

After the chambermaid left Amanda sat down primly to await Jared. He came to the door within minutes and beckoned silently for her to follow him. Picking up her hat box she trailed after him down the steps, secretly cursing the fact that he looked none the worse for last night's experience. He must have borrowed a clean cravat from one of his friends, and even in his same blue jacket he looked disgustingly well-groomed and at his ease.

The two men they had met the night before were standing in the shadows near the stables. The one called Kevin beckoned Jared to his side. "Did you see him? It wouldn't do at all to have him discover you here, especially," he threw a look toward Amanda, "with *her*. Wouldn't do for later on if he spies her now, if you know what I mean."

"Could you speak a bit plainer, Kevin? It's deucedly early for riddles."

"'Tis Freddie. Came in late last night. Don't like him," Bo volunteered.

Jared cast a quick look toward the inn. "Cousin Freddie? What the devil is he doing here? That's all it needed to make this farce complete."

Having safely delivered his message Kevin turned to Amanda and lifted her hand to his lips. "Good morning to you, dear Miss Boynton. I trust you slept well? My apologies for ignoring you in my haste to warn Jared of that odious toad's arrival. I'm never at my best before noon, you know. Can't get used to these country hours."

"I return your greetings, Mr. Rawlings, and excuse you. But pray tell me, just who is this Freddie that has everyone so upset?"

"Frederick Crosswaithe, Jared's cousin—several times removed, thank God, but none the less heir to the title until our friend produces some offspring of his own." He leaned toward her and whispered, "They don't get on, you know."

"Oh, is Jar—, er, I mean, is Lord Storm afraid of this Mr. Crosswaithe?"

"Afraid! That is a good one! Jared, Miss Boynton wants to know if you shake in your socks at the thought of Freddie."

Amanda noticed that while Kevin and Jared dissolved in mirth, Bo Chevington frowned deeply, his cherubic face a study in consternation. "Should be, Jared. Not a nice man. Not nice at all," he warned, which set Jared and Kevin off again into whoops.

"I—afraid of that popinjay? That would be like being afraid of *you*, Bo, though I assure you I do not lump you with such as Freddie!"

Amanda could see that Bo was serious and asked him to explain himself. "Punting on tick, is Freddie. Living on expectations. Don't trust him. Shifty eyes," informed Bo seriously.

Jared shook his head negatively as he met Amanda's worried eyes. "Don't let Bo frighten you, Miss Boynton. My cousin is greedy and a cad, but he would never dare raise a hand to me. Nice of you to look so concerned, I might add."

"Ah, yes," entered Kevin laughingly, "but you must remember: Freddie has been making noises lately about coming into some money."

"If dear cousin Freddie thinks I shall conveniently break my neck so that I can line his pockets, he is sadly mistaken. However, I do not wish to bump into my beloved relative while Miss Boynton is in my care. Do excuse us, friends, and we'll be off."

"What? Leaving already, without so much as a greeting for your relative? Shameful!" came a voice from behind Amanda—a voice she could only describe as slimy.

She whirled to see a small, pale, rather stringy-looking man dressed in flamboyant clothing bearing down on them as best he could with his ridiculously high heeled shoes wobbling at every step. His lime-green riding coat fit him badly, and there must have been three inches of padding in the shoulders.

His blond hair was thin, and he sported a large wart at the corner of his long, pointed nose. Beady, almost colorless eyes raked up and down Amanda and she shivered in repugnance. Bo was right! He was an ugly hateful little man. She moved closer to Jared and he put a protective arm around her waist.

"Ah, Freddie, I had heard you were here. You don't look well though, or is it because I have never before seen you in the daylight? I must say you surprise me, coming to the mill. I had thought you'd faint at the sight of blood. Or does the thought of seeing two hulking men stripped to the waist delight your senses?"

Freddie's eyes narrowed for a moment, but then he lifted one thin white hand to his face and dabbed at the corner of his mouth with a perfumed lace handkerchief. "I see the months since we last met have not dulled your vile sense of humor, cousin." He rested his eyes once more on Amanda. "But what have we here? Surely even you would not bring a lady to witness fisticuffs, even one so obviously fallen as this one. Is she just for you, or are all of you sharing her favors?"

"Told you. Not a good man," Bo supplied.

Amanda watched as a thin white line formed around Jared's tightly-compressed lips and a pulse began to beat rapidly at his temple. Before she could really take in what was happening Frederick Crosswaithe was sprawled in the dirt, a small trickle of blood running from the corner of his mouth, and Jared was towering over him with clenched fists at the ready.

"Get up, you jackass, and I'll serve you a little more home-brewed." Jared spat.

One look at the violent visage above him and Freddie chose instead to crawl on all fours until he was out from underneath Jared's spread legs. Then he took to his heels like a frightened rabbit as over his shoulder he cried, "The last laugh will be mine, cousin, and don't you forget it!"

"A wisty punch, Jared," complimented Kevin. "Worth missing a good seat at the mill to see that."

Bo stayed where he was and only Amanda heard him say, "Shouldn't have done that. Mean man, Freddie."

As the two set out for Storm Haven Amanda questioned Jared about his cousin, but Jared laughed off her fears, commenting only that he was flattered she should care about his safety.

"But Jared, he could do you some great harm. If he is in such dire need of money he might try to kill you."

Jared threw back his head and howled. "Freddie? He's afraid of his own valet—or in love with him. Besides, who do you think has been keeping him in silks and satins but me? He has not a feather to fly with without the allowance I send him. We hate each other, I grant you that, but Freddie knows better than to raise a hand to me."

"But Mr. Chevington . . ."

"Bo is an old woman. Forget it, Amanda. I'll race you to the top of that hill!" he called, and was off.

Amanda did not raise the subject again, but she stored Bo's warning away in her heart—though why she should be concerned over Jared's stupid neck she had no idea.

Jared made no mention of their intimacy of the night before when they stopped along the road for breakfast or again at luncheon. Doubtless the incident meant nothing to him. It was a subdued Miss Amanda Boynton who rode beside Lord Storm as they made the last leg of their journey to Storm Haven.

Chapter Four

AMANDA'S first sight of the Delaney ancestral home did nothing to lighten her mood. Although the immaculately-kept grounds reminded her of her beloved Fox Chase in the years before her father's death, Storm Haven itself was a dull grey stone monstrosity—cold and forbidding, although lit by the warmth of the sun that unkindly disclosed the details of its architecture. Even the green trailing ivy, so prevalent on English manor walls, seemed to shun the pale stones.

The center of the structure—obviously the oldest part—had very small windows, and Amanda could imagine the darkness within the rooms in that section. On either side of the three-storied main building were several additions that appeared to have been tacked on without thought to any overall design. The resulting hodgepodge could have been amusing except for the overriding gaol-like feeling that seemed to emanate from the walls.

Jared rode more slowly now, reining Devil to a walk, as if he really didn't want to reach the huge black wooden doors that stood closed and unwelcoming at the head of a circular drive. Amanda stole a look at him as the horses plodded along and she could see a slight tick working in his cheek. It seemed he shared her view of his home. Why had he brought her here if the place repulsed him so?

As they neared the doorway a groom appeared and hastened to hold Amanda's horse so she could dismount. But before she could do so Jared jumped from Devil's back and held out his arms to her. She rested her hands on his shoulders, and as he tightened his fingers around her waist and lifted her from the saddle his eyes searched her face for reactions. She forced a weak smile to her lips and he set her down gently, then held her for a few moments more than was politely necessary. On impulse she raised a gloved hand to his cheek and murmured, "It's all right, Jared. Really, it is."

His breath released in a rush, and he turned his face and pressed his lips against her exposed wrist. "I should not have brought you here. Whenever I'm away I close out the ugliness and forget how much I loathe this place. Seeing it again brings it all back. Forgive me?"

Forgive him? That was twice in less than twenty-four hours he had begged her forgiveness, and Amanda did not like the feeling it gave her. Such humility from the arrogant Lord Storm was almost too much for her. With a shake of her dusky curls she dismissed all sympathetic feelings from her mind and concentrated on Jared's ultimate plans for her. Pity Jared Delaney? What utter nonsense!

"Enact me no Cheltenham Tragedies please, my lord. It is but a house. Now, if you are done with your bout of conscience I suggest we go inside. I feel the need of a hot tub."

Jared released her as if he had just been stung. "Don't try me too far with your poisonous tongue, Amanda. We stand in my territory now—and you are completely in my control. You would be wise to measure your words."

"Please don't deign to tell me what would be wise, Jared. My stepfather said it would be wise of me to listen to him. Had I done so, I would by now be surrounded by lecherous old men who wanted a young wife in their beds. You said I would be wise to allow you to accompany me to Fox Chase, and look what has happened. I am so utterly sick of people telling me to be wise. They only mean I should do what *they* think is best. I am a woman grown, Jared, and it seems to me I would be wisest to start listening to *myself*. At least I could be sure *my* best interests would be served." She turned abruptly and mounted the stairs to the front door.

Jared followed and brushed past her to open the door, then bowed deeply and flourished one hand to usher her inside ahead of him. She inclined her head stiffly, looking as regal as a queen despite her stained riding habit.

With head lifted high she strode purposefully into the grand entrance hall, casting her eyes over high walls adorned in ancient flags and shields. Jared shook his head ruefully as he watched her.

Amanda was the most confusing woman he had ever met! She

appeared equally at ease when conversing with grooms in a stable as when defying the *haut ton*. He had seen her beautifully gowned; he had seen her dressed in outgrown muslins. But whether standing over him, laughing down while he lay sprawled in the mud, or facing him toe to toe in a verbal battle—or even lying beneath him in the first throes of passion—he could never override the feeling that she was first and foremost a lady of quality.

Any other woman would have succumbed to hysterics long before this. But then, any other woman would never have dared to so defy convention by running away from her guardian. How could anything so small and soft be made of such stern stuff? Look at her now, he mused, standing in this great drafty hall, surrounded by moldy antiques, alone and unknowing of her fate. Still her shoulders remained unbowed as she stood stripping off her riding gloves, gazing around her as if she were mistress of this mausoleum.

And here he was, asking her forgiveness for rescuing her from Denton and taking on a useless old man, not to mention a runaway orphan, to please her. He could have taken her at any time within the past few days and eased this burning in his loins. She should, in fact, right now be pleading for mercy, her eyes swimming in tears as she begged for him to deal gently with her.

Instead it was he who felt uneasy, he who felt insecure and faintly out of step. Well, no slip of a girl was going to have Jared Delaney dangling at her shoe strings! Wait until they were legally wed! Then he would be master and the imperious Amanda Boynton would be conquered.

Conquered? Even as his mind formed the word his heart laughed at his folly. Amanda would never be in anyone's power but that she let them. No, he could take her body, but her mind and heart would have to be freely given. Jared, my friend, he berated himself, you erred badly in thinking you could indulge in a lighthearted adventure with Amanda, marry her to maintain the conventions, then leave her at Storm Haven and return to London when your passion died.

It did seem a lark at the time they set out from London, but slowly and inexorably everything changed. Now he knew he wanted this girl as he had never wanted anything in his life. Possessing her body would not be enough for him. He wanted her to care for him, really care for him. Did he love her? Having never known love before, he wasn't sure. And to tell her that he did would only incense her. You don't treat someone you love the way he had treated Amanda these last days.

She would laugh in his face, at best. And at worst? He'd rather not think about that. No, he would have to win her heart. It would be a slow painful process, with only a faint hope of success. But first he would get her free of Denton's clutches. The marriage must take place tonight!

One of the heavy oak doors in the great hall opened, just as the silence between the two was becoming unbearable, and a small, thin, grey-haired woman glided gracefully into the hall and approached Jared.

"So you have finally condescended to arrive, Nephew. You try my patience sorely, young man. First you frighten me out of my wits with crazy boasts concerning that outrageous baggage at Almack's, and then you disappear. I awoke three days ago to face a maddeningly brief missive, brought to me on my breakfast tray, and which completely destroyed my appetite, Cook may quit, ordering me to make myself present here. I have done what you said, Jared, but I fail to see the purpose behind it. And who is this poor bedraggled creature who looks as if she's about ready to fall at my feet in exhaustion? Have you no sense of the proprieties? Bring the child into the salon and let her sit down."

Jared bowed over one blue-veined hand. "And greetings to you, dear Aunt. Thank you for that stirring welcome, and for deserting London at the very first flush of the Season, merely to indulge me. As for the poor little waif you see before you, you have not been formally introduced it is true—but you did see her the other night in King Street. Allow me to introduce Miss Amanda Boynton, the outrageous baggage you mentioned earlier. Amanda, my dearest—and, by the way, *only*—aunt, Lady Agatha Chezwick."

Jared had sent for his aunt? Why? Amanda shot him a questioning look, but he only grinned sheepishly and lifted his shoulders in a resigned shrug. Amanda sank into a demure curtsey and murmured a polite greeting.

Any other woman would have been dumbstruck to find herself confronted with a woman she had just condemned as "baggage"—but Lady Chezwick was not just any woman. "Upon my word, this pretty little child can't be the same girl who appeared in that odious gown." She crossed to Amanda and put a protecting arm around her waist. "Oh, you poor dear, what horrors your stepfather must have made you endure to force you to take such desperate action. And then to have Jared drag you all over the country—for even these old eyes can see you must have traveled on horseback—just to amuse himself. Thank goodness he had the belated good sense to bring you to me. I promise an end to these shenanigans, let me tell you!"

She directed Amanda's steps to the broad staircase and gave her into the care of a middle-aged woman who hastened down the stairs to help support the slight girl, whose shoulders were now shaking noticeably. "You just let Higgins take you to your chambers, my child. Jared insisted on the main chamber being made ready, and I assume it must have been with you in mind. Higgins, ring for bath water and get this child some hot tea and cakes, please. She looks quite done in. Now don't you worry, dear. I shall be up directly I finish boxing my nephew's ears, if I can reach that high. He shall feel the sharp edge of my tongue for this episode, I assure you. Don't you fret now, Aunt Agatha will set all to rights."

As Amanda mounted the stairs only Higgins knew—and only Jared suspected—that Amanda's shoulders were moving in suppressed mirth, not tears.

Only when they had disappeared down the upstairs gallery did Lady Chezwick turn to face Jared, a long lecture just forming on her lips.

But Jared cut her short. "Have the portmanteaux arrived?"

"What? Those large boxes that were delivered this morning? I didn't know what they contained but I had them sent to the servants' quarters. Such a motley-looking collection I have never seen."

"It would figure. Denton would not spend his blunt on anything that wasn't noticeable. That baggage contains Amanda's clothing. Have them sent to her chambers and let Higgins unpack. I felt sure Denton would see the advantages in obeying my instructions. We shall have no problems from that quarter at least. I do hope the dust-covers are off the furniture in here? Ah, I knew I could rely on you, Aunt Agatha." He walked into the main salon and rang for a servant. When the footman arrived he instructed him to set off at once for the village and bring back the parson. "Tell him to come prepared to perform a marriage ceremony in the chapel tonight."

Jared had finally accomplished what she had been striving unsuccessfully for many years to do. Having prepared to do battle with her nephew by demanding an immediate wedding, his aunt was entirely speechless. She staggered to a nearby chair and collapsed her body into it. "Jared?" she croaked in entreaty.

Jared left her dangling in suspense while he rang for brandy and ordered an early dinner served in the small dining room. When he gauged he had stretched his aunt's patience to the breaking point he put down his glass and explained his plans.

It seemed Jared had had a busy night of it after he deposited his aunt in Half Moon Street. After tracking down Lord Cunningham at White's and badgering him into issuing a special license, he had sent a note to Peregrine Denton advising him that he, Lord Storm, was marrying his stepdaughter at Storm Haven with only his aunt in attendance. Denton's absence was at the expressed request of the bride. The reason for such haste, if anyone should be so crude as to ask, was the ardor of the groom—though Jared doubted anyone would dare raise any questions, for Lord Storm was a law unto himself.

In addition, Amanda would require all her personal belongings sent on at once. They were traveling in a single coach, the note explained, with no room for her luggage because Lady Chezwick would serve as chaperone on the journey. He, Jared, was assured of Denton's blessings on the union, he wrote, and his man of business was drawing up a detailed marriage settlement that would be amenable to all.

Jared had then, he informed his awestruck aunt, instructed his valet to pack his belongings for him and travel to Storm Haven only after Lady Chezwick departed, for the sake of secrecy—and mostly to amuse himself at his aunt's expense, while he himself set off to intercept the young runaway. "It seems you took your time, dear Aunt, if Simmons has not yet arrived."

"At my age, Jared, I do not travel unless prepared for any contingency. Not everyone sets off on a journey with your helter-skelter attitude. But I am confused. That child—a runaway?"

Jared passed over her remarks and continued, "Nevertheless, Simmons should arrive directly. If not I shall be obliged to get myself riveted while in riding dress—but no matter." He leaned back in his chair and sighed deeply. "Ah, Aunt, I cannot tell you the excitement of the past days. I haven't felt this entertained in years."

"My felicitations, Nephew. I too have been known to kick up a lark now and then in my youth, but I must say you have far outdone anything I have ever known. Why, if you desired to wed that poor girl, did you have to go through all this pretense? She has no portion I know, but it is by no means a misalliance as she is quite acceptable—or was until three days ago. Where *have* you two been for the past three days?"

"Aunt, I wouldn't have missed these last days for the Gold Cup at Ascot. You have no idea the adventures we've had." He leaned forward in his chair and became suddenly serious. "I will admit to having certain misgivings now over handling the matter in just this way. At times I think Amanda has grown to like me a little, and then there are times when I feel she hates me entirely. Perhaps if I had stopped her flight before it ever got under way and approached her stepfather for her hand, things would be less complicated. But she would never have accepted anyone of her stepfather's choosing, I am assured. And besides, I am a full ten years older than she. Perhaps she would have refused me. The opportunity to do it the way I did was just too good to be missed."

"Jared, you seem to think I know what you are talking about. You must remember that I am not in your confidence. All I know is that you made a spectacle of yourself at Almack's with the girl, announced to me you would marry her, and then disappeared for three days—leaving only a note to meet you here. Now you show up with the girl in tow, no luggage or companion with you, and announce you are being married tonight. For the sake of her good name I entirely agree, but my head is reeling with questions for which you have given me no answers. Please, if you hold me in any affection, tell me what is going on!"

Jared poured himself another brandy and launched into a detailed explanation of the events leading up to the moment, omitting only his weaknesses in the meadow and at the inn, and telling only one outright lie. He told his aunt he had convinced Amanda to come to Storm Haven where he would protect her far better than her old nurse ever could, but completely deleted from the tale his threat to make her his mistress.

By the time he was finished recounting his third de-horsing, his aunt was dissolved in mirth and wiping her eyes with a fine cambric handkerchief.

"Oh, Jared, you have at last met your match! But I think you refine too much on Amanda's supposed hatred for you. I am a woman, too, and although I am well past the years of romance I believe the girl is not indifferent to you. You are a fine young man, Jared, and she is an intelligent girl. I understand now why you were so taken with her. You showed good judgement for perhaps the first time in your life, although you did fly in the face of all convention.

"But then you wouldn't be your mother's son if you did less. Ah, the adventures my sister and I had until . . ." Her voice trailed off and then she went on. "No, you would never be happy with any of those insipid girls I kept pushing at you, and I think I always knew it. This one will lead you a merry chase, and I look forward to sitting back and watching the fun. It will add a bit of spice to my declining years."

She arose and went over to place a light kiss on Jared's knitted brow. "Ah, dear heart, marriage will be the making of you. I must go now and help the bride-to-be with her toilette, as it grows late. You have me anxious to make her further acquaintance. Any woman who can put you into such a taking is a pearl beyond price." She got halfway to the door and then laughed aloud, "Held you off with a knife! Ah, to have seen that!"

Jared sat in the huge, depressing room for a long time after his aunt departed. His eyes raked over the ugly, dark furniture that he had known and hated since his childhood. Why had he never changed anything? It had been ten years since his father died, but his mark was still indelible in every room.

Jared had departed Storm Haven for London as soon as he could after his father's burial and had not returned for nearly five years—indulging himself in a life of gaiety and excess that was the talk of the city. His visits here since then were made only of necessity, and even then he never stayed above a few days. Perhaps he kept the house the same as a sort of punishment, a living reminder of his dark heritage. But it was time and more that he assumed the reins of his vast estate. Hadn't his man of business told him that often enough?

He would give Amanda a free hand in redecorating the place; perhaps she could force some life back into these dreary rooms. If his aunt had her way, she would tell him, a few young Delaneys running around the corridors would dissolve the gloomy atmosphere.

A scratching at the door diverted him from his thoughts and a footman entered to tell him his valet had arrived. With a last look at the bare wall over the fireplace, Jared turned and trod heavily from the room.

Amanda felt quite refreshed after her bath and the light meal Higgins had brought her. She was reclining between the silken sheets of the enormous four-poster bed in the attractive room, modestly attired in one of Lady Chezwick's old-fashioned dressing gowns. Higgins had drawn the curtains before she left, and Amanda felt her body relaxing into the comfortable mattress as she succumbed to weariness.

Her body was weightless as she hovered dreamily between awareness and the sweet call of sleep, secure in the knowledge that "Aunt Agatha," as she had called herself, would protect her from Jared.

"No, no, *no!* This will not do, this will not do at all! Get up, my dear, time is a-wasting!"

Amanda sat bolt upright at the commanding tones, every nerve tingling and her heart beating wildly in her chest as she tried to gain control of her sleep-muddled mind. She shook her head to clear it and turned to see Lady Chezwick in the process of throwing back the draperies so the last rays of the sun hit Amanda squarely in the face.

"Come, come, my dear, rise and shine. There will be plenty of time for lying abed after the ceremony. Oh, dear, wasn't that naughty of me! Never mind an old woman. You must help me go through these boxes now to choose a suitable gown. Pray heaven you chose your own ensembles, for if Denton had a hand in it they will all have to be discarded. Never did care a rap for that man." She stopped in the center of the room and tapped her small foot in exasperation. "Did you not hear me? You must get up!"

Ceremony? Gowns? What ceremony? Whose gowns? I must be dreaming, thought Amanda. She pinched her upper arm. "Ouch!" She wasn't dreaming. She heard a knock at the door and turned to see a footman bringing some battered portmanteaux into the room. They were hers! How did they get here?

She was not to be given time to figure it out. Lady Chezwick had already opened one trunk and was ruthlessly judging and discarding gowns. She dove into one box until it seemed she might disappear, and then a triumphant "Aha!" issued from its depths. She came up flushed and smiling, holding in her arms a white-silk gown purchased for Amanda's hoped-for court appearance.

It was far and away Amanda's favorite, a deceptively simple creation which molded to her figure and whispered when she walked. A further dive into the box produced a pair of white satin slippers and a soft white lace shawl that Lady Chezwick eyed with a speculative gleam.

"These will do nicely. Obviously Denton had the good sense to allow you to choose your own gowns. You have exceptionally fine taste, my dear. All the gowns are quite pretty, but this one is perfect for the ceremony."

Amanda ripped back her covers and placed her bare feet on the floor. As she felt the cold of the stone on her soles she was convinced she was definitely awake.

"If you please, Lady Chezwick . . ."

"Aunt Agatha, my dear, please, I see no sense in standing on formalities now that we are all going to be family, do you? And just when I had about abandoned all hope. We'll have to get Higgins to do something with your hair—you do have quite a bit of it, don't you? But never mind, we will contrive. Higgins is monstrously talented, you know."

Amanda held up her hands in mock despair. "Please! Lady Chez—er, *Aunt Agatha*—would you be so kind as to tell me what is going on? I am all at sea."

Lady Chezwick looked at her quite blankly for a moment and then remembered Jared's confession. She had been so caught up in the preparations for the hurried wedding, she had quite forgotten the bride still did not know she was indeed to be a bride. "Oh, I *am* sorry, Amanda—and I will call you Amanda, it is such a lovely name—but then you are a lovely girl, ah, my sister would have been so happy. In fact I'm sure she knows and is looking down right now and smiling at us. Not Carlton though. No, Carlton will be looking down and frowning, or should I say looking up, for I am sure he is not . . ."

"Lady Chezwick! Please!"

"What? Oh, I am sorry, my dear. You must stop me, I do get carried away sometimes. Jared says I am an incurable chatter-box. Why only the other day at Lady Flemington's . . ."

"*Aunt Agatha!* I am going to have a fit of the vapors if you do not tell me this minute just why my boxes are here and what ceremony you are talking about." Amanda was caught between an urge to laugh at this adorable old woman and an equally strong impulse to shake her until her teeth rattled.

Lady Chezwick returned to the point at hand and announced quite calmly, "Why, your marriage to my nephew, of course. We have less than an hour to prepare. I thought we could easily wait until tomorrow, but . . . why, my dear, you look positively dreadful! Here, sit down while I call Higgins. You *are* going to have the vapors," she cried accusingly, "and you promised you wouldn't if I told you about the ceremony."

Lady Chezwick helped the stunned girl to the bed, and as Amanda collapsed on it in a daze Lady Chezwick ran to the doorway and called loudly for Higgins. As her maid was waiting directly outside her ears were ringing slightly as she listened to Lady Chezwick's instructions concerning the smelling salts deemed necessary to revive the swooning girl.

Amanda had not fainted, however. Only to herself did she admit that she had certainly come close, but although the desire to sink into oblivion was enticing she knew she had to keep her wits about her.

While the search for smelling salts continued, Amanda sat up and announced her recovery. Inwardly shaking with rage or relief—she wasn't sure which—she asked for an explanation of Jared's decision to have an immediate marriage ceremony.

"It's really quite simple, my dear girl. My nephew has compromised you. Not only did he travel with you unaccompanied across half of England, but you were seen in his company by no less than twenty members of the *ton* at that horrid inn. There is no question, then, that you should marry as quickly as possible. Jared has procured a special license, and the curate will be arriving at any moment. Now, no more dawdling."

Amanda had no idea what a special license was. All she knew was that Jared was somehow being forced to marry her.

The fact that he had sent for her gowns did not surprise her. Obviously he had planned from the outset to bring her eventually to Storm Haven. Of course, even a mistress must have clothes. That Denton would have agreed to send them along just proved his threat that he would sell her to the highest bidder. It did not occur to her that Jared had no notion of that particular threat.

But nowhere in her mind could she explain Aunt Agatha. It was obviously she who insisted on the wedding, so why did he send for her? She decided to ask the woman in question.

"I am here at Jared's request, as you know," she answered honestly. "My nephew told me you had to go into the country to rescue a horse or some such thing. I must admit I didn't pay too much attention to that part of his story—something to do with tempests in a teapot or something, and old men and . . . a beggar, I think. I did like the part about the knife, though. That was very good." Lady Chezwick saw Amanda's face reddening and hastened to clarify her position.

"My nephew told me as we drove home from Almack's that he planned to marry you. He just wanted a little frolic first, I suppose. I imagine he has me here to stop the wagging tongues that would say you had eloped. As far as London knows, so Jared tells me, we three left London together and came directly here for the ceremony. The night at the inn will soon be forgotten, as not too many people saw you and none knew your name. Why, my dear girl, whatever did I say? You look positively incensed!"

Amanda was pacing the floor furiously. "So! He planned to marry me from the very first! He let me go through the past three days in constant fear, blackmailing me with Harrow and Tom, compromising me at a public inn, frightening me out of my wits by suggesting that I would become a scarlet woman. And all of it to *amuse* himself at my expense. He has been laughing up his sleeve at me all along! I ran away in all seriousness, but to him it was all just a joke—an excuse for a good time! Then he has the nerve to tell you what happened with the knife. Am I to have no privacy? Did he delight in telling you how he almost ravished me last night at a public inn? Of course he did, for how else would you know about the knife? And now he wants to marry me? Ha! Isn't it a bit late for him to be thinking of the proprieties?"

She stopped pacing abruptly and Lady Chezwick rubbed her aching neck, for the girl moved so fast it was getting increasingly hard to follow her. The child was making no sense. Jared had rescued her from her stepfather and was prepared to marry her. What could possibly be wrong in that? Ravish her? Jared made no mention of any ravishment. The girl was hysterical.

Suddenly Amanda picked up the lovely white gown and, bundling it into a ball, hurled it to the floor and ground her bare heel on it. "I wouldn't marry Jared Delaney if he were Prinney himself!" she announced baldly.

It was Lady Chezwick's turn to swoon, and she did it with the ease of long practice. When she roused it was to the smell of burnt feathers and the sight of Amanda hurriedly dressing in a dark green riding habit that had been pulled from one of the cases. Higgins helped support the old woman into a sitting position as she gasped out, "Where are you going?"

Amanda jammed a green feathered riding hat down on her dark curls. "Anywhere!" she shrieked. "Nowhere! Just as long as it's away from here! You're all quite mad, you know."

Lady Chezwick struggled to her feet. "Wait, Amanda! You don't understand. Jared wants to marry you, he just wanted to have a little lark in the country for a few days. You were running away from your stepfather, weren't you? He had no time to approach Denton to ask for your hand. Jared was smitten with you as soon as he met you, I swear he was."

Amanda stopped in her tracks. Lady Chezwick had twice now said that Jared had planned to marry her all along. Her lips curled as she remembered some of the lighter moments on their journey, and his kindnesses to Harrow and Tom. It would even explain Harrow's indifference to her plight. Jared must have taken him into his confidence.

She walked to the mirror and adjusted her hat. She studied her reflection and watched her color rise as she remembered Jared's kisses and his muttered "Not here. Not now." Was he waiting for their vows to be exchanged before he possessed her? She admitted to herself that, while part of her recoiled from becoming Lord Storm's mistress, another alien part of her trembled in anticipation.

But marriage? That was beyond her expectations. She could be Lady Storm, wife of one of the richest men in England. Her mind whirled as she pictured Jared by her side and small children gathered around her feet. Jared's children.

Would it really be so bad? After all, Jared had never intended to ravish her. He had assumed all along that they would marry. She brought herself up short. *Assumed!* That was it. That was what rankled her. He had been playing with her all along, amusing himself at her expense, and then he hadn't even bothered to ask her for her hand—he had just sent his aunt upstairs to dress her and inform her of the wedding.

The arrogance of the man! He was insufferable! Her chest heaved in her agitation as she considered the character of the man who had picked her for his bride. In an uncanny parallel to Jared's earlier thoughts, she likened herself to a horse.

It was to her as if he had looked over all the nags at

Tattersall's, and when one filly had taken his fancy he had taken her for a run in the country to see if she were saddleworthy. Well, Amanda Boynton was no sweet-going filly, and she was damned if she'd be a brood mare either! How dare he assume all he had to do was crook his finger and she'd fall on his neck in gratitude. She was right to leave. Ignoring Lady Chezwick's frantic pleas, she picked up her riding gloves from the vanity and left the room without another word.

Lady Chezwick was frantic. "Call my nephew at once, Higgins. If she gets away Jared will have both our skins!"

Amanda tore from the room, hesitating for only a moment to get her bearings, then headed for the staircase—and freedom. Halfway down the stairs she slowed her steps and cast a quick look over her shoulder to see if there was anyone in pursuit. There was none; Lady Chezwick must have taken refuge in another faint and Higgins was occupied taking care of her.

She felt sorry for the old woman, but she had to get away. On tiptoe she descended the remainder of the stairs and crept stealthily toward the door. Her hand was on the latch when the voice came.

"That's a devilishly fetching riding habit, Amanda, but I fear you have no time for a ride before dinner." As he talked, Jared approached her calmly and placed a hand under her elbow. "I'm sure you would rather return to your room and dress for the evening meal, as I am assured it will be delicious."

"I wish to ride, my lord," came the weak reply. He had frightened her half out of her wits.

"That is odd. I could have sworn eight hours in the saddle today would be enough even for you. If not, at least have a little consideration for your horse. Come with me to the main salon and I'll pour you a sherry. I think we have a few things to settle."

Realizing there was no escape, and suddenly too weary to argue, Amanda allowed him to lead her into the salon. As she sank into a chair her eyes searched the room and her pert nose wrinkled in distaste.

Jared saw her expression. "I quite agree, Amanda. It *is* horrendous. A veritable mirror of my father's personality, in fact. Here, perhaps some sherry will ease the burden of this unsightly view."

She accepted the glass thankfully, and they studied each other silently for a few minutes. How handsome Jared looked in his evening dress, Amanda thought. Why must he be so odious?

"Your aunt informed me of your plans for a marriage between us, my lord," she ventured at last. "I thank you for your concern for my reputation, but I assure you it will not be necessary for you to make so large a sacrifice on my behalf. My ruin was of my own making." She was keeping a tight rein on her temper and hoping to get through this discussion without losing hold of it.

"But what of our bargain, Amanda?" His twinkling blue eyes could not hide his glee at seeing her so obviously discomfited. "You promised to stay at Storm Haven with me until I tired of you."

Crash! Amanda's glass shattered in a hundred pieces as she hurled it to the floor in disgust. "For the sake of your aunt I tried to have an adult conversation with you, but it is impossible! Lady Chezwick has told me of your plans to marry me. For some twisted reason known only to yourself you made that decision the night we met. Everything that has passed between us since that moment has been utter farce and means nothing to me."

Jared raised one dark eyebrow and looked deeply into her eyes. They were both standing now, and the tension in the room was almost visible. "*Everything?* Amanda, do you really mean that?" His voice was low and husky. He appeared to be looking deep inside her, searching out her true feelings—feelings that must be kept hidden at all costs. If he knew how he affected her she would be forever in his power.

Amanda finally opened her mouth to speak; then closed it again without answering him. Surely he could hear her heart, it was thudding so loudly in her ears. She tried to tear her eyes away from his face but found she was powerless to move.

"Jared, I—" she ventured, but he stopped her with his mouth as it came down on hers with a force she didn't know he possessed. He held her to him in a crushing embrace as rockets exploded behind her closed eyes and bolts of lightning streaked down her spine.

What did it matter if he had tricked her? What was the harm in assuming she would be glad to marry him? It was true, wasn't it? She was here, wasn't she, here with him—where her heart had been telling her she belonged. She gave herself up to the moment and returned his ardor kiss for kiss until a voice pried them apart.

"Jared, I have a confession to—*oh, my!*—I see you have

found her. Well, I am assured the wedding will go off as scheduled. I also see that I am decidedly *de trop*. I would have to be a fool not to think so. Isn't this just wonderful! It is just as I had always hoped it would be for, oh, so many . . ."

"*Aggie!*" Jared broke in with a good-natured admonishment. "Get yourself the devil out of here before I break your neck!"

Miss Amanda Boynton became Lady Storm just two hours later.

It was a simple ceremony, unmarked except for the flustered stutterings of the awestruck young curate and the copious weeping of Lady Chezwick. But to Amanda it was the culmination of a life-long dream. She was married to a man she loved, and she would be as happy as her parents had been in their marriage. Oh, Jared had not said he loved her—it was too soon for that—but it was obvious he cared for her or he wouldn't have wed her. Of one thing Amanda was becoming increasingly sure: Jared Delaney did nothing under threat or force.

Likewise she had not told him she loved him, although she was sure her love was written all over her face as she gazed at him during the ceremony.

After Lady Chezwick's interruption there had been time only for a hurried meal and a quick toilette before she donned her hastily-pressed gown.

No, since that first embrace in the main salon private speech had been impossible, and the only words that had been exchanged were ones tame enough for Lady Chezwick's ears. But Jared's eyes spoke volumes, and that was enough.

Now, alone in her chamber except for Higgins, Amanda was suddenly attacked by a fit of nervousness. She had drained the wine glass Jared sent to her room, but it did little to ease her tension. She was so inexperienced—would she disappoint him? While she had mounted the stairs in almost unladylike haste, she now lingered over her evening toilette. As she sat in front of her vanity, slowly brushing out her long black hair, she spied Higgins in the mirror and gave a gasp of dismay at the virginal sleeping gown the maid brought out from the depths of one of the trunks. Denton had spent money on nothing but necessities, and her old gowns had not been replaced. Higgins held up the best of the bunch—a high-necked, long-sleeved, white lawn gown almost three years old, and embroidered across the bodice in Amanda's own childish design of rosebuds.

"Oh, Higgins," she wailed, "whatever will Lord Storm think when he sees that gown? I'll look a complete child. Quickly, braid my hair and pin it up. Perhaps that will add to my age."

Higgins sniffed loudly. What did the gown matter anyway? A man was a man, be he servant or lord, and if Higgins knew Lord Storm at all she was sure the gown was to be quickly discarded in any event. Poor little creature. Trapped into marriage with a rakehell like Lord Storm and then forced to live in this haunted house. Any child coming from a union under this roof would probably be born a monster.

After Higgins finally left the chamber Amanda was hard-pressed not to call her back and ask her to stay. Amanda's mother died before she and Amanda could have any serious discussions on love and marriage. Nanny's only enlightenments consisted mostly of words like "duty," "submission," and "your husband will tell you." She chided herself for her foolishness: Jared would be kind to her, she was sure of it. Wasn't kissing pleasurable, and his hands on her body? But that couldn't be all there was to it, she was sure. She snuggled farther down between the covers and tucked the blanket up under her chin. And waited.

Thus Jared found her, a tiny creature who barely dented the mattress, toes no more than halfway down the great bed. His eyes traveled the length of the coverlet to encounter a small white face filled with enormous golden eyes.

"You look quite lost, imp. Do sit up," he remarked.

She slowly edged her way to the backboard of the ancestral marriage bed, for that is what Lady Chezwick told her it was, and raised herself up—carefully keeping the bedclothes about her chin. She watched warily as Jared undid his dressing gown and slid beneath the covers next to her. She thought crazily to herself that she was glad he didn't wear a nightcap.

He also propped himself against the backboard and, turning his eyes to her, questioned, "Tell me, infant, do you have any idea what is to happen next?"

"N-n-no," Amanda stammered, inwardly cursing herself for her ignorance. "I only know that it is something like what I saw Cook's cat do to a stray beneath my window one evening." She averted her head and plucked nervously at the bedsheets. "At least, I think so."

Jared gave a throaty chuckle. "I agree, the basics are the same for all God's creatures, dear heart. But I assure you, we humans are by far more blessed in technique."

Amanda sat up straight in indignation. "Now you are making fun of me, my lord," she accused.

"God's death!" Jared exclaimed, taking in the concealing material of Amanda's best nightgown. "What do you call that contraption, madam? You look like a novice in a convent. And why, by all that's holy, is your hair drawn up like a governess? I feel you have armored yourself against me."

Amanda hopped from the bed in a fury. "You were the one—if I remember correctly, my lord—who insisted on this hasty marriage. I had precious little time to go collecting a trousseau. I realize you must be more accustomed to the nightwear, or lack of it, of your many lady friends. But until you wheedled my consent from me I was not contemplating marriage within the near future, and had no reason to change my style of sleepwear." She turned to face the warmth of the fireplace, little knowing that the glow of the fire silhouetted her figure beneath the threadbare gown and cast a golden halo around her sedate braids.

Gad, she entices even in such virginal attire! her husband thought. The thought of those beautifully rounded limbs, encased in filmy lace, made small beads of perspiration break out on Jared's brow. He rose slowly and crossed the room to his bride.

"Forgive me, imp," he said as he placed tender hands on her shoulders and reached down to tease the nape of her neck with his lips. Amanda remained ramrod stiff and unforgiving. "I am an unmitigated scoundrel to upset you, and I beg most sincerely for your forgiveness." His lips continued their gentle assault on her neck, and with the unaccustomed wine Jared had pressed on her both at dinner and after the ceremony clouding her mind, she found herself unable to remember the cause of her anger.

Slowly Jared turned his wife to face him and cupped her face between his hands. "I know you are frightened, Amanda, but I promise to treat you with all the consideration my bride deserves. I am not a complete bounder."

Amanda's eyes searched his face in the firelight. She looked deeply into his eyes and saw no trace of mockery. Slowly she lowered her eyes and gave an involuntary shiver—was it in fear or anticipation?—as with deft fingers he began to take down her hair. The ease with which he accomplished this feat was not lost on her, betraying as it did his expertise in the art, but instead of the anger she expected to feel she was relieved that he was so expert. A giggle escaped her lips, and Jared stopped in his unraveling of her braid to gaze at her in wonder.

"Imp?" he questioned.

Amanda blushed profusely. "I was only just thinking, my lord, that I am ignorant enough; if we were both of us of the same lack, tonight would be trying indeed."

Jared broke into a wide grin and exclaimed, "You are incorrigible, Amanda, incorrigible."

Amanda's laughter now sprang forth in earnest, and all tension vanished. As the mirth died, two sets of eyes met and held in a growing sense of wonder—the innocent surprised at her passion and the experienced astonished at his nervousness.

For a long time afterwards silence filled the room, until a log crashing into the grate brought them back to their surroundings. Two bodies slowly disengaged on the bed and Jared pulled Amanda's head onto his shoulder while he cradled her against him. At last the silence was broken as a sleepy, wine-befuddled voice whispered in wonder, "So that is how it is done, my lord. I do believe Nanny didn't understand the procedure at all." This proclamation was followed by a delicate hiccup, and then Amanda trustingly slipped her fingers into the soft mat of hair on her husband's chest. Before he could form a suitable answer to her announcement, she was fast asleep.

Sleep did not come as easily for Lord Storm. As he lay there, allowing his arm to go numb in fear of moving lest it disturb the small girl, he realized that he had never felt for anyone what he felt for this golden-eyed little minx.

He had lain with many women, more than he cared to recall, but never had he felt any emotions akin to the possessiveness and desire to cherish that overcame him now. With his free hand he eased the covers over them and placed a light kiss on her hair.

He had made a mistake tonight, but tomorrow he would have his aunt have a talk with Amanda about preventing any pregnancy. This one night could not make any difference—after all, he had been lying with Blanche for almost a year and there had been no problems. At the thought of his former mistress a hard look came over his face. Well, that part of his life was over. He would send her a draft on his bank in the morning.

He was not in the least tired. In fact, he felt he could remain awake all night, listening to Amanda's quiet even breathing as she lay curled up against him. Jared had known he desired Amanda, but now that the desire was satisfied he could barely wait until she awoke and he could hear again that sweet voice and see that engaging smile. With Amanda, even arguing was a pleasure.

Damn it all to hell! This wasn't in his plan. Slowly he moved Amanda back to her own side of the huge bed, and turning his back on her, he beat his pillows in frustration before resting his head in the dent he had made. He couldn't be in love with the brat!

He couldn't.

Chapter Five

ALTHOUGH Amanda had been awake for a few minutes, she felt strangely unwilling to open her eyes. It felt so good lying there between the smooth linen sheets as her body was warmed by their silken touch. Strange, she had never felt this tingling sensation of closeness before. She tentatively put a hand on her stomach and her eyes shot open wide in amazement. Where was her nightgown? She lifted the sheet and peered down at herself. She was naked!

Slowly the hazy events of the previous evening came back to her. She was married—married to Jared Delaney—and last night, in this very bed he had . . . .

Her face flushed wildly as the full force of her recent activities was brought into focus, and she lifted her head to see if her new husband was still beside her. That slight movement sent a blinding pain across her forehead, and she sank back into the pillows before trying the maneuver again, this time more cautiously. He was gone, thank goodness. She needed time to think, but first she craved to quench her burning thirst.

As if at a signal, the door opened and a young housemaid bustled in bearing a tray with a steaming cup of chocolate. Amanda hurriedly dove deeper under the covers in embarrassment.

"Mornin' milady, 'tis a beautiful mornin', tis it not? Me name is Sally. Lady Chezwick said I wuz to let yer sleep as long as yer wanted, but I got ter thinkin' yer might want yer chocolate now, it bein' after eleven and all." She set the cup on the table next to the bed, curtsied briefly, and scurried out, giggling behind her hand.

After eleven! Amanda sprang from the bed, ignoring the crashing cymbals in her head, and hastily donned her nightgown

ch still lay on the floor near the fireplace. After sipping her
chocolate she rang for Sally once again, bathed quickly, and
dressed in a white muslin morning gown with green tracings on
the bodice and hem. Armored in the trappings of a young
woman of fashion, she set off in search of her husband.

She found Lady Chezwick firmly ensconced on a sofa in the
forbidding main salon, talking to herself under her breath.

The throbbing in Amanda's temples had faded and she was
feeling remarkably better, well enough to enjoy the spectacle of
her newly-acquired Aunt Agatha holding a fierce argument with
herself.

"I won't do it, I don't care what Jared says. It's indecent.
That's what it is, indecent. But on the other hand, what if he's
right? Could I ever live with myself if I failed him in this? Oh,
what am I going to do?" The fine cambric handkerchief in her
lap was in shreds due to her agitation, and impetuously Amanda
crossed to her and planted a kiss on her cheek.

"Why, Aunt Agatha, whatever can be the problem on such a
glorious morning as this? I'm sure if Jared wants you to do
something it is definitely for the best. My husband," her heart
swelled in her breast at the word, "is a very clever man, and I'm
sure he has your best interests at heart."

Lady Chezwick looked up at Amanda, her face full of hope.
"Do you really feel that way, Amanda? Oh, that relieves my
mind considerably. I never realized Jared could be as adamant
as he was with me this morning. Why, he fairly raged at me when
I refused to do as he commanded. I always knew Carlton had
hurt him deeply, but I never supposed it would come to this."

Amanda could see the woman was upsetting herself again and
quickly changed the subject to the one that interested her most
at the moment—the whereabouts of her husband.

"Oh, he was here with me all morning, arguing I fear, but
then a footman came in to tell him someone had arrived at the
stables. Farrow? Arrow? Why, Amanda, where are you going?
You haven't eaten."

"I'll wait until luncheon now, Aunt Agatha. I must get to the
stables," Amanda tossed over her shoulder as she hurried out
the door.

Once outside she located the stables easily and, hiking her
skirts to an unladylike height, set off at a run. As she came in
sight of the stables she skidded to an abrupt halt at the sight of

her husband's shining black head towering over those of Harrow and Tom. She didn't think he would appreciate his new wife carrying on like an overjoyed schoolgirl at the sight of him.

Jared was the first to see her, and he searched her face for any sign that she had talked with his aunt. After giving him a shy smile she turned away, seeking out Harrow to share her newfound happiness.

To Amanda, Harrow was the father she had lost, the brother she did not have, the playmate she had been denied. Tutor, companion, comforting shoulder, the relationship of mistress and servant had never occurred to either of them, so she was brought up short by Harrow's deferential "Good morning, my lady."

"Harrow?" she questioned. "Is that any way to greet me?"

Harrow colored under his weathered skin and shifted back and forth in his dusty boots. "Yer the Lady Storm now, Miss Mandy. I'm just a groom, and not even head groom at that."

Amanda turned her face to her husband's. "Jared, is this on your orders?"

"It certainly is not. I imagine Harrow thought this up all by himself on his way here. How about it, Harrow? Is that any way to greet your Miss Mandy?"

"My lord?" Harrow was looking decidedly uncomfortable. "It wouldn't be proper to treat her ladyship as if she were still a child. If I am to live here, I must know my place."

Jared saw the tears in Amanda's eyes and addressed Harrow sharply. "You, sir, are trying my patience mightily. My wife considers you her friend and so do I. Your position here is without question: You are the new head groom, as I'm sending Barkham to London, charged with maintaining my stables and breeding for me the best horses in England. That shouldn't be too hard with Tempest in the stables. Miss Amanda and I also entrust you with the care of that young scamp there, and hope you will train him as your successor before you choose to retire. Tom seems to enjoy horses and he appears an intelligent, if rather dirty, child. Now, if that is satisfactory to you, I would appreciate it if you would properly greet my wife and wipe that unhappy frown from her otherwise appealing face."

"Yes, my lord!" Harrow exclaimed, and opened his arms to Amanda as he had done when she had arrived at Fox Chase. And as she did then, Amanda flung herself upon him and hugged him fiercely. "Oh, Harrow, you old dear, you scared me so. I love you."

Then she placed a kiss on Tom's grimy cheek and ruffled his hair as he looked adoringly up into her eyes. "I love you, too, scamp, but I wonder what you look like under all that dirt. When I return here this afternoon to take Tempest out for a run I expect to be able to see your clean face, do you understand?"

"Aye, milady, aye, even if it hurts, milady," Tom agreed, dreading his first contact with soap in over two years.

As Jared and Amanda fell into step on the way back to the house for luncheon Jared inquired, "You slept well, Amanda?"

Suddenly shy again, Amanda averted her eyes as she confirmed her good night's sleep. "But my head ached abominably this morning, my lord. Why was that, do you think?"

"That, my infant, is the price you must pay for being foxed."

"Me? Foxed? Oh, Jared, I was *not!* How dare you say such a thing."

"Well, maybe not completely foxed, but certainly a trifle tipsy."

Amanda was embarrassed and took refuge in anger. "Well, if I was it was all your fault. Plying me with wine all evening, and then that brandy you forced on me after the ceremony. Filthy stuff."

Jared's blue eyes were twinkling in amusement. "I did it for your own good, my little sweetheart. Brandy is good for the nerves."

"Oh," Amanda answered in a small voice. "Thank you."

Jared stopped just outside the main doors of the house and put his hands on Amanda's shoulders. "Did the brandy just help make last night endurable, or did you enjoy it even a little bit?"

Amanda averted her eyes. "I should be asking the same of you. Did I—did I disappoint you?"

Jared crushed her against his broad chest and cradled her head with his hands. "Disappoint me? Oh, Amanda, you could never do that. If last night pleasured you only half as much as it pleasured me you would be the happiest woman in England."

She pushed back her head so she could see his face. "It pleasured me, Jared. It pleasured me very much."

She could feel him tremble under her hands, and it amazed her to know that she had the power to affect him this way. Just before their lips met he groaned, "I want you, Mandy. I want you so much." They clung to each other for untold moments, bodies straining for a closer union, and only the sound of the big doors opening brought them back to earth.

"Good heavens, I seem to have done it again!" screeched Aunt Agatha. "Jared, you must find a better place to indulge in these torrid embraces. Think what would happen if the servants found you like this." The hovering butler was dealt a threatening look and disappeared from behind Lady Chezwick to inspect some silver or something. "It is normal to indulge in a little madness—we all do sooner or later—but it might be wise if you exercised a little restraint during the daylight hours."

Jared raised his mouth for only a moment, a devilish look dancing in his eyes. "Shove off, Aunt Agatha, as my young friend Tom would say, or I'll give you a pop on your noggin."

"Jared! To talk to me like that! I wash my hands of you."

As Amanda tried desperately to keep a straight face Jared replied wearily, "If only you would, Aunt, if only you would. But I doubt it highly."

The beleaguered lady turned on her heel and stalked off in high dudgeon, while Lord and Lady Storm hung together in guilty glee.

"We must go after her and apologize. I'm sure she is highly upset." Amanda tried to be serious. "Poor Aunt Agatha," she lamented solemnly, and then giggled.

"Serves her right, the old busybody, though I love her dearly." Suddenly Jared was serious. "Did you talk with her this morning, pet?"

"Oh, she was telling me something about having an argument with you, but I'm afraid I wasn't attending properly. And when she said Harrow had arrived I deserted her entirely. Why? Was it important?"

Jared's eyes darkened. "Yes, sweet child, it is very important. Please find time to talk with her after luncheon. I will busy myself getting Harrow and the boy settled and I'll join you for a ride about three o'clock at the stables. I think we can miss tea this one time, don't you?"

Amanda's brows drew together in a frown that he quickly kissed away. She gave him her promise and they went in to find Lady Chezwick, to do their best to placate her hurt feelings.

* * *

Lady Chezwick patted the space beside her on the sofa and urged Amanda to join her. "This is an exceedingly delicate conversation we are going to have, my dear, and I trust you will allow me to build myself up to it gradually. You see, it all has its roots with my sister Lavinia, Jared's mother."

Amanda listened attentively, for anything having to do with her new husband interested her greatly. Lady Chezwick went on. "Lavinia was the most beautiful girl I have ever seen, and the most lovable." Her eyes misted as she drifted back in time. "Jared is very like her, you know, with his blue eyes and dark hair. Perhaps that made it even worse for Carlton, I sometimes think.

"But I digress. Lavinia was almost twelve years my junior, added to the family rather as an oversight I imagine, but we got on famously. She was always so alive, so vital—ah, the pranks she played on us all! I was already married when she met Carlton. He was much older. I had met him when I first came out myself, and must say I wasn't overly impressed with the man.

"He was handsome, I guess, in a watery sort of way, all blond hair and white skin. And those eyes! Oh, I never did like his eyes, they were so light they were almost colorless. He looked like he had faded in the sun. He and Lavinia looked like night and day when they stood together, but they made a handsome couple.

"But it wasn't his appearance that set me against him, it was his vile temper. When I met him socially he seemed quiet and reserved, but I had heard tales—married women do get to hear more gossip—of his wild rages whenever he was crossed. I tried to tell Lavinia and warn her off him, but she told me he was the model of kindness to her. I don't think she ever did see him angry, and they were married for over five years. I like to think it was her influence that kept him controlled. He certainly reverted soon enough when she was gone."

Lady Chezwick produced a handkerchief from a pocket in her gown and wiped at her eyes. Amanda laid a hand on her arm and whispered, "I understand if you don't want to continue with this, Aunt Agatha. I can have Jared tell me everything himself. It was heartless of him to ask you to do something that obviously upsets you so."

"Oh, no, my dear, please do not," Lady Chezwick pleaded. "He has no idea I am telling you all this. He just expects me to tell you one thing, but I feel you have a right to know the reasoning behind his request. I'm quite all right, really. It is imperative you know this as soon as possible.

"As you may have guessed, Lavinia and Carlton were married at the end of her first Season, much to the distress of the many fine young men who had been courting her devotedly." She spread her hands to encompass the room. "He brought her here as soon as they were married and she never returned to London. He was very jealous, you see, being so much older and quite aware of my sister's beauty. But she never minded. I was very surprised, let me tell you, when I visited here, because Lavinia seemed quite content. She was still so bubbly and full of life, and Carlton doted on her every whim. I guess it is true that opposite natures are drawn to one another.

"Lavinia's only unhappiness was that she seemed unable to bear a child. Twice she had carried for a few months, but she lost both the babies very early. I know it is indelicate of me to speak so plainly in front of a young girl like you, even if you are married, but it will help you to understand."

She rose and walked to the fireplace. "Carlton had my sister painted just after she learned she was pregnant for a third time." She lifted her eyes to the blank wall over the fireplace. "It was a very good likeness of her: I saw it just before Lord Chezwick and I departed for India. The portrait is in the attic where Carlton put it, and I wish it could hang here again as I last saw it."

She turned and studied Amanda's pale face. "You resemble her a bit, Amanda—small and slight with that black hair so like hers. But as I said, her eyes were a deep pure blue, like Jared's. And, ah, what glorious love shone from those eyes out over this room. It wasn't always like this, you know. Lavinia filled the house with color and delicate furniture, but Carlton had it all burned except for what is in the beautiful chamber that is yours now. Yes, when last I saw Lavinia she was the happiest woman in the world."

Suddenly Lady Agatha looked her years. "We were in Bombay when she died. Carlton's note was brief, just saying she had died in childbirth and the child had lived. He didn't even bother telling us whether it was a boy or a girl. I wanted to come home right away, but Lord Chezwick became ill and only after he passed away two years later was I able to return. By that time Storm Haven looked as you see it now, and Carlton was a madman. I know that description sounds harsh, but it is true.

"He wouldn't even let me see Jared, turned me away at his

front door, he did. I tried ever so hard to have Carlton give Jared over to me to raise, because I never did have any children of my own, you know, but he ignored my letters.

"I first saw Jared at his father's funeral. My heart went out to him, and he came back to London with me that very day. I've lived with him now for over ten years and I love him like the son I never had. He was a wild one back then, as if he was alive for the first time and meant to live every moment to the fullest. He almost went through his entire fortune, but finally I beat some sense into his head—and for the last five years he has calmed down considerably. He never talked about his life with Carlton, but I know he suffered badly."

She went over to Amanda and took her hands. "That is why I am so glad he has married you, even if he went about it in a very unconventional way. I am assured he will settle down now and make a wonderful husband. He has all of my Lavinia's wonderful character and love of life. He also has a bit of his father's wild temper, and sometimes frightens me by his dark moods, but they pass quickly. And I'm certain, now that you are here, they will vanish entirely."

"Thank you for telling me all this, Aunt Agatha. It does help to explain my husband's personality," Amanda told her as she wiped her tears away with the back of her hand. "But this has all been a strain for you. Let me ring for some tea and then you should go to your room and rest a bit."

"*No!*" she exclaimed. "I am not finished yet. I have to tell you Jared's wishes. Anything I said until now was only to prepare you for what is to come. You see, my dear, Jared does not wish you to have any children."

There was a hush over the room for some time before Amanda felt herself capable of speech. "But—but that is ridiculous, Aunt Agatha. I am young and inexperienced, that is true, and I am aware that a few women do die in childbirth. Many more live. To assume I will die as his mother did is preposterous."

"I agree with you, my dear," Lady Chezwick said placatingly, "but unfortunately Jared is adamant. He fears for your life and refuses to take chances with it. Obviously he is very much in love with you. In a way you should be quite flattered."

"*Flattered!*" The word was an explosion. "I assure you, Aunt Agatha, I am anything but flattered. He did not treat me last night as if he were in fear of my life. Oh, no, when his animal lust came to the foreground he was more than ready to cast aside my welfare. What if there is already a child, dear lady? What if I have already conceived?"

Such plain speech was a bit much for Lady Chezwick and she burst into tears. "Oh, my child, such language, I implore you."

Amanda's chest heaved in her agitation but she commanded herself to be calm. "Dear Aunt Agatha, do not put yourself into a taking. I will listen to what you must tell me and then I shall make my own decision."

Lady Chezwick then haltingly described a method of prevention to the young bride. Amanda barely hid her disgust at so unnatural a conclusion to what was supposed to be a moment of love.

"And if I refuse, Aunt Agatha? Then what do you suppose Jared will do? Will he desert my bed and satisfy himself once more with his London ladies?"

"I—I don't know."

"Then perhaps I shall confront my husband and find out for myself!" Amanda rose from her seat and made to retire. "I appreciate the pain you felt in reliving the past as you did, Aunt Agatha, and I thank you for sharing your knowledge of my husband's childhood."

She drew herself up to her full height. "However—and I mean this as no disrespect—the subject of whether or not I am to bear children for my husband is not one that shall be decided for me. I fully intend to talk to Jared as soon as possible."

Amanda's composure lasted until she reached her chambers, where she flung herself face down on the bed and gave way to a storm of weeping.

She cried for the long-dead Lavinia, who never held the son she had wanted so desperately. She cried for Carlton, whose love twisted into hate when his wife died. She cried for Jared, his unhappy childhood spent locked in at Storm Haven with his father's twisted grief. Mostly, however, she wept for the children she seemed destined to be denied.

She hadn't really had time to consider bearing Jared's sons. Her love was too new for her to think of sharing it with another person, even a child of their own making. But to be suddenly denied even the prospect sent a knife-sharp pain through her breasts which suddenly, unaccountably, ached to feel the small body of an infant against them.

Her life had taken so many turnings in the last few days. From an unhappy life she had been catapulted into the arms of a wonderful man who showed all signs of adoring her as much as she adored him. She was free of her stepfather and surrounded by people who only wished her well. So short a time ago as when they had faced each other over the luncheon table, Amanda had been tempted to pinch herself to make sure the handsome face in front of her was indeed real. She had thought herself the most fortunate of women, and now—and now?

There was nothing for it but to confront Jared. She had to convince him that she was a young, healthy female who could bear him many children without mishap. Part of her was gratified by his concern for her, but another part was outraged that he could make such an important decision without consulting her wishes. It was just another sign of his arrogance.

She would wait until they took their afternoon ride and talk to him then. Surely he could be made to see reason. On that thought she fell into a troubled sleep and did not wake until it was time to get dressed and meet her husband.

They rode for miles, their mounts covering distances at a gallop as they raced each other across the fields. Amanda rode astride, her long hair flying behind her as it quickly loosened in the wind. For her the wild ride was a purging, a release of her pent-up emotions. She was still a bit wary of her husband and knew she faced a difficult discussion with him as soon as they returned to the house. She rode as if she would ride forever, wanting nothing but the bliss of her husband riding beside her, off into infinity.

Jared could tell by the faint puffiness under her eyes that she had been weeping, and he was sure of the cause. His aunt had warned him that Amanda took his decision badly and he was mentally preparing himself for her anger. He should have told her himself, but he felt she would be too shy to take that sort of instruction from him. If he could have waited a few weeks, until they knew each other better, it would have helped—but the urgency of the discussion was brought home to him clearly by his failure to contain himself last night. That kind of mistake could not happen again.

They were nearly home when out of the corner of her eye Amanda spied a small, enclosed cemetery at the crest of a low hill and turned Tempest toward it. It was surrounded by tall, shady trees, and she was fairly sure that this was the Delaney family cemetery. Lavinia must be buried here! Knowing she was doing a foolish thing she urged Tempest up the hill and had dismounted before Jared could reach her.

"Dismount and join me, Jared. It is peaceful under these trees."

"I'd as lief ride on if you don't mind, Amanda. I don't like to come here." She noticed the tic was back in his cheek.

Amanda continued to walk closer to the fence, perversely ignoring her husband. Her heart was pounding in her chest and she felt her steps would falter, but they didn't. What better place to lay old ghosts but in a graveyard?

Jared came up behind her and tried to turn her away. "Come on, imp, before the ghosties get you." His words were light, but his grip on her arm was just a bit too tight for comfort.

She turned to face him and lifted a hand to his cheek. "I am not afraid of ghosts, Jared. My only fear is that you will allow those ghosts to color our future. I know about your parents, darling. Your aunt told me everything."

He cast her hand away sharply. "You know nothing, Amanda. My aunt was not here when my mother died, and she wasn't here when my miserable father told me how she died."

"She died in childbirth, Jared—*your* birth. Now you are concerned that the same thing could happen to me, but that's ridiculous. My mother bore me with no harmful effects, just as the majority of women in England have given birth." She put her hands on his arm and begged, "I may never be lucky enough to bear your child, Jared, but don't deny me the chance. I cannot understand how such an intelligent man as yourself could think the way you do."

Jared grabbed her hand and dragged her over to the fence. He pointed to a large stone topped by an angel with widespread wings. "Read that," he commanded harshly. "Read that and read my heritage."

Amanda opened the creaking gate and went over to the monument. Lavinia Delaney lay under the stone that noted the brief years of her life. Then Amanda gasped as she read the inscription her husband had had placed there:

> *"Here lies a sainted woman,*
> *murdered by the devil child*
> *of her husband's lust."*

Amanda sank to her knees before the stone. "Oh, my God," she whispered. "What a vile thing to do. How could he believe she would ever blame him or you for her death?"

Although Jared was standing right beside her now, his voice was very low and distant. "He only blamed himself for a little while. He soon transferred all the guilt to me. After ignoring me until I was five, he suddenly discovered a new outlet for his grief—me. He died telling me what he told me every day since my fifth birthday—that I had killed my mother."

"Wh-where is he buried?" Amanda asked quietly.

"You're kneeling on the bastard."

Amanda hastened to move away. "The grave isn't marked. I didn't know."

Jared gave a low laugh. "My one revenge, Amanda. Either that or I couldn't think up an inscription worse than the one you just read. Come away, infant, I think we have spent enough time with my ghosts."

She followed him meekly back under the trees and watched helplessly as he sank to the ground and put his head in his hands. "I thought it didn't hurt anymore, Amanda, but it does. Ten years the man has been dead, and still he has the power to wound me."

Amanda knelt beside him and cradled his head in her arms. "But he *is* dead now, Jared, and his hate died with him; he can't touch us unless you allow it. Don't let him reach out from the grave and destroy our happiness. He was a sick man, crazed by grief and loneliness. What happened to your mother could have happened to anyone. You didn't kill her."

Jared's eyes were glazed with remembered pain. "You don't know what you're talking about, Amanda. I was there. I lived with it for almost all of the first eighteen years of my life. He told me all about it, you see, down to the last detail. Over and over I heard the story of my mother's death. I used to climb up to the attic and look at her portrait and try to imagine her laughing face all twisted up in agony, her body washed in her life's blood."

He pounded his clenched fists into the dirt. "It's true, I killed her. And a child of mine is not going to take you away from me!"

Could this be her husband? Where was the laughing man who rode with her across England? What had happened to the light-hearted companion who teased her and laughed with her—and who had only last night made her his wife in every sense of the word? She did not know this man. She remembered his aunt telling her he had some of his father's black moods, but this was more than that. He was fatally convinced that he, as an infant, had killed his own mother. What madness!

"Tell me about it, Jared, please, so that I can understand," she said softly.

Jared rose abruptly and walked a few steps away from her. He was silent for a long time, staring into her frightened eyes. And then, as if the words were torn from him, he began to speak. "I know my aunt told you everything she knows about my mother's death, but she was in India when it happened. I never had the heart to tell her anything more.

"According to my father, my mother was never very robust, and carrying me robbed her of a lot of her strength. When her time came he insisted on staying with her, holding her hand and trying to keep her comfortable."

He spoke in a monotone, as if repeating something learned by rote. "She labored for three days and nights and each day she grew weaker. My father was frantic; he cursed himself for ever allowing her to get pregnant. He would have laid down his life gladly to make her terrible pains go away.

"At the end of the third day the pains suddenly stopped, but he stayed by her side throughout the night anyway—even though he was exhausted himself. Toward dawn she woke up and grabbed his hand. 'I love you, Carlton,' she told him, but before he could answer her eyes grew wide in her head and she started to scream. She screamed and screamed as the bedding around her turned a bright red.

"The doctor tried to make my father leave the room, but he refused. After a long while her screams stopped and she closed her eyes. She was dead, of course."

He took a long breath and continued. "The doctor wanted to use a knife on my mother's body to slice me from her stomach before I died, too. My father saw and tried to stop him from cutting my mother open. The doctor knocked him unconscious with a candlestick, and when he came to his senses he heard the doctor tell the midwife I had been too large ever to have been born normally.

"As my father staggered to his feet he saw the mutilated body of his wife and the huge, disgustingly healthy infant who lay squawling in the midwife's arms. He picked up the knife that had been used on his wife and tried to push it into me, but the doctor and some servants held him back. After that he calmed down and made everyone leave the chamber. He stayed with his wife without food or drink until the following day, when he finally turned her over to the women to prepare for burial.

"I was given to a servant to take home and wet-nurse, and it wasn't until one day when my father was out riding five years later and chanced to see me that I was brought back to Storm Haven."

Amanda tried to stop Jared from saying any more, but he shook his head and continued. "Then it started. He would see me in the halls, or I would deliberately try to get his attention, I wanted to know my father, and he would lock himself in his study and drink himself into a rage. Then he would call for me and tell me the story of my mother's death. The only respite was my time spent with the village curate who gave me my lessons. As I grew older, the mere telling of the story was not enough and he began to beat me as well.

"Strangely, I never raised a hand to him—not even when I was older and stronger than he. There was something in his pale eyes, some torture that kept me from it. I don't know why I didn't run away. Other than my first five years, Storm Haven was the only life I had known and maybe I just accepted it as normal. After all, I was guilty, didn't my own father say so?

"Anyway, as I grew older I began to notice some of the prettier servant girls. When I was nearly eighteen I decided to take one girl up on her offer to teach me about life. My father found us out behind the stables one day, and something inside of him must have snapped. He took up a horsewhip and started to beat me, screaming all the while that I wasn't to kill anymore. Any child of mine would do as I had done, kill its own mother. I had never thought of that before, but it was very possible.

"If it hadn't been for my unusual size, my mother would have come through the birth unhurt. Any child of my body would be like me. The thought stunned me so that I just lay on the ground and let him beat me. He brought the whip down on my back over and over again, screaming all the while, until suddenly he dropped the whip and started clawing at his throat and gasping for air. I still remember his colorless eyes, bulging half out of his head as he fell forward to land on the ground next to me.

"That's my heritage, Amanda: that stone you just saw, that damned house I brought you to, the story you just heard, and this—" He ripped off his shirt and turned his back, showing her the scars from his beating. "There is my constant reminder, the brand of shame that I shall carry with me to the grave, a badge of dishonor placed there by my own father with his last strength." Jared slumped to his knees in front of her and shook his throbbing head. "Are you satisfied now, Amanda? Have I bled enough for you now?"

What could she say? How could she comfort him? Her whole body quivered with compassion and love. She was horrified by what he told her. To think that he had endured all those years of pain and anguish, and still come away from it without his mind being completely twisted or destroyed, showed the true measure of this man she had married.

She understood now his reckless approach to life, his constant joking and naughty pranks. It was his escape from the nightmare of his youth. She would devote the rest of her life to making him happy, erasing all the shadows and filling his world with love and light.

She did not believe Carlton had told his son the truth. It was unfortunate he heard the doctor say what he did, but she refused to believe that Jared's size alone caused his mother's death. Jared had told her she wasn't a strong person, and she had lost two children already. She, Amanda, was young and disgustingly healthy. Nothing like that could ever happen to her. But how could she make this poor tortured husband of hers believe it?

"Jared, darling," she ventured, "please don't go on like this. You are frightening me. Hold me, Jared, hold me and everything will be all right." She held her arms out tentatively, and he pulled her toward him in a desperate embrace. They clung to each other for endless minutes, and then Amanda raised her mouth to his.

They were both so full of tension, both looking for the comforting cessation of all thought. The reaction of their clinging lips was explosive and they hung together frantically, trying to ease their pain.

It was over almost as soon as it had begun, and Jared thrust her away from him roughly. "Why did you do it, Amanda? Why?"

"I love you," was all she could answer. "I love you, and I want to bear your child so that your ghosts can be laid to rest once and forever."

A violent expletive sprang to his lips and he shook his head in dismay. "Then you refuse to use precautions, Amanda?"

Her head came up proudly. "I do."

"You stupid, stupid child!"

They dressed in silence after that, and didn't speak until they were again crossing the grass to the house. Jared broke the tension at last by asking, "You will not reconsider?"

Amanda searched his face for some sign that he understood her reasons for refusing him, but she found nothing in his features but pain. "I cannot," she whispered quietly.

"Do you like it here at Storm Haven?" he asked suddenly.

What was he talking about? "Yes, Jared. The countryside is beautiful."

"Then I wish you joy of it, madam. I leave for London tonight!" He turned on his heel and was gone.

Chapter Six

THE THREE men joined arms as they staggered down the steps of the White House, London's most famous brothel, and out into the street. As they walked haphazardly toward the corner two of the men burst into song:

"When I get you Nell—ee, I'll get you in the bell—ee.
 You do me, oh, so well—ee,
 I want to take you home . . ."

"God in Heaven, won't you two stop your caterwauling? Do you want to be picked up by the Watch, you drunkards?"

Kevin disengaged himself and swept into an elaborate—if somewhat unsteady—bow. "I beg your pardon, my lord, but are you in-insinuating my friend Bo and I are—such a distasteful word—drunk?"

"Not so. Sober as a judge. *Hic*," added a bleary-eyed Bo.

"Ha! And I'm Richard the Lionhearted, at your service," retorted Jared. "There's my coach, gentlemen. Where to now?"

"Home for me, I think, Jared, old friend. Nellie's charms have fatigued me and I crave my bed."

Bo agreed. "Go with you, Kevin. Don't feel too well. Feel dashed queer, in fact." He then proved his point by making a mad dash for the gutter.

"What a pair of deadheads you are. Very well, I will drop you off if you are so chicken-livered . . ."

"Don't, please. No chicken livers. Couldn't right now, thank you," Bo pleaded as he rejoined the group.

After leaving his two friends at Kevin's lodgings, Jared directed his driver to take him to Lady Wade's. Blanche was sure

97

to be home, for it was almost three in the morning. Maybe with Blanche he would find the release he was seeking. After all, she had never failed him before. It was his last hope.

Damn Amanda anyway! When would she go away and leave him in peace?

As his coach made its way to High Street, Jared's disgustingly clear head went back over the last six weeks. Six weeks of drinking and gambling, of parties and women. Kevin and Bo had welcomed him back into their bachelor circle without question, although he knew they were bursting with curiosity. All he had told them was that his wife was at Storm Haven with his aunt. Something in his eyes sidelined any further questions, and for that Jared was grateful.

For the first few weeks he had amused himself at his old haunts, culping wafers at Manton's, inspecting the new stock at Tattersall's, trading punches with other male members of the *ton* at Cribb's Parlor, and drinking himself into oblivion at the Daffy Club. At night he would gamble at White's or Watier's, and—much to his agitation—he rarely lost. He fell heavily into his bed each dawn after drinking himself past remembering, only to wake from nightmares in which Amanda always took the leading part.

He had seen Blanche one night at a small dinner party, but she ignored him. It was obvious she had heard of his marriage and her temper was evident. He really didn't care about her one way or the other—she had been well paid—but it rankled him that her escort was none other than his cousin Freddie, who, Jared thought at the time, wouldn't know what to do with someone like Blanche even if she did invite him into her bed.

The hatred in Freddie's eyes when he spied Jared stemmed from several reasons, he knew. Even if he could be sure Jared was never to father an heir, he still would hate his cousin with all the malice he could muster—which was considerable.

Yet on the night of the dinner party Freddie had merely offered his congratulations, and withheld any sly innuendos as to the bride's absence. Wasn't a bit like Freddie to do that, Jared thought at the time, but maybe their last encounter had taught Freddie to hold his tongue.

Finally getting some brains in his pointed little head, Jared concluded as the carriage halted in front of Blanche's residence. A fine sweat broke out on his upper lip as he ascended the front steps. What if he had the same result with her that he had with the whores at the White House? The first time he had failed he blamed it on drink. But now he was really worried.

Blondes, brunettes, even that little Chinese girl tonight, he could raise not a jot of desire for any of them. Soon he would be the laughingstock of London. He hadn't told anyone of his problem, not even Bo and Kevin, and had paid each of the girls handsomely to keep them quiet. But he knew word would get around soon enough. There wasn't a woman born who could hold her tongue. Amanda had bewitched him, spoiled him for other women.

Damn her, damn her, damn her!

A sleepy butler opened the door, recognized Jared, and let him in as if it were a matter of course—which for several months it had been.

"I know the way, Smythe, thank you." He unhooked his evening cape, handed it to the man, then made his way upstairs. Blanche was sitting on a chair in front of her dressing table, combing out her long blonde hair, when he entered her room. The brush dropped to the floor when she saw him enter.

"So, Jared, you think you can come back here as if things were as they were before. Go home to your little bride, Jared. Or is she already as sick of you as I am?" She got up from her chair and gave him a full view of her body, visible through the diaphanous nightgown. Her green eyes were blazing as she heaved a hand mirror at him. "Get out!"

Jared dodged the mirror neatly, and it splintered into a thousand pieces against the door. "Oh, that *is* too bad, darling. Now you shall have bad luck." As she let out a stream of curses he added, "Careful, Blanche, your background is showing." He advanced toward her, smiling in a way she had never seen before, and she remembered her one-time notion that he was deeper than she knew. The first flutterings of fear beat against her breast as she backed away from him, but then a slow smile curved her lips.

Her body was what he wanted, and with her body she would gain control of him once again. Jared was very generous to his lady-loves. She changed her tactics. "Jared, darling, I *have* missed you. No one has ever satisfied me as you do. So what if you married some simple schoolgirl? It's me you came to tonight, isn't it? Did you miss me, Jared?" She undid the tie at her neck and let her gown fall to the floor.

Jared stopped in his tracks as his eyes raked her from head to toe. Where once she had looked voluptuous she now looked over-blown. Amanda's small, perfect body rose in front of his eyes and he felt he was going to be sick. Blanche smiled at him and she looked distorted, as if he viewed her through flawed glass.

When she drew nearer he could smell her overpowering musk, so different from his wife's sweet lavender smell, and he compared the hard, glittering green eyes that laughed up at him now with the smoldering gold of Amanda's.

Blanche was talking to him, but he couldn't hear what she was saying for the pounding in his ears. All he could see was Amanda's little pointed face as she looked up at him and declared him to be her love. He shook Blanche's hands off him as if they were dirty, and she went crashing backwards to the floor.

"You disgust me! You cow!" he spat, groping in his breeches for some banknotes. He emptied his pockets and threw the money at her before he turned and fled from the room like a man trying to escape his fate.

"Jared! *Jared!*" she screamed. "I'll kill you for that, you black bastard! Did you hear me? *I'll see you dead!*"

He grabbed his cloak up from the startled Smythe and crashed out of the house and into his coach. "Take me home, Simpson!" When he reached Half Moon Street he entered his study and spent the rest of the night consuming all the brandy in the room.

"Aunt Agatha, how do you think the roses look here against the new walls? Would they perhaps be better in the music room?"

Lady Chezwick dutifully inspected Amanda's handiwork, and between them they decided to leave the roses where they were. The older woman looked around the once dreary room, now flooded in sunlight and lit by the creamy flocked walls and light blue furniture. "You have worked a miracle with this room, my dear, and the crowning touch for me is to see my dear sister's portrait back where it belongs."

"Thank you, Aunt Agatha, I do think using the blue of her gown for the furniture was the right touch. But I had no idea how lovely everything would look without those dreadful heavy curtains at the window."

Lady Chezwick returned to her seat near the fireplace and

beckoned Amanda to join her. "I still cannot get over your boundless energy, my dear. Ever since you had me summon the workmen from London there has been nothing but hammering and banging from morning till night. Even the servants quarters were not left untouched. Are there any rooms still to be done, do you think, or will you not rest until you have laid an Aubusson carpet in Tempest's stall?"

Amanda laughed at her aunt's joke and hastened to assure her the worst was over. "I think all is in readiness now, but I shudder to think what Jared will say when he gets the bills." Her smile faded as she remembered her husband's last words to her before he mounted his horse and rode out of her life: "Why not play house, Amanda? You seem to wish to be domestic."

She had taken him literally, and entered full-force into renovating Storm Haven—leaving only the ancestral marriage-bed unchanged. There at night she would relive her wedding night and weep into her pillow.

Sometimes she would ride Tempest to the old cemetery and sit next to the two simple stones she had had erected over Jared's parents graves. She had received a perverse pleasure from watching Lavinia's former marker taken away, and had ordered it smashed to bits. So much for old ghosts!

Lady Chezwick had asked her many times why she was driving herself like she was. But Amanda would just smile at her and continue choosing upholstery fabrics, or watching over the painter's shoulders as they mixed colors to her orders.

She had hired a few new staff members from the village—although the house was fairly adequately manned—and renovated the stables to meet Harrow's specifications. She met daily with the estate manager, and had taken over the keeping of records. Every afternoon she spent an hour with Tom, who had turned out to be a fairly handsome youth under his grime, teaching him his letters and sums. She sampled Cook's sauces in the kitchens, counted the linen with the laundress, and polished silver with the butler.

In the three months since her marriage and subsequent desertion by her husband she had firmly entrenched herself as chatelaine of Storm Haven. The staff adored her. Didn't she regularly send baskets of food and materials to the village, and order the re-thatching of all the cottages on the estate? Wasn't it Lady Storm who knew all their names, and all their children's, and never hesitated to pass an hour with one of the old ones?

It was only at night in her bed, when she let herself relax, that she gave in to her fears and memories. Lady Chezwick kept assuring her that Jared would soon come to his senses and return home, but then Lady Chezwick did not know what Amanda knew. It would kill the old lady to learn exactly how her sister died—and Amanda wisely kept her own counsel.

On this warm summer day, after a cold collation in the smaller dining room, Lady Chezwick retired to her room for a rest and Amanda went out into the garden. This was her favorite spot, the formal gardens full of summer flowers, and she had made no alterations there—a decision which endeared her to the old gardener. She spent a few minutes talking to the elderly man now, exchanging hints on pruning the ancient rose hedge, before she moved off to her private haven—the kitchen garden.

There was a peace there that she could find nowhere else: the homely smells of rosemary and thyme calmed her senses. She had scandalized her aunt by working in the garden herself, often returning to the house with grubby hands and stains on her gown. Amanda smiled to herself now as she dropped to her knees and began pulling some weeds that threatened the young parsley, a childhood song coming to her lips as she worked.

When she raised her head the world tilted dizzily for a few moments and she grabbed a nearby bench for support. "I am aware of your presence, child. You can stop reminding me, thank you." She quickly looked about her to make sure she had not been overheard, then placed her hands on her still-almost-flat stomach as she addressed her unborn child.

"I have waited patiently for your father to get over his anger and come home. I don't know if it was the possibility of bearing him a child or the fact that I disobeyed him which sent him from me. Your father is such an arrogant, headstrong man. Before I knew I was to become your mother I was content to put his house to rights and wait for him to come to his senses. He cannot live in the past forever, for the future belongs to those who are brave enough to face it. I would wait longer, my precious, but your advent has taken Jared's decision from him.

"We'll keep our secret a little while longer, but soon you will make yourself known regardless of my wishes. I will give your father another fortnight to come to us, but if he does not I think I shall not have the strength to go on."

She often wondered when her child had been conceived. Was it on her wedding night? Or was this baby the result of their violent coupling under the trees near the cemetery? Either way the child was conceived in love, of that she was sure, but she would rather think it had happened on their first night together. Amanda was not superstitious by nature, yet the thought of a child conceived next to a graveyard did not rest easily on her heart.

She was not in any fear of her life, for all her fears were directed at Jared's reception of her news. He loved her—she was sure of that now in only the way a woman can be sure. After all, only a man deeply in love would deny himself the fierce pleasure of their physical union just to prevent a child. It was because he loved her that his father's words frightened him so badly. Poor, poor Jared. She could still see his haunted eyes as he told her the story of his childhood. She was so young, and she did not have the words to convince him—to make him understand he worried for no reason.

She got up from her knees and returned to the main salon to stand under the portrait of Jared's mother. "I need your help, Lavinia. Your son needs it, too. Help him to banish his fears and come home to me, where he belongs, to me and to this child I carry within me." A single tear spilled down her ashen cheek. "Oh, Lavinia, I love him so much!"

Lady Chezwick had been just about to enter the main salon to fetch her embroidery, but at Amanda's quiet words she put a hand to her mouth and backed silently from the room.

"Dash it all, Jared, you've got to snap yourself out of this. You are living like a damned recluse. Look around you, man. How do you survive in such filth?" As if to give credence to his words, Kevin swept a week's worth of newspapers off a chair, along with two empty brandy bottles, and sat down with a thump. "I cannot believe you are a sane man. Even Bo would not act like this over a"—he searched for the proper word—"*female!*"

Jared did not so much as raise his chin from his chest, but his blue eyes sparkled in anger. "Why don't you shove yourself off—and take that other long face with you." He pointed to Bo, standing next to the fireplace and shaking his head in dismay.

"Can't do that. Our friend, you know. Must help you," Bo explained.

"I suggest you save your concern for those who may value it. For myself, I wish only my own company, thank you."

Kevin cursed under his breath and threw an empty bottle into the hearth, where it exploded like a pistol shot. "You miserable derelict! Look at you. Just look at you! You haven't shaved in days, your shirt is filthy, and—quite frankly, Jared—you smell bad. Your man tells me you refuse all food and just wallow here swilling brandy. Ever since you met that girl you have been a stranger to us.

"First you run off with her, then you marry her, and then in just two short days you bury her in the country with your aunt. Then you come back to London, acting like the world was going to end tomorrow and you were going to enjoy your remaining time to the fullest. For weeks you near drove Bo and me mad, bull-rushing all over the city, and for the past month you've taken to your rooms like a sulking schoolboy. You may be my friend, but quite frankly, you disgust me!"

"By George, Kevin, that's a bit strong," warned Bo.

Jared waved a limp hand in dismissal. "Let him go, Bo. It's probably the only bit of pleasure he's had in months." He raised his bloodshot eyes to look at his friend. "Is that the end of your homily, or must I listen to more before you feel satisfied?"

"There's a hell of a lot more, Jared, but I'm too tired to waste my energies on a drunken dolt. I'm off to Storm Haven in the morning. Perhaps I can find some answers there."

Jared swayed as he rose to his feet. "The devil you are, Kevin. You keep your damned nose out of my business!"

"Ah, so there is some spirit left in that self-pitying body! What secret is there at Storm Haven that you are protecting so fiercely? Did you murder the chit and bury her in the cellar?"

Jared lunged toward his friend, but his movements were sluggish and Kevin had ample time to sidestep the blow and grab his friend's shoulders. Jared slumped against him and muttered an apology before darkness overcame him. He would have slipped to the floor had it not been for Kevin's strong grip.

"Good," commented Kevin. "Now we can put him to bed and get his man in here to clean away this mess. Bo, pull the rope and order some food for our fallen friend here while I put him between the sheets. We ought to be able to sober him up enough later to find out what's going on."

In short order the maid had cleaned up the room, and after Kevin forced some soup down his throat Jared allowed his man to shave him. His friends tried to keep him in bed, but he insisted on bathing and getting dressed. When the three friends were finally settled in the downstairs study he apologized to them for his behavior. They shrugged it off.

"Only one thing, Jared. We do want to help. Do you want to talk about it?" Kevin asked.

Jared's lips curled in a sardonic grin. "Not particularly, Kevin, if you must know. But don't worry that the moment you leave me I'll crawl back inside a bottle. By the way, if you ever have a problem you don't wish to face, don't try to forget it with women and liquor. Take it from an expert—neither works." He lit a slim black cheroot and tossed the match into the fireplace. "No, a man has to face his problems—and that is what I must do."

"Would money help? Glad to make you a gift."

"Thank you, Bo, but no amount of money can buy me out of this one. Besides, my drawers upstairs are stuffed with banknotes accumulated during my first weeks in town." Almost to himself he added, "Lucky at cards, unlucky in love."

Kevin heard him and exclaimed, "Aha, as I said before, this all has something to do with the young lady we met so briefly. How could one small girl put you into such a bad case of the dismals?"

"Obviously you didn't have more than a passing association with the imp or you wouldn't ask that. My wife is not one of your little society misses, content to spend my money and let me go on about my business. Oh, no, Amanda wants complete surrender. It's all or nothing for her."

"Surrender? Surrender what?" Bo never could understand Jared, though he liked him immensely.

"She wants children."

This didn't affect Bo unfavorably. "So? Like them myself. Don't you?"

"Damn it man, of course I do! What kind of a monster do you think I am?"

Kevin was thoughtfully tapping a finger against his lips. After a few moments his eyebrows flew up and he asked quietly, "Your mother died in childbirth, didn't she?"

Jared nodded mutely.

Kevin winked broadly at Bo and exclaimed, "By Jove, Bo, you were right. He is besotted!" He got up and went to Jared and clapped him on the shoulder. "You're in love with the puss, ain't you? Ah, Jared, the bogeymen we can find when we are in love. Go to her, man, and give her the child she wants.

Childbearing is what women do best, makes them softer and more pliable."

Jared's voice was dull. "She could die, Kevin. I can't risk that."

"And you, my friend, could get run down by the mail coach on your way across the street. Life is never sure. Are you willing to give up all chance of happiness because of what happened to your mother? I didn't know you were such a coward."

Jared's head came up at that. "Do you really think that's what I am? A coward? Is that what Amanda thinks? She looked at me queerly when I rode off."

Kevin had the upper hand now, and he played it to the hilt. "Wouldn't care to make a judgment on that, Jared. But it is she who's going to have to bear the brat, isn't it? Fine fool you look, being afraid where a little girl isn't, you know."

Bo had been self-consciously casting dice, right hand against left, as the conversation had taken this delicate turn. Now he turned beet red and let out a laugh. "Jared Delaney bested by a female? Hah, Kevin, that is good!"

"Shut up, both of you! Leave me, I must think. Go on, I will be all right. Come back tomorrow morning, prepared to spend some weeks in the country." Slowly a smile lit his eyes. "You shall be my guests at Storm Haven since you have seen fit to champion me. Perhaps the two of you can protect me from my little lioness."

Since the Season had drawn to a close weeks ago anyway, the two friends agreed to the move. "Better than Bath," Bo offered. "Can't stomach the waters."

They had only been gone from the room some fifteen minutes when the butler announced, "Lady Agatha Chezwick, my lord," only to be swept aside by that same lady as she countered, "You're as dead as a red brick, Boggs. You don't announce *me;* I *live* here!" As Boggs beat a hasty retreat she turned to her nephew in a fury. "I am here to take you back to Storm Haven, you naughty boy. You are behaving like a spoiled child and I am thoroughly disgusted with you."

"You and Kevin should form a club, Aunt," Jared said, amused at the sight of his agitated relative.

"What? Oh, fiddlesticks, I never could understand you when you were tugging my leg with your fancy jokes. I mean what I say, Nephew. You have been the light of my life these past ten years, but in your latest pranks you have shamed me deeply.

You look awful, by the way. I'm glad to see you've been suffering, for it may mature you."

"I live only to please you, Aggie." Jared grinned.

"Well, in this instance, you have fallen far short of the mark, let me tell you! How dare you leave that poor little thing pining her heart out alone at Storm Haven while you kick up your heels in London? Oh, yes, I have friends of my own, you know— Honoria for one, and believe me, she has taken quite a bit of delight in keeping me informed of your activities.

"Why, the very day your wedding announcement was in the *Gazette* you were seen at Covent Garden, with two Cyprians dangling on your elbows. Where is your sense of shame? Where is your honor? Where is my cup of tea? I have been standing here a full five minutes and you have not made one move to see to my comforts. Are you beyond salvation after all?" Her breath exhausted for the moment, Lady Chezwick sank into a chair and began fanning herself with her handkerchief.

Somehow she contained her anger until a pot of tea and some cakes were placed in front of her by an awestruck footman who looked wonderingly on this intrepid old woman who dared to beard Lord Storm in his own den. Then she continued her assault.

"Now, Jared, I wish to have some plain speech with you. I admit to being a bit shocked when you brought Amanda to me, but I must tell you I have never been so pleased with a child in my life. She is a bit unconventional, I have to say—riding astride and all of that, not that she would do it in Town—but she has taken hold of my heart with her sweetness and charm. I will not stand by and let you treat her so shabbily. Do you know what that girl has done these past three months since you went off to sulk?"

"No, Aunt, but I rest easy in the knowledge that you will not allow my lack in this area to continue."

"Don't be fresh. That dear little girl has taken it on herself to completely re-do Storm Haven, as if it didn't need it. Why, you wouldn't believe the changes she has made—all for the better I might add, and her taste is unexceptional. Everything has been done in the highest degree of style, and the end result is charming, simply charming."

"I certainly hope so, Aggie, for the bills are large enough for her to have refurnished Carlton House. Will Storm Haven now put Prinney to shame?"

"Bother the bills, it's results that count. The house never looked better, and even the village and stables have been redone."

Jared crossed to his desk and pulled out a thick sheaf of papers. "Really, Aunt? Tell me, do any of the eight chandeliers hang in Tempest's stall?"

"Indeed they do not, though I must admit I myself teased Amanda about putting carpet in the stables. The chandeliers hang in the main rooms of the house, Jared, and what fun it is to watch the butler lower them on chains to light the candles, then raise them up from where they send down the most flattering light."

"Ah, that would explain this bill for candles. A hundred and fifty pounds for candles. How silly of me, I should have known. Chandeliers, of course."

Lady Chezwick dismissed the bills with a flip of her hand. "The house itself is but a minor part of Amanda's work. She has bewitched the villagers with her kindness, and even that crotchety old gardener is eating out of her hand. Cook amazes me nightly with her dishes, most of which Amanda taught her to prepare, and she even works on the estate books—I don't know how, for I can never even total up my bill from the milliners."

"Go on, dear lady, I am enthralled by all this. What other pies does my enterprising wife have her fingers into?"

Lady Chezwick was obviously enjoying herself and continued. "Let me see. Well, she is teaching Tom his lessons—he *is* a sweet child—along with five or six other young scamps from the estate who seem to wander by every afternoon. Work is underway on an orphanage outside the village and, oh, yes, she has ordered a greenhouse built on the south lawn." She settled back in her chair and gave a triumphant smile. "I think that is about all."

"Thank heaven for that! If she doesn't soon stop I shall be bankrupt."

A cloud seemed to pass in front of Lady Chezwick's eyes. "Oh, Jared, I think I had better tell you of two other, er, little changes she has made."

A crease appeared between Jared's eyes. "Go on, Aggie, you have come this far. Spit out the rest, since you obviously feel the need."

She shifted uncomfortably in her chair and began. "Do not

rush me. Let me say first, I agree wholeheartedly with what she has done. It is time and enough that the past is left to bury itself. As I always say—and you know I always say it—evil deeds are best forgotten, and only the good things should be remembered. Amanda feels the same as I, and I suppose that is why she did what she did. But regardless, she has lightened my old heart considerably."

"Aunt, do try to bring yourself to the point, please."

"Very well, Nephew. I feel I must tell you that your sweet mother's picture is back in its place of honor over the fireplace in the main salon, only we call it the blue room now. I cannot tell you how it warms my heart to see it there. It was always a pretty picture, and a good likeness of my darling Lavinia. Amanda has taken the blue of her gown and used it to cover the furniture. Let's see, there are three sofa's and five—no, six—chairs, some simply lovely rosewood tables and . . ."

"Aunt Agatha, relax. I do not mind having my mother's picture back in the main—er, the *blue*—room. I thank Amanda for doing it, as a matter of fact. But what is the second thing you are afraid I won't like?"

She averted her eyes and mumbled, "She had new stones put on the graves."

A tic began to work in Jared's cheek and his knuckles grew white around the stem of his glass. "*Two* stones, Aunt?"

"Y-y-yes."

"One for my father also?"

"Yes! I told you, two stones! She had Carlton's monstrosity broken up into a hundred pieces and scattered into the quarry, and then put up two simple stones that have nothing but names and dates on them. Oh, Jared, please do not look at me like that. I know I should have tried to stop her, I knew you would be furious and you are, but she told me your mother would rest better this way. She said Carlton was a sick man and could not be blamed for what he did. I asked her just what he did, but she wouldn't tell me any more than I already know.

"I watched the stones put up, Jared, and when I went back to the house I could have sworn Lavinia's picture was smiling at me, almost as if she knew. Your mother loved him very much, dear, and it is fitting they should finally rest in peace. Please, Jared, darling, don't be angry."

Jared was quiet for a long time, thinking about what his wife had done. Even though Carlton had threatened her happiness from beyond the grave, she had been forgiving enough to give his burial-place a marker. Didn't it matter to her how he, her husband had suffered? Of course it did. It just wasn't in Amanda to hate—and who should know that better than he? What an innocent she was! She needed a keeper!

Slowly Jared realized that he really wasn't angry. In fact, he was curiously relieved that the damning stone was finally gone. So what if his father's grave was finally noted after lying unmarked for ten years? His mother had loved the man, and he had made her very happy. For that alone Jared could forgive him. He felt a sudden lightening of his shoulders, as if a weight he had carried for a long time had suddenly been taken from him.

It had been quite a day for him. First Kevin convinced him to try to set aside his fears for Amanda if she should someday bear him a child. Now his aunt had told him there was nothing of the past left at Storm Haven to haunt him. He could barely wait to get home!

He bent and kissed his aunt's white cheek. "It's all right, dear. Although I am astonished by my reaction, it seems not to matter to me at all. Amanda used good judgment. I remember her saying something about laying old ghosts to rest, and I imagine that is what she thought she was doing. Surprisingly, I think she accomplished what she set out to do."

His face grew serious again as he asked, "You have been busy telling me about my wife's exploits in my absence, but you have neglected to tell me how she is going on. She hasn't worn herself to a shadow with all her good works, has she?"

"Actually, Jared, Amanda's health is the main reason I have journeyed to London. I wanted to discuss her condition with you."

Jared paled and gripped his aunt firmly on her upper arms, shaking her as he yelled, "Well, you took a dashed long way around getting to the main subject! What's wrong with her? Is she sick? Did she fall off that damned horse? Speak to me, Aunt!"

Lady Chezwick shook off his hands and tried to secure her hair with the few pins that Jared's rough handling had left in her head. "I can scarcely talk to you while you rattle the very teeth in my head, Nephew. Calm down and I will tell you."

Jared sat impatiently on the edge of a chair and urged his aunt to continue.

"Amanda hasn't said anything to me, you see, Jared, so it is possible I am wrong. I only know she hasn't been riding Tempest lately, and she is slightly off her food."

He jumped up in a fury. "Then she is ailing! I must go to her at once."

"I doubt if your presence will alleviate the problem, Jared, although it will go a long way in settling the poor child's nerves. Many a night I have heard her sobs through the walls. Your concern would touch me more if you had shown it sooner, Jared. How can I be sure you will act in Amanda's best interests if I tell you her condition?"

Jared dropped to his knees in front of his aunt. "I love Amanda, Aggie, I swear I do. Only since I am in London have I realized how very much that vexing creature means to me. She haunts my every moment. I have never been in love before and, frankly, the experience has shaken me badly. Please, Aunt, I beg you to tell me what is wrong with my wife. I promise to be gentle with her."

Lady Chezwick was suitably impressed with Jared's confession, and she took a deep breath before saying, "Very well, Nephew, I will tell you: Amanda is going to offer you a token of her affection."

Jared frowned. "A token of her—*what?* Aunt, if you love me, speak plainly! What has a gift to do with Amanda's condition? What can she give me? I don't—" Slowly the truth dawned on him and he began to tremble. "She's pregnant? Is Amanda pregnant? Tell me, Aunt! *Is my wife pregnant!*"

Lady Chezwick nodded her head violently, scattering her remaining pins all over the carpet.

Jared's mind was reeling. "But you said she didn't tell you anything. How can you be sure?"

"I, er—well, you see, er, she told Lavinia."

Jared slapped his palm against his forehead in exasperation. "Aunt, I vow you will be the death of me. How could Amanda tell my *mother* she is pregnant?"

"Really, Jared, there is no need to become so incensed. It is quite simple. I walked into the blue room one day last week just as Amanda was standing under my sister's portrait and talking to it. She asked Lavinia to help her to bring you home to her—to her and your child." The old lady's face grew pink as she added, "I also heard her tell your mother that she loved you very much—not that you deserve her."

"For once I agree with you, Aggie. I don't deserve her at all.

Now, you go off upstairs and rest until dinner. Tomorrow morning we all leave for Storm Haven. Bo and Kevin will be meeting us here after breakfast."

Lady Chezwick was dumbfounded. "Bo and Kevin? Do you mean to stand there and tell me that you had already made up your mind to come back? How dare you let me run off all this time when you had already decided! Jared, I do not ever recall being more put out with you. To think I traveled all this way, in the heat, and in my advanced years, just to have you tell me you would have come home tomorrow anyway. That is the outside of enough!

"I had to tell Amanda I was coming to have some fittings and would be gone at least a week. It was the only thing I could think of to get away without too many questions. Now I can't go home with you or Amanda will know I put my nose in where it wasn't wanted—or needed, come to think of it. Just for that, you young scamp, the bills for my new wardrobe—and they will be considerable—will come directly to you!" And she swept from the room as haughtily as her small frame would allow.

Jared stood looking out over the square for several minutes, and when he finally quit the room there was a bounce to his step that his butler hadn't seen in months. The news of their master's change of mood spread quickly belowstairs, and Lady Chezwick was treated to a new respect by Lord Storm's suitably impressed staff.

"Bless the old dear," one footman was heard to say. "I ne'er knowed 'er 'ad it in 'er!"

There was a loud yell coming from the entrance hall. "Ho, ho! Time to be up and off, friend Jared. What is keeping you, sleepyhead? We have a tale for you."

"Quiet, you idiots! You'll wake my aunt!" Jared returned loudly.

Lady Chezwick appeared in her doorway, her lace sleeping-cap falling down over one eye. "Not really, Nephew," she yawned. "You have succeeded where they failed. What is going on?"

"Go back to your bed, dear lady. It is only Bo and Kevin, ready to leave for the country. They must have stayed up all night and come here with the dawn, drat them. I shall see you in a week, Aunt—and again, thank you for coming to me, for your intentions were of the best." He dropped her a quick kiss that landed somewhere in the vicinity of her left ear, and loped off down the stairs.

"Give Amanda a kiss for me, Jared," she called down to him, and returned to the comfort of her bed—not to leave it again until at least noon.

Jared entered the study and called out, "Let us be off, gentlemen . . ." Then he stopped in his tracks and exclaimed, "Good Lord, what have you two been up to? Fighting again, Bo? Aren't you getting a trifle old for that sort of thing?" He turned to face a lanky figure draped negligently over a chair, one booted foot swinging in mid-air. "And you, Kevin, you will have a bruise on that cheek for certain. What happened?"

"I refuse to answer any questions until I have a glass in my hand." Jared hastened to comply with Kevin's request, pouring a goodly amount of brandy into two beakers. Then, deciding he might need it, he poured a third for himself.

"Now, dear friend, that is more the thing," Kevin drawled after sniffing his glass appreciatively. "Bo, my boon companion, my chin aches abominably, so you tell our dear Jared how we championed his lady."

"True, true. Knights of old, Galahad. Smashing go! No swordplay though. Planted a facer; Kevin, too. Worst to them. Cheers!" Bo lifted his glass and drank deeply, then held the cool tumbler to his rapidly coloring eye.

Bo's conversation was at best hard to follow, but Jared, in his agitation, could not make heads or tails of a single word. "Bo, you addle-pated buffoon, speak plainly. What are you talking about?"

"Take offense, Jared. Quite clear I thought. Freddie and Denton at White House. Talked about your lady. Couldn't have that, could we? Waited outside, Kevin and I. Smashing go it was. Bad one, Freddie. Told you so. No left hand, either."

"Kevin!" pleaded Jared, turning to appeal to his friend.

"Very well, I see I have to explain, since you care little for my aching jaw." He crossed the room to refill his glass. "Bo told you we were at the White House," he said, and turned a searching eye toward Bo. "At least I *think* he did. We were discussing our trip to Storm Haven when your dear cousin, the toad, croaked out some rather unkind things about your bride. Denton said little but he smiled a lot, the sponge."

"Quite right . . . toad and sponge," nodded Bo.

"Quiet!" gritted Jared.

Kevin continued. "As I said, Denton was with him, and the two went on at some length about the, uh, bizarre circumstances of your marriage. Freddie was pretty well in his cups and said a few things about you personally that I am not going to bother to repeat."

"Cad. Boor. Never liked him above half," came from the corner of the room.

"Shut up, Bo!" warned Jared.

"Well, now, Jared, you can't call out a man who is not quite sober, much as I wanted to. Not good *ton*, you know, so Bo and I waited outside until Denton and your cousin came out. Waited a dashed long time, too. It seems it was Denton's birthday, and Freddie was treating him to a little fun. I hope it wasn't Nellie; she's too good for him. Anyway, we waited a dashed long time. We stood back until they turned the corner, then Bo here tapped Denton on the shoulder."

"Right. Explained his error. Jared our friend, wife our friend, though we don't really know her, do we? Told him to button his yapper."

"That's when Denton hit him," Kevin broke in. "Freddie then made a move—I disremember whether it was toward me or toward flight—but he did move, so I felt honor-bound to hit him. I don't remember many more of the details, Jared, because Freddie's valet appeared from nowhere—he's a big fellow you know—and my mind becomes hazy once I am on my back in the gutter."

Jared's face was white with rage. "I'll kill them!" he squeezed between his clenched teeth, and made for the door.

Kevin was there before him. "No need, Jared. Place was nearly deserted when they made their remarks. No one heard but us, and I'm sure that is the only reason Freddie spoke. Besides, what reason can Denton have to hurt you? Can't call a man out for no reason."

"I won't call them out for no reason. Denton doesn't bother me: I can shut his mouth with a few shillings, the pompous fool. It's Freddie I want."

"Be reasonable, Jared. If you call Freddie out you'll bring your wife's name into it. You don't want that."

"I won't call Freddie out because of Amanda, Kevin, how much of a loose-screw do you think I am? I'll insult his coat, God knows that's easy enough. Anything will do for an excuse, but I'm going to kill him!"

"And then what? Flee to the continent with your wife? Or would you leave her behind? Use your head, man! Freddie won't open his mouth again."

"Quite. Can't, you know. Broke. I heard it."

Two heads turned toward the portly Bo. "What broke, Bo?" Jared asked quietly, as if he were addressing a backward child.

"Cousin's jaw. Clear shot, heard it go. Worth my eye, it was." He raised his glass. "More brandy?"

Jared and Kevin stared at each other in disbelief. Then Kevin said, "That settles it, Jared. You can't call out a disabled man. You have to wait until he heals, and that could be months. Freddie won't be talking in the meantime, either." He turned to Bo. "You never cease to amaze me, Bo. I didn't know you were so good with your fives."

"Not good. No left hand, Freddie. None. You don't listen; told you that before."

Jared laughed with his friends before swearing them to secrecy about the real reason for their bruises. It would not do to upset Amanda. As for Freddie, perhaps he had overreacted. Once he returned to Storm Haven the scandalmongers would find other fuel to fan the flames of their gossip. As for himself and Amanda, they would become models of circumspection. A nagging thought stirred in the back of his mind, though. What were Freddie and Denton doing rubbing shoulders? A more unlikely duo he could not imagine. He decided he was reading into things, and his forthcoming confrontation with Amanda was much more important.

As the three friends rode through the early morning mists on their way out of London, their valets and luggage to follow later in Jared's town coach, they were blissfully unaware of the bustle occurring in High Street—where the Lady Blanche Wade made a most unlikely nurse, raining down curses on the moaning figure of her patient.

Chapter Seven

I T WAS just past noon when the three horses drew up at the sight of Storm Haven in the distance. The midday sun winked back at them from the sparkling windows that appeared larger than before, their massive frames all newly-painted a dazzling white. Summer flowers bloomed in profusion on the grounds, and large planters of miniature evergreens mixed with geraniums banked the cheerful red-painted front doors, making the grey stones mellow instead of forbidding.

"By Jove, Jared, can this be Storm Haven?" Kevin gasped. "I thought you told me it was depressing. I find it quite delightful—don't you, Bo?"

"Indeed, Kevin. Very nice. A bit large, but very nice."

Jared said nothing, but just sat on his horse and stared at his birthplace as if he had never seen it before. Amanda *had* wrought a miracle. Why, there were even a few shoots of ivy bravely making their way up the walls. He cleared his throat and told his friends, "You two stay here and rest in the shade for an hour. I wish to go alone to my wife. Then come down and I will properly introduce you to the new Lady Storm; that is, if I have not been thrown out on my head."

He rode off at a canter, leaving his befuddled friends behind to call out, "Send someone up here with a bottle, friend, and we promise not to intrude on your homecoming scene."

Jared dismounted a few yards from the main doors and walked his horse quietly to the entrance, where he handed the reins to a footman. "Where is Lady Storm, James?"

"Her ladyship be down by the stream, m'lord, learnin' the young'uns their lessons."

"Thank you, James. I shall join her ladyship there. Kindly take some refreshments to my friends up on the hill, and have two rooms prepared for them, please." He started to walk away, and then added, "Oh, yes, and see that my wife and I are not disturbed."

James squinted in the direction of the hill and saw two gentlemen waving gaily at him. "The gentry is surely queer," he muttered as he scratched his head and moved off. "Surely queer."

Jared first saw Amanda as she sat on the ground like a young girl, her muslin skirts spread out upon the grass. Her long, black hair was held back from her face by a pale yellow ribbon, and hung in silky curls down her back as she bent over what looked to be one of Jared's old schoolbooks. One arm was curled around the shoulder of a thin little boy who looked vaguely like Tom.

As Jared watched, Tom tried to read aloud, and his efforts were rewarded by an affectionate pat on the head and a kiss of dismissal before the lad rose with a grin and loped off—presumably on his way back to the stables. Amanda followed him with her eyes, then sighed deeply and started to gather up books and papers that lay strewn on the grass.

Jared stood transfixed, watching his wife until a slight sound at his feet brought his eyes downward—where he saw a young grey-striped kitten rubbing against his boot. He reached down and picked up the small body. "Come along with me, tiger, and I shall make you a peace offering to my wife." Jared circled widely and came quietly behind Amanda before dropping the kitten into her lap.

"Well, where did you spring from, Sampson? You certainly are a long way from the kitchens. Are you lost?" She picked up the hysterically delighted animal, which quickly buried its head in her hair and made her laugh as its small paws started a kneading motion on her neck. "Stop that, Sampson! You are tangling my hair, you naughty puss!"

"May I be of some service, my lady, as it was my idea to present you with the beast in the first place?"

Amanda's hands froze in the process of removing the kitten and the animal cried out in pain, dealing her a slight scratch as it wriggled to free itself.

"Allow me, imp. You are crushing the poor creature." Quickly Jared removed Sampson from Amanda's nerveless fingers, and only then did she look up into her husband's bright blue eyes.

"It's true," she murmured. "You are back. I thought I must be hearing things." Amanda didn't know what to do. She longed to throw herself into his arms and hang on for dear life, but her pride stopped her. What was he doing back here? Had Aunt Agatha sent him? Well, she didn't want him back on orders from his aunt! Besides, how dare he just waltz back into her life with no explanations? Look at him—standing there grinning like the village idiot!

Jared saw the emotions coming and going on Amanda's face and hastened to explain. He dropped to his knees beside her and picked up her icy hands, pressing them to his mouth one after the other as he felt her shiver beneath his touch. "I rehearsed a long speech on the ride here, darling, but it flew out of my head the moment I saw you. All I can say is you were never out of my thoughts for a moment while I was gone, and the last three months were the most miserable ones in my life. And with my background, you must admit that is quite a statement. I have missed you terribly, and I am here to offer my heart to you in complete surrender. I swallowed my pride the moment I met you."

Amanda allowed a slight smile to cross her lips, but it vanished just as swiftly. "I am gratified by your admission, but that does not explain your return today. Was there any special reason for you to be returning just one day after your aunt reached London?"

"There is not, although I am glad my aunt came to see me. I had already planned to return today; I decided the moment my dull brain finally made me see reason. I was always a slow study, you know." He relaxed a little as she gave a small laugh. "I love you, Amanda. I must, nothing else makes sense. And I want to be with you forever."

A single tear ran down her cheek, and she hastily wiped it away. "And children, Jared? What about our children? Are you still of the same mind about that?"

This was it. He knew he had to say just the right thing to make himself sound believable. He put his hand under her chin and lifted her face to his. Slowly and clearly he said, "I cannot lie to you and say I am not afraid for you to bear my children, but I am very proud that you wish to do me such a signal honor. I promise you, Mandy, I will accept the will of the gods in this matter and stop running from my ghosts."

Her deep golden eyes searched his face and she gave a

shuddering sigh. "I believe you, Jared, and I thank you for it. But it seems my foolhardiness has already sealed our fate. I was ever one to rush my fences: Our first child is due to be born just a few weeks after Christmas."

Jared acted suitably surprised and exclaimed, "Are you sure, imp? Are you quite sure?"

Amanda put her arms around his neck and kissed him on the cheek. "As sure as I can be, having never carried a child before. Are you displeased?" Inwardly she was shaking with a fear he could feel through the material of his riding jacket.

Jared swept her quickly up into his arms and swung her around him in the air before stopping quite still and gazing into her eyes. "Displeased? I look at you and you are even more lovely than before. I see the light in your eyes and the bloom on your cheeks. Displeased? No, brat. I am not displeased. A little frightened, yes—perhaps even a bit jealous of another person being capable of making you so happy—but if you promise to always love me I shall survive." Suddenly he stopped talking and set her on her feet. Gone was his play-acting as the truth was brought home to him like a stunning blow to his mid-section. His aunt had been right: Amanda was pregnant. She had just confirmed it.

It was all well and good to try to convince his wife that he was not overly concerned for her health, but the reality that he was—at eight and twenty—to become a father, was a bit too much for him to comprehend. "Oh, my God, have I hurt you?" he exclaimed. "Here, Mandy, sit down and I'll call someone. Why didn't you stop me? You shouldn't be so active. And what were you doing sitting on the damp ground? You could have caught a chill . . ."

Amanda pressed her fingers to his mouth, laughing delightedly at his concern. "You goose, I am quite fine, really. I am breeding, not ill, you silly man." The laughter left her eyes and they became dark with remembered passion. "Oh, Jared, I missed you so much."

Jared kissed her palm and then lowered his mouth to hers, kissing her with a gentleness she had never felt from him before. It was a gentleness that grew slowly into passion, and they held each other as if they would never let go—telling each other of their fears and longings, proclaiming again and again their undying love. When at last they separated Jared's voice was husky and there were tears in his eyes. "Amanda, my love, I want you so, but I don't want to harm the child."

She slipped her hand into his and squeezed it. "I do not think we need fear that, my Lord Storm. The child will soon tell us when such activity is no longer possible."

Jared lifted her once more in his strong arms and headed for the house. As he made their way toward the broad staircase Bo and Kevin came out of the blue room, glasses in hand.

"What have we here, Bo? Could that be Lord and Lady Storm we see tripping stealthily up the stairs?"

Jared looked over his shoulder at his two friends and grinned. "Make yourselves comfortable, gentlemen. Lady Storm and I will do the civil by you at dinner tonight, but for now we have some pressing matters to attend to."

"Jared!" Amanda choked out, highly embarrassed.

Her husband merely laughed and called out, "My friends, you will excuse us, I know. But you see my wife has just informed me that she wishes to be alone with me to discuss, er, estate business." Amanda buried her flaming face against his shoulder until he delivered her to the top of the stairs.

As the sound of a door being kicked shut came to the pair waiting below, Kevin lifted his glass to the empty stairs and exclaimed cynically, "Drink to the occasion, Bo, old boy. You have just seen *true love*."

Bo looked confused but drank deeply anyway. "Dashed early to go to bed. And with one's wife, too." He shook his head. "Ring for the servant, Kevin. I'm hungry."

The setting sun cast its fading light over the tangled clothing that lay in an untidy trail leading to the foot of the huge bed. From its depths rose the lilting laugh of a well-loved female.

"Did my lovemaking amuse you, pet?" came a deep voice striving in vain for sternness.

"Oh, no, my dearest. I was just recalling the look on your friends' faces as we passed them on the way up here. I doubt I will ever be able to face them. Why are they here, Jared?— although I do not mind."

Jared pressed a light kiss on her forehead and explained, "I asked them to come along as protection, my love. I assumed you could not throw me out if I had brought guests."

121

"Why, Jared Delaney! Do you mean you were afraid of *me*? That is silly."

"Yes," he agreed, "it seems so now, though at the time it appeared a good idea. But now that they are here we shall have to entertain them. Have any of our near neighbors dropped by?"

Amanda ran her fingers into the black cushion of hair on Jared's broad chest. "A few: Squire Bosley and a Lord Close. They seemed a bit upset to hear you were not in residence, but I explained you had business in London, you reprobate. Their wives are nice, although we have little in common. But young Anne, Squire Bosley's daughter, is becoming a good friend. I think she and Bo would deal famously together as she is also quite shy."

"None of that, my love! Bo and Kevin are here as my guests, to hunt and ride at their leisure. I will not have you matchmaking. I lived with Aunt Agatha's schemes too long to inflict such punishment on my friends."

"Yes, my lord," Amanda murmured meekly, and was silent for some time. "Jared," she finally asked, "when did you know you loved me? I still find it hard to believe."

He tapped a fingernail against his teeth in a parody of deep thought while Amanda busied herself exploring his chest with her fingers. "Let me see, when did I first feel affection for you, brat? Was it when you turned on me in anger after I saved you from those footpads? No. Was it while you held a knife to my chest that I found my heart melting toward you? No, it was a strong emotion I felt at the time—but as I remember it was total exasperation, not love. No, it was neither of those times. *Stop that, it tickles.* Let me think. Well, if you must know, I fell in love with you—*I warn you, stop that*— when we kissed for the first time, in the meadow. Perhaps I was still stunned from my fall and mistook the stars in my eyes for love. When was it for you?"

"It seems we fell in love about the same time, Jared. I only bested you by a few moments. I really thought I hated you until you stupidly fell from your horse, but as you lay there it suddenly meant very much to me to see you open your eyes. I knew then that I loved you, but I would not admit it. You looked so very young and vulnerable lying there in the clover, rather like a lost little boy . . . *ouch! Don't do that!*"

Jared had leaned over and taken a playful nip at Amanda's soft earlobe. She retaliated by pushing his supporting elbow out from under him. They rolled back and forth on the huge bed,

Amanda pushing vainly at Jared's hands as he tickled her unmercifully.

Grinning wickedly, he intoned in mock severity, "I believe it is time I schooled you in showing the proper respect for your husband, chit. A husband is never 'stupid' and I for one never look vulnerable." Amanda held him close and covered his neck and shoulders with kisses. "Oh, my husband, how I do love you," she whispered as he replied in kind.

When Jared finally rolled away he gathered her into his arms and questioned shakily, "Are you adequately chastised, madam?"

"Indeed, yes, my lord. In fact, I think I shall rack my brains weekly to discover ways to receive further instruction in the respect due my husband," she replied unashamedly. "I do believe dinner will be a bit late," she added with a twinkle in her eye.

"Imp, I shall ever be amazed at your brazen tongue." He leaned over to drop a kiss on her nose. "And ever grateful," he added huskily.

Bo and Kevin were having a drink before dinner when Jared and Amanda finally made their appearance in the blue room. Dressed in a golden gown that nearly matched her eyes, Amanda glowed with health and shared love. Her smile of welcome to her husband's friends was genuine. Jared looked exceedingly handsome and well pleased with himself in his suit of blue superfine, and his eyes clouded only for a moment when they encountered the portrait of his mother. He leaned over and whispered to his wife, "She looks very content, doesn't she?" and was rewarded by Amanda's grateful smile.

Kevin saw them first. "By gad, Jared, could this be the little ragamuffin we saw at the inn? No wonder you were in such a rush to wed her and, may I add, why you continue to wear that insufferably smug look. She's a beauty." He took Amanda's hand and pressed it to his lips. "My most bewitching madam, let us murder this oaf and run away together. I am by far the better man."

Amanda's delighted laughter brightened the room like sunlight. "We meet again, Mr. Rawlings, and I see your tongue is even more silken than before." She daintily withdrew her hand and crossed to confront Bo. "And you, Mr. Chevington. I am delighted to see you again, but pray, what has happened to your eye? It looks excruciatingly tender."

"Amanda, it is not polite to inquire on Bo's appearance. You should ignore his obviously ill-gotten injury as if it were not there," chided Jared with a grin.

"Nonsense," returned Amanda, slipping a hand through Bo's arm. "You come and sit down, and let me call for my maid, Sally. She knows how to deal with these things. Poor man, you should not be standing about."

A thoroughly-enamored Bo was led to a nearby chair as Jared resignedly rang for Sally. As they waited for the maid they watched while Amanda fussed over the embarrassed Bo. Kevin turned to Jared and pleaded with a smile, "Be so good as to punch me, Jared, I feel quite neglected. Perhaps a bruise or two would find me some of your wife's sweet consideration."

"I will not hit you, you fool, but I will refill your glass if you like." He paused to glance at his wife and friend, now wrapped in earnest conversation. "I'll be damned, Kevin, if the imp doesn't understand his every word."

But Kevin was gone, hastily finding a seat near Amanda and vying for her attention as the maid dealt swiftly with Bo's injured eye. By the time dinner was announced Jared found himself walking alone to the dining room, as Amanda had given an arm to each of his friends—Bo because he had asked nicely, and Kevin because he had issued a promise to shoot himself if she did not let him escort her. As Jared watched their departing backs he decided Amanda should be allowed to introduce the pair to the local society, perhaps that would keep them away from his wife!

After dinner, Bo and Kevin turned down brandy and cigars in favor of returning to the blue room with Amanda. Once settled on facing sofas, Jared quickly maneuvered himself to sit by her side, and Amanda asked, "Was the Season a success, gentlemen? I'm afraid I left London during the first week. I imagine the city is quite empty this time of year."

Kevin answered, "It was its usual crushing bore, my lady: endless parties deemed a success only if the place was so crowded you could not find the supper room, and the selection of eligible females—ah, Jared picked the rose from the thorns so quickly we none of us had a chance, and I for one refuse to settle for second-best."

Jared remarked, "What about the Chatsworth girl? I saw her at Almack's."

Kevin wrinkled his nose in distaste. "Which one, friend? The one with the squint, or the blonde one with the spots?"

"One more, Kevin. Has chicken teeth."

"Bo, your ignorance is showing again," Kevin returned. "A chicken don't have teeth."

"Oh? Really? Chicken mouth then. Charity Chicken, right?" he ended, undaunted.

"Charity?" Amanda interposed. "Charity Chatsworth? Oh, how perfectly awful a name. Why ever did they name her Charity?"

Jared leaned over and patted her hand. "They had to, pet. The first two horrors were named Faith and Hope. Charity just followed, and she squints. Hope has the chicken teeth. But do not waste your worries on them, for they have very hefty marriage portions and shall find themselves husbands by and by."

"Some dark night," Kevin suggested.

"Mr. Rawlings, you are a mean man."

"Indeed, no, my lady, it is you who are unkind. Calling your husband's good friend Mister. Please, call me Kevin, for I wish to be as a brother to you."

Amanda looked inquiringly at her husband, who only smiled. "Very well, Kevin. My wife shall call you both by your Christian names, and I do think you have her permission to address her as Amanda. But I warn you: I am a very jealous man."

The new friends spent the rest of the evening in lighthearted banter, Kevin and Bo both agreeing to make it an early night after their activities of the previous evening. After they had retired, Amanda told her husband how delighted she was with his friends.

"Yes, imp," he replied, "but I must warn you not all members of polite society are as open and above board as those two. You must not be too trusting of everyone you meet. Bo and Kevin have been my best friends for many years—although I must admit they are both rather rackety—but for a woman to be on such good terms with the male members of the *ton* would raise quite a few eyebrows. So, when we give our little parties, you must address them by their proper names."

Amanda clapped her hands in delight. "Then I can invite

some of our neighbors over for a party. Oh, thank you, darling. I can hardly wait to show off all this pretty furniture and prove myself to you as a good hostess. Can we open the ballroom?"

"Madam, my friends are here to relax, and you are not to try to marry them off. Don't deny it; I can see it in your eyes. I agree to some activities, but they will be here only three weeks and in that time I expect no more than two parties. Have I made myself clear?"

Amanda looked quite crestfallen. "But, my love, we are so happy. Surely you wish nothing less for your friends?"

Jared took her hands in his. "There is only one Mandy and she is mine. Bo and Kevin will just have to stumble along as best they can on their own."

"Yes, Jared," Amanda murmured meekly. "Only one small dinner party and one tiny dance. I promise." Her mind was working swiftly. She would have her dinner party the very next night and after word of two eligible young bachelors residing at Storm Haven got around, there would be few idle evenings. She kissed her husband demurely and walked up to their bedroom silently, planning the menu for her opening salvo.

Amanda awakened slowly and reached out her arm to Jared's side of the huge bed, only to find it unoccupied. Had she dreamed yesterday? Was she still alone and unloved at Storm Haven? As if in answer to her question there was a slight knock at the door and Sally entered, a broad smile on her otherwise homely face.

"Good mornin', milady, an' a fine day it be, with the master 'ome and all. Ach, look at this mess, your ladyship's fine gown all in a heap on the floor." She bent down swiftly and came up with Amanda's gold gown in one hand and Jared's discarded neckcloth in the other. "No need to be askin' wot went on in 'ere last night, if you'll pardon my sayin' so. And you breedin' an'all. Tsk, tsk!"

Since Sally had more than once cradled a weeping Amanda against her ample bosom, her mistress only blushed furiously and asked the whereabouts of Lord Storm.

"Hiz lordship 'as taken 'iz two friends down to the stables to see that bloody 'orse. From the devilish gleam in 'iz lordship's eye, I'm thinkin' it's trouble he's brewing."

Amanda rushed through her toilette, refusing breakfast, and

hurried down to the stables. She arrived in time to see Kevin and Jared holding each other up as they howled with laughter while a flustered Bo was assisted to his feet by Harrow. Calmly chewing on some field grass was her red stallion, surveying the scene with horsely disdain on his white-blazed face.

"Oh, Jared, that was unkind! You should have warned Bo about Tempest's little trick." She went to Bo and offered him her arm. "Don't you let them upset you, dear friend. Come away with me and we shall walk down to the pond out of the sight and sound of these two bullies."

"Er— yes, er, thank you, Amanda. Enjoy that, I would." Bo answered as he swept his carroty hair out of his eyes. He threw an impish grin over his shoulder to his tormentors and supplied innocently, "Thank you, gentlemen. Amuse yourselves. Don't know when we'll be back."

Kevin roared again and slapped Jared heartily on his back. "Bested you in that round, old friend."

"Oh, shut up, Kevin. Come on, we'll ride out this morning for a few hours. Amanda plans a dinner party for tonight and I have a feeling I won't see much of you after she launches her matchmaking schemes."

"Ah, do you mean there are some comely country wenches in the neighborhood?"

"If there are, they have escaped my notice. Amanda talked of Squire Bosley's Anne, but she is already picked for Bo, poor fellow."

"Bo? With a female! I cannot wait to see this grand romance. He will probably trip over his own feet and put his head in the punch bowl. I believe I look forward to this evening, Jared. It will be amusing at the very least."

Kevin was correct that it would be amusing. To him. To Bo it was both a nightmare and a dream. When Amanda brought the small blonde Anne Bosley to his side, he colored deeply and tried to hide behind his hostess. But as Miss Anne was turning a decided pink herself and was—instead of either giggling at him or dismissing him with scorn—looking into his wide blue eyes with sweet innocence, he soon left his refuge and bowed shakily over her hand.

Miss Anne was as slight as Bo was pudgy, coming no more than to the tip of his slightly double chin. She looked up into his freckled face and he could tell by her soft green eyes that she was a creature as frightened as himself. With Amanda to draw Anne's hand through Bo's arm and direct them to a secluded sofa that she had positioned earlier, the young couple was destined to spend the greater part of the evening in one another's company. Placed side by side at the dinner table, they continued their stilted conversation that—to an outsider—would have appeared highly one sided.

"Cool for July, Miss Bosley."

"Indeed, yes, Mr. Chevington. How astute of you to notice. Is it so cool in London, sir?"

"Yes," replied Bo, and the two lapsed into silence as the main course was served.

"The beef is quite tasty, is it not, Mr. Chevington?"

"Yes."

"I do so admire Amanda's dining room decor. She did it all herself, you know."

"Yes. Very nice."

"Do you stay long in the country, Mr. Chevington?"

"Yes."

"Do you admire the country then, sir?"

"Yes."

Any other woman would have thrown up her hands in disgust, but then Anne Bosley was under terrific maternal pressure. Her mother had been harping on her all day about her lack of social presence, and she did not wish for a repetition of her sermon on the morrow. Throwing caution to the winds she made one last try, although her mother had warned her never to discuss this particular interest of hers in masculine company. "Did you perhaps notice the *Dizygotheca elegantissima* in the library, Mr. Chevington? It is really a fine specimen."

Bo was silent for so long the girl nearly slid out of her chair in embarrassment. Her mother was right: She was a hopeless case. Her failure at polite conversation had been bad enough, but adding the bit about the *elegantissima* was striking the very depths. As her mother had said, she was destined to spend the rest of her life being a prop for her parents in their declining years.

Suddenly Bo, who had been studying her with some intensity, spoke. "Did not see it. How about the *Brassaia actinophylia* in the blue room? Surprised to see it outside a greenhouse."

Anne's little heart-shaped face lit up in a smile capable of melting the strongest heart, and Bo was good and truly lost. They both rushed into speech at the same time, laughing and urging the other to go first, and in the end had to be called to attention twice by their host before either realized it was time for the ladies to retire from the table.

Bo watched as Anne left the room with the other women, and waved shyly to her as she turned at the door to look at him once more. As soon as possible he sped to the blue room, where the two quickly resumed their conversation of the possibilities of grafting two particular rose bushes.

Kevin, deliberately eavesdropping, rushed to Jared's side and exclaimed, "I don't wish to alarm you, friend, but Bo is saying foreign words—him who has barely mastered the King's own. Do you think he is making untoward advances?"

"I highly doubt it, Kevin, but what foreign words did you hear him speak? Were they French?"

"I truly don't know. It sounded like *Chlorophytum comosum,* or *sam picturatum,* or some such drivel. Do you suppose he's asking her to see his etchings?"

Jared was well and truly puzzled. He called his wife over and asked Kevin to repeat himself, which he did—with even less accuracy than his first attempt. As he finished a slight smile lit Amanda's face and she allowed her eyebrows to rise in shock. "Indeed, gentlemen, did I not tell you Bo was deeper than you knew? I believe that is Latin for 'your green eyes glow like stars.' And you said they wouldn't hit it off!" She snapped her fingers in Jared's face, quipping, "That to you, husband," and tripped off to hide her grin in an effervescent exclamation over the beauty of Lady Close's new fan.

Out of the corner of his eye Jared saw Bo lead young Anne through the French doors, out into the garden. He nudged Kevin and brought his attention to their shy friend's new-found *savoir-faire.* "Never known Bo to steal a march on you, Kevin. There must be something in that chit you overlooked when you were introduced."

Kevin's forehead wrinkled as he realized his reknown as an irresistible lady's-man was in jeopardy. He quickly scanned the room and singled out Lord Close's daughter Elizabeth as the least horse-faced of the group, and set out to redeem his reputation. As Lady Elizabeth would make her debut next Season she was more than willing to practice her wiles on the handsome young dandy.

This left Jared to his own devices, as Lord Close and Squire Bosley and the other men were deep in a discussion of the proper time to manure their fields—a subject not close to Jared's heart—and the ladies were all in a group planning the best date for Amanda's *soirée* and a suitable guest list.

By the end of the evening Bo had promised to call on Miss Anne the following day to inspect her greenhouse, and Kevin was committed to driving out with Lady Elizabeth. That this suited Amanda was a foregone conclusion, and when Jared realized it would leave him alone with his wife he too liked the arrangement. And so he told his wife later as they ascended to their bedchamber.

"I am relieved to hear that, my dear, for I felt you might be bored to distraction here at Storm Haven. Are you sure you won't miss the social round if we stay in the country until after our child is born?"

Jared dismissed the waiting Sally with a wave of his hand and answered, "If I had my dearest wish I would lock out the entire world for at least a year and spend all my time with you, for as I have mentioned before, you affect me in many ways—but boring me is definitely not one of them."

Amanda threw him an impish grin. "Indeed, my lord, and just how do I affect you?"

"You know damn well, you vixen. Now stop fiddling with that necklace and come to me. You talk too much, when your place is in bed."

She dropped her hands from the intricate clasp and pouted. "It was you, not I, who sent Sally away. Besides," she lifted her chin impishly, "I do not believe I am yet sufficiently fatigued to retire. Perhaps I will go down to the library and get a book."

"Amanda, I am not a patient man. All evening you have been making cow eyes at me across the room, nearly driving me out of my mind. Now, come here, wife!"

"Cow eyes! *Cow eyes!* Oh, how charming! And you, sir, must be casting yourself in the role of bull. How apt, for bull-headed you are in truth. Well, I refuse to come meekly to you when you crook your little finger. I languished here alone for three long months before you deigned to remember me. Now I would like to be courted—not ordered—my lord. Heaven knows I've had precious little of the former."

A slow grin appeared on Jared's face as he surveyed Amanda's pouting mouth, and he made her an elaborate bow.

"Ah, my dear Lady Storm, forgive my boorish haste. First allow me to compliment you on your charming appearance this evening. I intend to write a sonnet tomorrow about your lustrous ebony curls, and the glorious golden jewels which are your eyes—not to mention the enchanting bloom of spring ever-present on your creamy cheeks . . ."

Those creamy cheeks were flushed now as Amanda retorted, "Do not make sport of me, Jared. I know I was flirting with you downstairs this evening in hopes of some light courting, but you are making it a bit too thick and rare. Can you never be serious?"

He wagged a finger in her direction. "Please do not interrupt me, madam, I was not yet finished. Let me see, where was I? Oh, yes. I had finished with your hair, eyes, and complexion; now I must find a way to describe your pert little nose and that tempting mouth. Ah, I cannot think. Better to dedicate my sonnet to your most enchanting of all features: your bewitching breasts—I stared at them all the night long, and if your gown had been but a bit lower, madam, I do believe I would have seen them peeping back . . ." He broke off to dodge a china cup full of hair-pins as it came flying by. "Oh, naughty puss, you will be sorry for that."

"I am sorry—sorry I missed! Stand still so I can aim."

Jared advanced smilingly toward her, saying, "Put down the vial, Amanda. If you break that perfume we'll not be able to stay in this chamber for a month for the smell."

Amanda looked down at the bottle in her hand and agreed with him. But just as swiftly as she put the perfume down she picked up her hairbrush and launched it at his head—only a second too late for it to have done any damage.

"That did it, madam! Now you shall be punished. Don't you remember my telling you at the inn that I would retaliate in future? Or perhaps you wish for another spanking?"

Her eyes widened as she remembered the solid whacks Jared had administered and she picked up her skirts for flight. "You will have to catch me first!"

Before Jared had time to move, Amanda was poised behind one huge bedpost, her hands clasped lightly around it as she prepared to lunge either right or left. As Jared committed himself she jumped the other way, only to find herself caught between the wall and the bed.

"Zounds! Treed, by gad!" Jared chuckled.

Amanda dove across the pillows and scrambled off the far side of the bed and her hair broke loose from its pins and cascaded down her back. As she stood on the other side of the bed, watching for his next move, Jared calmly began walking around the room as if she were not there—extinguishing all the candles until only the small fire in the hearth remained, for the old house was chilly even in the heat of late summer.

Amanda could barely see anything, but Jared was guided by the winking of her diamonds in the firelight and he stealthily circled until suddenly Amanda found herself attacked from behind.

She squealed as he lifted her as if she were weightless and deposited her unceremoniously on the hearth rug. "Jared," she pleaded, "be gentle with me, I am a mother now." He knelt beside her, and as she watched he drew his brows together as if he were considering the matter.

"Very well—*mother*—like all criminals you plead your belly. But I warn you, in six months I shall demand payment."

The firelight cast a rosy glow on Amanda's bare shoulders and sent small lights dancing in her riotous curls as she settled herself into the soft fur of the hearth rug and allowed the tip of her tongue to lick her upper lip. She had won! She never took her eyes from those of her husband, and her heart sang at the sight of the naked longing apparent in every line of his face. Slowly she raised her bare arms to pull him down to her as she whispered, "Court me, Jared. Woo me, please."

"You plague a man out of his mind, brat," he muttered as their lips met in a hunger not to be denied. The chase over, the two antagonists became lovers, as fierce in their lovemaking as they had been half-hearted in their disagreement. Mouths clung as bodies intertwined, hands struggled wildly with cumbersome clothing as burning limbs strained to be released.

"Damn," cursed Jared as he met with yet another intricate feminine fastening. With one swift pull gown and chemise were rent to the hemline, and two bodies joined in a frantic coupling that left them both gasping for breath on the other side of the glorious mountain they had climbed together on the wings of passion and love.

Finally Amanda rose to her feet and surveyed the damage. "Oh, Jared, look what you have done! My beautiful new gown is ruined beyond repair, and it just arrived from London a week ago. How will I ever explain this to Sally?" Suddenly she left off complaining and broke into giggles. Could this be her husband? This disheveled man who sat on the rug with his breeches hanging about his ankles and his shirt and neckcloth twisted halfway round his neck? "Look at you," she exclaimed, "the fashionable Lord Storm. Is this to be a new rage, my lord?"

"Look at yourself, imp, sporting nothing but your diamonds and one satin slipper." He paused a moment and his voice was low as he added, "Yes, my fine lovely wife, just look at you. With your curls caressing your rosy skin, your tawny eyes shining brighter than any jewel—you are my Venus, Amanda."

He kicked away the last of his clothing and reached out his hand to grasp hers. "Come, goddess, let us retire to our cloud where we can touch the stars at our leisure."

July slipped uneventfully into August as the guests at Storm Haven extended their stay from three weeks to nearly six. The foremost reason for this was the blossoming romance between Bo and Anne. The pair spent endless hours in the gardens at Storm Haven—much to the displeasure of Jared's possessive gardener—discussing the local flora and perhaps one or two other subjects.

Kevin, however, was beginning to get restless. The Lady Elizabeth was becoming, in his words, a damnable leech, and he had no intention of being made her tame pet. Lately he had been making noises about returning to London for the Small Season, and Amanda knew that Bo would feel bound to follow. This Amanda could not allow, at least not until Bo worked up his courage sufficiently to approach Squire Bosley for Anne's hand.

To this end she planned another small dinner party, putting her well over Jared's expressed limits. This time she invited only the Squire and his family, cajoling Kevin into allowing himself to be invited to dine at the residence of Lord Close. Lady Chezwick deemed this an optimistic move on Amanda's part, but one that she herself considered a bit short of the mark.

"Compromise 'em, I say," she told Amanda the afternoon of the party. "That fool boy will never speak up, don't think he's capable of it, to tell the truth. Anyone with half a brain in his head can see they're bosky over each other. Why, the fool near drools when little Anne comes into a room—and she, poor misguided soul, thinks the lad hangs out the stars. I commend you, Amanda. You and Jared are obviously devoted, I thank

God, but you seem to have learned to control yourselves in public."

Amanda disregarded her aunt's comments on her personal life and instead concentrated on Lady Chezwick's first recommendation. "Compromise them, dear lady? Do you mean to surprise them one night in the garden in a passionate embrace? If so I fear you are overly romantic. Jared and I were taking a stroll through the greenhouse the other evening and Bo and Anne were over in a corner with their heads together. Needless to say, we thought we had interrupted a proposal, but as we approached—there was no sense in pretending we were unaware of them—they stepped back and there between them was a wilting fern they had been transplanting. Compromise them? I doubt it, Aunt."

Lady Chezwick wrinkled her aristocratic nose. "Playing in the dirt like a couple of children. I wouldn't be surprised if they made mud patties and had little tea parties under the trees." She threw up her hands and exclaimed, "Sometimes I want to pull his flaming hair out by its flaming roots! How can he be so dense?"

Jared came into the room in time to hear his aunt's last words, and as he kissed his wife's cheek and settled himself beside her he said, "I assume you are discussing the backward beau, if you will forgive my play on words. Pray do not harm the lad, Aunt, for he comes by his density quite naturally. Not that he is entirely vacant in his upper story, but he is by nature a very deliberate person. I have it from his own lips that he intends to wed the girl—at least I think that is what he said—he just has to build up his courage to approach the Squire."

Lady Chezwick was not impressed. "Ha! If I know Francis Bosley he'll not only agree to the match but kiss Bo's hands in the bargain. Anne is the last of six daughters and he's been trying to marry her off for three years. They'd take Bo if he were completely to let in the attic, which personally I think he is. By the way, where is the fellow—out pinching the ladybugs off the roses?"

Jared made an elaborate business out of repositioning a curl that had sprung loose at Amanda's nape while he calmly announced, "As a matter of fact, I have no idea where he is. He rode out earlier to pay a morning call on the Squire but he should have been back by now."

"Oh, foul! Foul!" exclaimed Amanda as she jumped up from

the sofa and turned on her husband. "You knew all along that Bo was going to ask the Squire for Anne's hand this morning and never breathed a word of it to us. You are the most—" She searched for a word which her aunt quietly supplied. "Yes, despicable, thank you, Aunt, despicable man I have ever met. And stop grinning like an ape, Jared, for you know how long I have planned for this moment." Slowly the indignation left her face and she reached out her hands to Jared and smiled happily. "You are just as thrilled by this as I am, aren't you, darling?"

He squeezed her hands as he replied, "Yes, infant, I am, although I must say it pains me deeply that you should be so successful on your first attempt at matchmaking. I shudder to think of poor Kevin's fate once you spy out a wench for him. He won't stand a chance of escape."

"Jared, that is unkind. I did not force Bo and Anne to fall in love. I merely introduced them and, er, let Nature take its course."

Jared rose and put his arms around her waist. "Certainly, dear heart, you yourself did little to forward their romance, only a slight nudge or two in the right direction every now and then. Like the time you invited Anne over and then deliberately left her alone with Bo for an hour, pleading a crisis in the kitchens. You were very subtle, Amanda—as subtle as a house falling on his head."

Amanda's lower lip came out in a pout, but she was too happy to be subdued for long. Still in the circle of Jared's arms, she turned to Lady Chezwick and appealed for her help. "Was I too heavy-handed, Aunt Agatha?"

"Good heavens, no, my dear. Compared to me you were light-handed indeed. Why, in trying to get Jared bracketed to Miss Farnsworthy I deliberately stepped on the hem of her gown at a picnic so that I could offer her the use of our coach to return home and change."

"Yes, indeed, Aunt," Jared interjected, "and once you had the chit and her abigail firmly entrenched on the seat you came to me and forced me to accompany her because you—you won't believe this, Amanda—were feeling ill on your stomach and were afraid of the poor springs of my coach upsetting you further. Bad springs indeed, on a coach of mine! It took me three months of being downright rude to the dratted gal before she accepted Viscount Whitterby in my stead. Then there was the time . . ."

"Stop your prattlings, Nephew. I did not ask for a recital of my sins."

A drawling voice issued from the doorway. "Sins? Oh, good, we are baring our souls are we? For me, my greatest transgression of late was to be called on to compliment Lady Elizabeth on her needlework. I do hope she won't present me with handmade slippers this Christmas, for I refuse to wear anything so shoddy and my valet is much larger of foot than I."

"Oh, shut up, Kevin Rawlings. Your tongue betrays the void between your ears," said Lady Chezwick. "I have known you since before you were out of short petticoats and you become more like your mother every day, always primping and posturing and worrying about your outside while totally ignoring the vacancy in your upper rooms. Sit down, you popinjay, and fasten your lip. We are discussing important things here today."

Kevin assumed a crestfallen expression and took up his position at the liquor table, saying, "I retire from the lists and leave the field to you, madam. I dare not argue with someone who admits she is at least thirty years my senior."

Jared had been putting a glass to his lips as Kevin spoke, and Amanda was soon quite busy—thumping him soundly between the shoulder blades as he choked and coughed on the brandy that was halfway down his throat when his aunt called Kevin a son of a female hound. "A-aunt," he got out after another round of coughs, "where did you ever pick up such a, um, candid expression?"

Lady Chezwick busied herself with her needlework while she informed her nephew that, contrary to what he believed, her time in India was not all spent at ladies' teas. "I saw a bit of the rough and ready, if you know what I mean."

A now thoroughly chastened Kevin approached the offended lady and bowed deeply over her hand as he issued a long and rather complicated apology—which ended only because Bo chose that moment to enter the room. Immediately all eyes were on him and silence filled the chamber.

Bo looked around at the four staring faces, muttered something unintelligible, and turned to leave. Amanda was after him like a shot and dragged him back into the room, where she proceeded to ask him six questions without once waiting for an answer.

As Amanda stopped to catch her breath, Lady Chezwick stepped into the breech and launched her own volley of questions, which sounded very like the ones Amanda had just asked. As Jared was fully engaged in laughing up his sleeve at the sight of Bo's confusion, Kevin felt it was up to him to step into the fray and save his befuddled friend from this female attack.

"I say Bo, stop opening and closing your mouth like a demmed fish and take a deep swallow of this. The ladies are a bit impatient about something and it is impolite of you to ignore them. Here, drink deep and I promise to call them off until you are ready to face them."

Then he turned and addressed the two impatient women. "Ladies, I implore you to consider this poor boy's feelings. Look at him—" and they did, "look at his high color, a sure sign of a fever, I'd say. Note his trembling hands: possibly he has sustained some bad shock." He leaned over and peered deeply into Bo's rather vacant eyes. "You know, you're really not yourself, Bo. I'd take something for it. I really would."

Amanda appealed to Jared to make Kevin stop his taunting, but Jared was so dissolved in mirth she gave it up as a bad job and tackled the tormentor herself—a move which completely disabled both Jared and his aunt—by simply stepping up to Kevin and kicking him soundly in the shin, sending him sprawling full length on the carpet, one leg held high in the air as he howled in pain.

"Why, Kevin," she exclaimed in all innocence, "That was a most lamentable accident. You really should be more careful."

"Brat," commented Jared, trying to be stern and failing miserably. He held out his hand to his friend and helped him to his feet. "Get up, Kevin. You're making a cake of yourself."

To Lady Chezwick it was obvious this entire scene was getting out of control. She clapped her hands for attention and announced, "Silence! Silence all of you! Good heavens, I feel like a nanny whose charges have run amuck in the nursery. Now sit down, all of you, and let us get to the business at hand. We are all waiting to hear the outcome of young Bo's visit to the Squire this morning." She sat primly on the edge of her chair, hands folded in her lap, and soothed, "All right, dear, we are all attention now. Please tell us what happened."

Naturally this speech made Bo the immediate center of attention and his usually florid face grew almost excruciatingly red. In his agitation he ruined his already poorly-tied neckcloth with his fumblings, and tried to calm his nerves by reaching for his brandy—which unfortunately slipped from his shaking fingers and landed upside down in his lap.

"Oh, poor Bo!" cried Amanda.

"Get you a napkin," offered Jared.

"Sapskull," commented Kevin.

"Brightest thing you've said all day," said Lady Chezwick.

In the end Amanda handled the affair in a question-and-answer-type interview—which, Jared commented, "would have put the Lord High Justice firmly on his mettle."

"You went to call on the Squire, Bo?" Amanda purred.

Bo nodded.

"And was the Squire at home?"

Another nod.

"Ah, we proceed," whispered Kevin to Jared, whose shoulders had started to shake.

"And did you and the Squire have speech?" continued the Lord High Inquisitor, after throwing a quelling glance at the two men.

Once again the head moved in the affirmative.

"And what did you talk about?"

"The weather."

Jared groaned and sank down in his chair, earning him another speaking glance from the love of his life.

"Did you speak of anything *else?*" Amanda pleaded.

"Napoleon."

Kevin put his hand to his mouth and loudly whispered to Jared, "Gad, that must have been a deep debate. I'd have given my best bay to hear the farmer and the fool discuss politics."

Amanda was rapidly reaching the end of her tether. "Was there anything else, dear Bo?"

Bo nodded and turned a becoming shade of scarlet, whereupon Amanda took a deep breath and asked, "Did you discuss Miss Anne?"

Another nod. Kevin jumped to his feet and shouted, "Good God, we could be here until Christmas with all this dancing around the outside of the question." He turned to Bo and asked, "Are you going to marry the chit or ain't you, Bo? It's getting on for dinner and I have things to do."

Amid the general uproar from the ladies this candid questioning caused Bo's garbled "Yes" to be barely heard, so he repeated it. He then repeated it a third time, whereupon all other speech quickly died—just as he took a long breath and admitted, "I love her!" so that his declaration echoed in the silent room.

"No need to shout, man," remarked Kevin. "We all heard you. Don't say that I like it a bit, the two of you deserting me like this. All I know is that after tonight I shall be shoving myself off to London before Lady Elizabeth corners me in the garden." He crossed to his friend and shook his hand. "Getting yourself riveted, are you Bo? My condolences." And he quit the room, taking up the brandy decanter as he went.

Amanda watched him go with a sad expression on her face. "Poor Kevin, he is feeling quite alone. I really must . . ."

Jared cut her off the only way he knew how. He kissed her soundly and then added, "Connubial happiness is not the only happiness, although it suits me perfectly well. Leave Kevin alone. I'm sure he can find his own companionship in the city."

Amanda would have answered him with a remark on Kevin's idea of a suitable companion, but the butler came into the room to announce the arrival of guests.

"Who could it be?" asked Jared, happy for the interruption.

"It is I, darling—or is it, 'It is me'? No matter," came the self-supplied answer as Lady Blanche Wade swept into the blue room, followed closely by the puffing figure of Peregrine Denton.

Blanche put her hand through Denton's arm and looked down into his plainly adoring face. "Peregrine has honored me with a proposal of marriage—a proposal which I accepted, of course. Aren't you going to kiss your step-mama to be, Jared dear?"

Chapter Eight

AMANDA was busy in the morning room, arranging
flowers with an intensity of purpose that was literally destroying the fragile blooms. After cutting one stem too short and
finding she had run out of carnations entirely, she was about to
give it all up as a bad job when Blanche floated into the room on
a wave of musky perfume. Immediately Amanda tensed,
breaking yet another delicate stem.

"Oh, what a pity, dear child," lisped Blanche as she hastened
to remedy the damage. "Do not feel badly. Some of us are just
less talented in the artistic things. Here, let me help you. Hand
me the scissors, please, dear. I just need a few blooms here, here,
and—behold! A perfect bouquet! Now you go sit down, dear,
and I shall call a servant to clean up your mess. I must say you
are looking a trifle off this morning."

"Thank you, Lady Wade. I have sat here in my new gown
since breakfast waiting for just such a compliment. Now my day
is complete."

Blanche looked over her shoulder as she went to ring for a
maid. "Oh, are we out of sorts? Has my naughty stepson-to-be
been ignoring his little bride?"

Amanda restrained an impulse to yank Blanche's golden hair
out by its—she was sure—brown roots, and crossed to a sofa to
sit down. She looked innocently up at her uninvited guest and
commented, "If only that were the case, *dear* Lady Wade, but
Jared scarce leaves me any time to myself. He is extremely
attentive to my every wish, for after all, as you say, we are newly
wed. Perhaps when I am as long in the tooth as you he will not be
so eager."

Amanda smiled sweetly as she watched the color drain from
Blanche's face. She could not resist adding, "Surely my

stepfather, being closer to your years, keeps you sufficiently amused, Lady Wade?"

"Why you—I mean, *please,* Amanda—cannot you find it in your heart to address me more informally? After all, I am soon to become one of the family."

Amanda's eyes danced as she inquired, "Will you wish me to call you Mama?"

Blanche was fast losing control of her temper but held it on a tight leash as she answered, "Indeed, no, my dear. I would certainly never dream of replacing your mother. Please, just call me Blanche."

Amanda grudgingly gave up the fight and agreed. As Blanche turned to the maid, who was clearing up the flowers, and ordered some light refreshment, Amanda took the time to study the woman who had entered their lives so presumptuously three days before. Jared's shock, and then barely-suppressed outrage, was clear to her and—except at meals, where they were forced into one another's company—he made a wide cut around the Lady Wade. Amanda was sure they had been known to each other in London. Hadn't Blanche addressed him as "darling"? But Jared refused to talk to her about it.

Amanda had questioned her stepfather at length about both his visit and his intended bride, but the besotted Denton only told her that Blanche had expressed an interest in meeting his stepdaughter and he could refuse her nothing. That Blanche was not in love with him was obvious to Amanda, yet since she must know her future husband was supported largely by the marriage portion he received from Jared, and since he had no title, what could have made her enter into such an unadvantageous alliance? Amanda was sure Blanche did nothing without a self-serving reason.

Look at her, thought Amanda. The gown on her back even now must have cost well over a hundred pounds. And the diamonds she wore at dinner last night had set someone back a small fortune. She had noticed Jared's eyes on that necklace more than once and didn't like the way her own mind was moving.

The woman *was* beautiful, though in a cold way. Even as overdressed as she was, there was no denying her appearance was one that would cause male eyebrows to rise appreciatively. Yet Kevin had shown no interest in her, and had departed Storm Haven directly after Amanda's dinner party. And Bo, he had slipped from the blue room after rudely cutting Blanche dead, and even now his luggage was being moved to Squire Bosley's where he would stay until after the engagement party next week—saying it was more convenient that way.

Oh, if only she could make Blanche leave before the woman ruined little Anne's big night, for Anne had been forced by courtesy to extend both of Amanda's houseguests an invitation!

Blanche was watching the emotions coming and going on Amanda's expressive face, and she deliberately preened herself as she enjoyed the girl's discomfort. Cheeky little tart! So this was the chit Jared had dropped her for. His bad taste surprised her. The whole thing was insulting. Freddie was right, though: The way to get at Jared was through this green girl, for Jared was obviously bewitched by her.

Blanche never could abide Freddie—no woman who thinks herself irresistible can understand a man who finds his joys in the arms of another man—so when she heard of Jared's marriage she had sought him out to tease him about his lost inheritance.

She had always known Freddie disliked his cousin, but she had been surprised at the vehemence of his hatred. When Jared left her, after his final insult, she had studied long and hard on a way to make him sorry. And Freddie, with whom she had already spent long hours ruing their combined ill luck, had naturally come into her mind. It was Freddie who suggested she take up with Peregrine and get herself invited to Storm Haven, but once there she was on her own.

She meant what she said to Jared that last night. He *would* pay for his insult. Oh, not with his life, as she had threatened, but destroying Jared's insipid little marriage would go a long way toward soothing her own outraged ego. As her first move Blanche had made it plain that once she and that stupid Denton—so like her late husband—were married (as if she would ever marry that buffoon!) they would hope to spend at least three months a year visiting their dear relatives. Yes, so far she had succeeded in embarrassing Jared, but her revenge was far from complete.

Blanche smiled as she remembered the look on Jared's face when she heard her plans at dinner last night, and she had deliberately fingered the diamond necklace that was his last present to her. No, it was far from the last, for if her plans went as she expected he might be talked into paying her to stay away from Storm Haven.

This was all amusing, but now the girl was showing her milk teeth, daring to spar with her. It was time things came to a head. She decided to stop this prattle and ventured boldly, "By the way, Amanda, I have something of Jared's upstairs in my room. I had hoped to return them to him at a more," she pretended to search for the proper words, "*intimate* moment, but he seems to be scarcely ever at home. You see, Jared left London rather unexpectedly and I had no time to return the gloves he left in my bed—er, my entrance hall the last time he visited me. The poor darling was always leaving one thing or another behind— gloves, hats, cravats. I shall have my maid place them in your chamber." Blanche reached for her teacup and hid her triumphant smile behind a raised napkin while searching Amanda's face for her reaction.

The room began to spin dizzily before Amanda's eyes. There was no denying what Blanche so crudely implied. Jared had been Blanche's lover—her lover *since* their marriage! While she languished here at Storm Haven and cried into her pillow missing him, he was rolling about in Blanche Wade's bed.

How can I sit here sipping tea while my world crashes down around my ears? she mused crazily. I breathe, I see, I hear, my heart beats—yet I am dead inside. Then her mind began to churn at a furious pace. She would not give in without a fight! Jared had never discussed his months in London with her, not since that first day when he confessed he had been miserable without her.

Well, obviously he found some surcease from his pain in Blanche's perfumed embrace. And those diamonds! Of course, how could she have been so stupid! They must have come from Jared. Why else had he been so uncomfortable when Lady Chezwick had commented on them. Oh, it was all coming together for her now.

Amanda looked around her distractedly. I must not let her know she has upset me, she warned herself. I must remain calm. Later I shall certainly indulge in a riotous storm of weeping, after which I will confront Jared with what I know. But for now I must deal with this—what was the word Aunt Agatha used?— bitch. Yes, that was it, this blonde bitch.

Amanda had no idea of the events of Jared's last meeting with Blanche in London, but she knew he was definitely not overjoyed to see her at Storm Haven. She was sufficiently sure of his love now to believe he would not stray in Blanche's direction again, especially after she confronted him tonight. With this half-formed thought in mind she unwittingly sealed her husband's fate as she airily replied, "La, yes, Blanche, Jared told me *all about* his last meeting with you in London. I am only surprised you would wish to mention it, since, as we have now both said, it was his *last* visit to you."

Blanche sat speechless with shock while Amanda rose and made to leave the room, turning only to add, "You may not be aware, but Jared and I are to start our nursery in the new year. With our new informality, would you wish the child to address you as Grandmother? Good heavens, the handle has quite snapped off that teacup! I shall send a maid to wipe the stain from your lovely gown before it is ruined."

As the livid Blanche dashed from the room, holding her sodden skirts, she shouted, "Send that stupid Denton to me at once! I wish to return to London!"

Jared crept rather stealthily into the house by a side door, hoping to avoid any meeting with either Blanche or the idiot Denton. Though he did not really harbor any animosity toward Denton, three days of mealtime conversation had proved Amanda correct—he was too stupid to arouse hatred, just exasperation. Blanche was another matter entirely.

He had been racking his brain ever since her arrival to figure out her motive in coming to Storm Haven. He remembered her last words to him, screamed as she lay naked on the floor of her bedchamber with his money fluttering around her, but he doubted she had come to place a knife between his shoulders. More probably she wished to put a pistol to his head—figuratively—and he was more than ready to pay her any amount to be rid of her. But marriage to Denton? She was really pushing credulity a bit too far if she thought she could smoke him with that story. No, Denton was just the dupe—a role he seemed quite fitted for—and Blanche was up to no good.

As he passed the small salon he heard a loud *"Pssst!"* and stuck his head in the room to see his aunt beckoning frantically to him to join her.

"Why are you hiding in here, madam? Have you run afoul of our guests? I'll share your hideaway if I may."

Lady Chezwick wore a pained expression as she whispered, "Keep your voice down, you dolt, and close the door before you have the whole house down on us. I am only trying to save you, though heaven only knows why, for you have never appreciated my help. Ah, that's better. Now, come sit down next to me while I tell you of this day's events. Guess, just you guess, what has happened!"

"My dear lady, I have no time for games. My mind is over-occupied as it is, trying to find some way to kill off our houseguests and bury the bodies where no one will find them."

"But that is it exactly! However did you guess?"

"What is it *exactly?* You mean Blanche and Denton are hidden under the daisies?"

Jared's attempt at humor was rewarded by a smart slap on his wrist from Lady Chezwick's fan. "Don't be more of a fool than you can help, Nephew. This is serious."

He rubbed his hand as he agreed. "I totally concur, Aunt. Murder always is."

"Murder? Murder! Jared, I feel we are talking at cross purposes, but I refuse to go back and figure out where we left the main road and started down this side path. What I called you in here to tell you is that Amanda's odious stepfather and his hussy have left for London. If you had been at home, instead of hiding out all day with Harrow pretending to inspect the estate, you would be aware of the fact."

Jared jumped up and said loudly, "That is about the best news I have heard since my horse won at Newmarket! Why didn't you tell me sooner? I must go congratulate Amanda and order a special dinner from Cook. However did my sweetest wife accomplish this great miracle?"

Lady Chezwick was nearly purple with rage as she pulled on his coat sleeve to gain his attention. "Keep your voice down, Jared, or I shall leave you to your fate. If Amanda were to learn you are home before you and I put our heads together, you would not have a head left. The girl is incensed, I tell you!"

She now had his undivided attention as he sat down and motioned for her to proceed. She settled herself comfortably on the sofa and launched herself on a dressing-down she felt was long overdue. "Now, you wretched boy, your past has come back to haunt you. I always told you it would one day, and you know I am right more than I am wrong—although I must admit

I have been in error once or twice, like when I misjudged dear Amanda, but not more than that, I am . . ."

"Aunt, keep to the point, if you please. I believe you were about to chastise me for my checkered past."

"Do not interrupt! I will get where I am going in my own way, Jared, and I would appreciate your attendance to my words." At his meek nod she continued. "As I was saying before your rude interruption," she threw him a wicked glance, "your past has indeed come back to haunt you. I never cared for Blanche Wade, told you so innumerable times, but did you listen? No, you did not. I knew when she waltzed in here the other day she was up to no good, but I did not believe you could have been so much a loose screw as to have visited her since your marriage to that sweet, innocent, adorable—"

"Her name is Amanda, Aunt."

"I know that, but when I saw that poor betrayed girl upstairs today, sobbing her heart out over a blackguard such as you, I realized you are still ignorant of her many virtues."

"Crying? My wife was crying?" He rose as if to quit the room. "What did that tart do to upset Amanda?"

"She only told her the truth—that you had visited her when you ran away from Storm Haven like a delinquent child and stayed in London. I know it is true, for I can see it in your face. The guilt is plain to me and it will be just as plain to Amanda." The old lady's face crumpled as she wailed, "Oh, why, Jared? Why did you do such a terrible thing? And with a hussy like Blanche Wade!"

Jared put his arms around his sobbing aunt, and after some minutes she gained control of herself and allowed her nephew to explain. He owed the poor woman the truth, and her face brightened considerably as Jared told her of his one meeting with his old mistress. But then her face clouded once again.

"Now what is the matter, Aunt?" asked Jared.

"You certainly cannot tell that story to Amanda."

"Why not? It is the truth."

"*The truth!* I gave you credit for more sense than you must have. Do you really think it makes a difference to Amanda whether or not you achieved what you went after? No, the mere idea that you *wished* to bed the creature will be enough to send Amanda up to the treetops. Lie to her, Nephew, lie to her! It is the only way!"

"Aunt, you never cease to amaze me. Do you really think my wife is too small to accept the truth, such as it is? After all, in a way the truth flatters her."

Lady Chezwick shook her head vehemently. "That don't signify a scrap, Jared. You must not admit to setting foot in that woman's house since the day you laid eyes on Amanda."

"But that is almost the truth. I only saw her that one more time."

Lady Chezwick sighed in deep exasperation. "Jared, my favorite nephew, believe me in this. *Lie to the girl.* It is your only hope of salvation."

"All right, Aunt, I bow to your judgement. But if you are wrong, I promise you I shall lay all blame directly on your doorstep. Just promise me you will not give me away at some future time."

His aunt sniffed at this unheard-of possibility and then suddenly broke into delighted laughter.

"Now what has tickled you, Aggie?"

"It's just—it's just that I have suddenly seen how funny it all is. You see, I never did tell you why our guests left so hurriedly. Goodness, Denton was really quite put out by his intended bride's haste. Oh, it is too good!" She clapped her hands in glee.

Jared grinned as he enjoyed a joke he did not understand and pressed his aunt to explain.

"Amanda told me of her discussion with Lady Wade this morning—the one in which she found out you had left your gloves in that hussy's bedroom on your last visit. Amanda coolly replied, I don't know how she had the courage, that you had told her *all about* that last visit and that it was indeed just that—your last visit. That is when Lady Wade spilled her tea all down the front of her atrocious gown and flew upstairs on her broomstick to pack her things. Jared? Don't you think Amanda was quite clever? Jared, whatever can be the matter now? You look positively ill."

Jared stalked to the door and pulled it open before turning to his aunt and saying coldly, "Your brain is to let, madam, if you think Blanche Wade will take that kind of insult lying down. Nothing but my blood will satisfy her now!"

He charged hurriedly up the stairs, only to stop himself and walk slowly toward the main bedroom where he was sure Amanda was waiting—her battle lines clearly drawn. The news that she had so effectively set down Blanche filled him with concern; it was, however, a concern he could not let his wife see.

But then, just what could Blanche do? She would seem to have taken her best shot in coming to Storm Haven, and her ignominious retreat without so much as a pound of silence-money from him should be the end of it. Yet had he ever imagined she would have gone as far as engaging herself to a dullard like Denton, just to exact revenge on an old lover?

She must have seriously believed I would marry her, Jared thought. Why, even before Lord Wade was cold in his grave she was making noises in that direction. He remembered how startled she was when he had mentioned Bertram's untimely end. Could she have—no, it was impossible. Not even Blanche would do murder. Would she? And if she did, what was to stop such an unscrupulous woman from wreaking havoc on Amanda? He had no thoughts she would be stupid enough to try to do him physical harm. After all, she was only a woman.

But Amanda? Of course! Why had he not thought of it sooner? It was Amanda she was out to destroy; Amanda was her reason for coming to Storm Haven. And through Amanda she could hurt him, more than she could possibly dream. Thank God no one had mentioned the baby. At least Blanche was ignorant of that!

As he entered the bedchamber, Amanda dismissed Sally—who was arranging her hair—and turned to her husband with a set look on her face. "I am honored, my lord, that you are still in residence. I had thought you would be on the road to London by now, to bid a fond farewell to your doxy."

"Amanda, sweetheart, let me explain . . ."

She cut him off when she exclaimed, "Explain! *Explain?* Whatever is there to explain? You and that jade were lovers—most probably before, and definitely since, our marriage. Deny it, sir, if it is untrue. But please, do not bore me with explanations."

"Then I deny it! Well, I deny part of it—the last part. But I *can* explain all of it. Dash it all, woman, look at me when I talk to you! It's deuced uncomfortable talking to your back."

Amanda whirled on him, her amber eyes dark with pain. "Does it make it easier to lie to my face, my lord?"

"No! I mean, yes! Oh, dash it, shut up Amanda!" He was not doing well in this exchange, and he knew it. He had never found any difficulty in dealing with a woman before—except his aunt, of course—but then he had never cared for a woman as he did this slip of a girl. "Think of the baby, Amanda. You might harm the child."

"Ha! All this concern over one little child. How many children have you from the wrong side of the blanket, Jared? Will my baby have many bastard brothers?"

Jared crossed the area separating them more quickly than Amanda could register his movement, and she found herself clutched tightly to her husband's chest. "Stop this, Amanda. Stop it now."

In a voice cold with anger she replied, "Let me go."

"If I let you go I shall probably hit you, and I don't want to, so kindly shut your mouth while I try to get us out of this muddle." When her struggles to free herself ebbed and she promised to be good, he let her go and paced back and forth while he pleaded his case.

"I am eight and twenty, Amanda, and I told you once before I was a bit of a hellion. I'll not deny I have known many women—Blanche Wade among them, more's the pity—but there are no by-blows of mine running the countryside. You of all people should know that, for the love of heaven." He ran a shaking hand through his once-neat hair, then turned to her and implored, "I refuse to lie and tell you I sported a lily all my life, because I know you could not believe it. But I do not lie when I tell you I have not made love to any woman but you since first I laid eyes on you at Almack's. If Blanche told you I was her lover in London these months past she is lying, and may I die tomorrow if what I say is untrue. I leave the next move to you, madam!" He turned abruptly and made to leave the room when Amanda stopped him with one sentence.

"Forgive me."

He raised his eyes to heaven and vowed a new ruby bracelet to his wise aunt before he opened his magnanimous arms to a weeping Amanda.

"Oh, my poor darling," she cried. "How could I have been so corkbrained as to believe that odious woman? Please forgive me. I love you so much and I was eaten up inside with jealousy. Of course you couldn't have been within a mile of that trollop while you were gone. Anything you did before you met me does not concern me, although I must say I am surprised in your poor taste if you ever thought that fleshy thing attractive."

Jared buried his face in Amanda's hair and murmured, "Indeed, I have wondered the same thing a hundred times over since she arrived here. I must have been deep in my cups to find that obvious female attractive. You are my heart's delight, dearest, and from the moment I met you every other woman in England has looked to me a crone." He nibbled one small ear as he whispered, "You are a witch, Amanda, and I am under your spell."

Amanda felt her last doubts melting away. It was far easier to forget than to keep up an argument with a man you loved so entirely, and she turned her face for his kiss. Jared could feel her trembling in his arms as he teased her with his tongue and then sucked lightly on her lower lip. His hands reached out to untie her dressing gown and he traced a pattern of kisses down her throat until he reached the curve of her breast.

Suddenly he felt a movement and put his head up in mock shock. "Madam, you take liberties uncommon in a well-bred female."

Amanda giggled and denied any forwardness.

"I distinctly felt you reach out and touch me. There! You did it again!"

Amanda held up her hands to proclaim her innocence—and he felt the movement a third time. She tried to suppress her mirth while she took hold of one of his hands and pressed it to her gently-rounded stomach. "I know my dresses still conceal the fact—thank the French for their styles!—but you as my husband must be aware of the child's growth. It is your own son who has nudged you, my lord." She kept his hand pressed to her and was soon rewarded by a very healthy kick.

Jared drew his hand back as if he had touched something hot, then slowly replaced it. He lifted one eyebrow and remarked, "Champing at the bit to get out here with us, isn't he? Doesn't that hurt, Amanda?"

"No, silly, I enjoy it immensely, but this is the first time he has performed for you. Are you upset?"

In answer he scooped her up in his arms and deposited her lightly on the bed where he quickly joined her. "Upset? Infant, I am confused and bewildered by just how pleased I am. I must admit I thought of the child as an enemy when I was not busy trying to ignore his existence. But you are right, you know: It is definitely a son, and now I find myself quite proud of his amazing strength at such a young age. You are quite sure it doesn't hurt?"

Amanda was delighted at her husband's new interest and

hastened to explain that all babies kicked their mothers though definitely not as lustily as a child of Jared Delaney was capable. His next question was not quite as easy to answer.

"It is time we stop our lovemaking, pet?"

Suddenly she was quite shy—an emotion she had not felt in some time around Jared. To admit she would miss his love-making terribly would seem brazen, she thought, yet she did not want it to stop no matter how advanced her pregnancy. Finally she cast down her eyes and stammered, "S-surely, t-there are—*ways* that would n-not injure . . ."

Jared's face lit in a wicked grin as he reached for her and whispered into her ear.

"Oh, Jared! Oh, my goodness, *really? . . .*"

Amanda and her aunt were sitting in the small salon, intent on placing invisible stitches in the hems of some dresses for the coming baby, when Jared entered with a letter in his hands.

"That is unfortunate," he was heard to remark aloud, upon which his wife asked him to what he referred.

"Kevin writes to say he cannot be with us for Bo's party tonight; it seems he has been called to his uncle's bedside in Sussex. The old man has been dying these last twenty years or more, but this time it seems he really means it. Kevin is his only heir, you know, and will inherit a packet and the title once the old codger sticks his spoon in the wall."

"Hrummph!" commented Lady Chezwick. "Poor old man, the vultures always gather at the end."

"I would not waste my pity on the old earl if I were you, madam. He always was a bit of a rum touch." He went back to his letter and remarked, "Blast me if Kevin didn't sponge on me for a second sheet! He refuses to cross his lines, you know. I wonder what he has to say that could be so important." He read for a few moments and Amanda could see the confusion etched on his face.

"What is the matter, sweetheart? You seem upset."

Jared folded the letter and slipped it into his pocket. "Nothing to concern you, my love. Kevin sustained some heavy losses at White's and begs a few pennies, that is all. Oh, yes," he said rather offhandedly, "he also mentions he saw my cousin Freddie at Manton's Gallery, I wonder that Freddie knows which end of a pistol to point, and he told Kevin he heard you are increasing. How could he know, I wonder?"

"Heavens, I have not the faintest idea. Is he by any chance known to my stepfather?"

"Denton? I do believe he might be," Jared answered, remembering Bo's and Kevin's encounter with the pair. "Why?"

Amanda colored prettily as she recalled her last words to Lady Wade. "I just remembered that I asked Lady Wade if she wished our coming child to address her as *Grandmother*. It is possible she mentioned it to my stepfather and he repeated it to your cousin."

"The devil you did! Good God, Amanda, could you not hold your tongue?"

Lady Chezwick put a restraining hand on Amanda before she could reply angrily and observed, "You must have a reason for all this concern, Nephew. Perhaps you would do us the honor of sharing it with us before you find your wife's needle stuck in your gullet."

Jared dropped heavily into a chair made for a lesser weight and tried to gain control of his temper. It would not do to unnerve the ladies. "It is nothing, I assure you, but an immature urge to be the one who presented my cousin with his usurpation by means of the birth announcement of our new heir. I know it is petty, but then I am by nature a mean man."

Lady Chezwick seemed mollified by this, but Amanda was more shrewd. She remembered Bo's opinion of Freddie and instinctively spread her hands over her stomach protectively. "Your cousin would not try to harm the baby?"

Jared had been so intent on his preoccupation with Blanche's intentions that he had not really given Freddie much thought, but he did so now. Could Blanche mean to enlist Freddie in her cause? A vision of his cousin as he had last seen him passed through his head, and at the thought of the effeminate little dandy a sneer appeared on Jared's face. Freddie? Never. No, his problem lay with Blanche, and other than to make another try to cause a breach between him and Amanda she was really quite powerless. Blast! He was behaving like an old woman, starting at shadows.

He hastened to reassure his wife. "Freddie is an impotent twit, my love. At best he will indulge in a tantrum when our son is born, and then hide himself away from his creditors. Do not concern yourself with him. And stop frowning! Our child will be born wrinkled enough!"

"But Jared, he hates you. And once we have a son—"

"Enough, love. I refuse to let the thought of my cousin ruin an otherwise perfect day. Have you chosen your gown for the party this evening?"

"I did. I do not wish to outshine dear Anne, so I am wearing the green silk—with just a few of those marvelous Delaney emeralds you gave me. I am sure Anne's new white brocade will be the prettiest at the ball. Besides, my figure is no longer one to captivate any audience."

"Untrue, my love. Your roundness becomes you, does it not, Aunt?" He winked in Lady Chezwick's direction.

"Fiddlesticks, you rapscallion! You would adore her if she were the same size as Cook, and by the fish-eyed way you two are looking at each other now I can see I am not needed here. Excuse me, my dears, for I wish to rest before Higgins does my toilette. The older one gets, the longer it takes to hide the ravages of time."

Amanda gave her aunt a kiss. "You are the loveliest of women, dear Aunt. I only hope I can be half as beautiful at your age."

Lady Chezwick surprised them both with her stammered denials, and they were quite pleased with themselves as they remained closeted in the morning room discussing subjects not in the least connected with Freddie or Lady Wade.

At Squire Bosley's that evening, a glowing Amanda was content to watch from the sidelines as pretty little Anne and her ungainly swain circled the room under the benevolent eyes of the assembled guests. The pair was oblivious to the presence of others in the ballroom and several times continued to dance after the musicians had put down their instruments.

Jared finally dragged Bo off to the library to share a bottle and give him some rather bawdy instruction on the care and feeding of wives, while Amanda and Anne settled themselves in a corner to have a friendly coze over some ratafia.

Anne pressed her friend's hand and gushed, "I cannot thank you enough, dear Amanda, for everything you have done. We are so happy, Bo and I, but if it hadn't been for you and Lord Storm we might never have met."

Amanda modestly waved aside all credit and pointed out that it took the love of an intelligent woman like Anne to discover Bo's heretofore hidden depths. "Jared told me he never knew of Bo's interest in plants, and he has known him these many years. However did you manage it?"

Anne blushed and told of her desperation in trying to hold a conversation with the retiring Mr. Chevington. "I brought up the subject of plants as a last-ditch measure. We discovered we had a mutual interest, and ever since that first evening there has not been an uneasy silence between us."

Amanda looked up in time to see Jared and the soon-to-be bridegroom approaching. "It would seem Bo cannot exist without you for more than a moment, dear, for he is fast beating a path to your side."

The two ladies made room for the gentlemen on the settee, but Jared decided he would rather stand. "It seems we have a slight problem, my love. Bo is quite convinced the—oh, blast, I cannot remember the name of the thing. Anyway, some fool plant is set to bloom tonight in our greenhouse, and he wishes to take us back to Storm Haven to witness the great event. Are you willing?"

The four-mile journey was not one Amanda relished in her condition if she had to return again to the party, and it was certainly too early in the evening to retire. "Darling," she sighed, "do you mean to say you are so dense that you believe Bo desires our company? Loan him our carriage and let the two of them sneak away. Perhaps they have more to discuss than the maturation of some greenery. I can witness this great feat on the morrow."

"Can't, you know. Only blooms at night. Pity you won't go."

Amanda patted Bo on his chubby cheek. "I am desolated, I am sure, dear, but Anne shall make up in enthusiasm what you will lack in numbers. Won't you, dear?"

In answer the girl blushed and busied herself in finding a suitable place to hide her unfinished glass of ratafia. She then rose and held out her hand to her betrothed. "I should love to accompany you, Bo, dearest."

Jared and Amanda went with the pair to search out Harrow, who had been pressed into coachman duty for the evening, and the lovebirds were soon off for what seemed their first hours alone since the engagement had been announced.

The night was warm and pleasant, a perfect evening for a

drive, but had it been otherwise the happy couple would not have noticed. They held hands, and every few minutes Bo would lean over and press a light kiss to Anne's lips. "Love you," Bo whispered more than once.

"Me, too," would come the answer. There was more conversation but it was of interest to—and probably understood by—only them.

They were almost within sight of Storm Haven's gates when a shot rang out and two horsemen broke from the trees, shouting, "*Stand and deliver!*" Harrow was alone on the box and had to restrain the startled horses before he could reach for the blunderbuss kept under the seat. But before he could cock it, one of the robbers mounted the box and pressed an ugly-looking weapon between the servant's bony ribs.

Inside the coach, Bo tried hard to disengage the clinging Anne in order to reach into the pocket of the carriage door for Jared's pistols. "Pray, Bo, dearest, you will not try to be a hero!" Anne implored. "Let them take our valuables and go. If you make them angry, they may hurt you."

Bo sighed, and only grudgingly relinquished this chance to play Galahad to his fair lady. He replaced the pistols and kissed the distraught girl on the forehead. "Buy you another ring, love," he promised, and while Anne held him back by convulsively clutching at his coattails he tried vainly to stick his bright red head out the door to inform the robbers of his peaceful intentions. "I say, dumpling, can't step out to wave the white feather. Do let go my coat. Deuced difficult otherwise, you know."

Anne relinquished her hold just as Bo turned the handle of the door, allowing her swain to tumble pell-mell into the muddy roadway—where he landed, rump skywards and perched on his pug nose. "Oh, dear," she cried, "that was unfortunate," and scampered out to give her fiancé assistance. But first, in a mad moment of daring, she secreted one huge pistol in the folds of her cloak. After all, as any woman knows, there is a fine line between employing the path of least resistance and allowing oneself to be led to the slaughter!

She would not allow Bo to leap headlong into battle with heaven knew how many vicious footpads, but if the villains were out to do murder after they had pocketed their booty, little Anne—who formerly would have swooned dead away at the mere sight of a highwayman—was now possessed of the fierce determination to protect her man.

Meanwhile, her hero was busy pushing himself up and away from the muddy road and onto his knees. "*Yecch*," he slurred thickly. "Drunk too deep, I wager. Lost m'balance." He climbed clumsily to his feet with Anne's clucking assistance and staggered drunkenly over to the carriage, where he anchored himself to the left forward wheel—bewildering Anne by appearing to be badly castaway.

"Bo," Anne gasped, "say you're not *drunk!*" Whereupon that gentleman—so unjustly accused, puffed himself up to his unimposing height, adjusted (and thoroughly muddied) his twisted cravat, and (doing his best to look imposing while droplets of muddy water dripped from the end of his nose) demanded to know if the lady had the audacity to suppose that he could not carry his wine.

The two footpads, with Harrow now securely trussed up like a Christmas goose and harmlessly stuffed rump-down into the space beneath the driver's seat, showed all signs of mightily enjoying Bo's little show.

"Drunk as a wheelbarrow," the big one commented.

"Ain't met a flash cove yet what could 'old 'is drink," the second concurred.

While their would-be robbers laughed uproariously at their own would-be victim, Bo took the opportunity to wink at his beloved, letting her know he was bamming. Anne frowned, not quite seeing the necessity for such outlandish buffoonery, but—as she had a contingency plan of her own—she saw no reason to belittle Bo's efforts.

Suddenly the bigger and dirtier of the two robbers bellowed, "Stow the shilly-shallying. We's gots a job o' work ta do, Clem, so let's 'ave at it. The gentry mort what 'ired us says ta make it look like robbery. Do ya want to lift the goods now or pick em from the corpses?"

From his undignified position in the driver's footwell, Harrow could hear every word. He began struggling against his bonds—a movement that only knocked his knees into his shoulders and settled him more firmly into his prison, where he could do no more than bang his head against the wood again and again in frustration. But the stamping of the startled horses drew the eyes of the robbers away from the seemingly harmless

Bo and Anne for a moment, a moment Bo knew would not likely come again.

He pushed his chubby body away from the carriage wheel, and with a fierce yell that would have done a savage American warrior proud, he launched himself at the scoundrels who would dare harm his beloved.

Clem, most secure when limiting his capers to mild bits of pickpocketing, felt the tiny hairs on the back of his neck lifting at the terrifying sound and ran for his horse as if the Hounds of Hell were after him. His companion, however, was made of sterner stuff. As Bo vaulted into the air to hurtle himself broadside into his foe, the man merely shifted one large step to his left—leaving Bo to renew his acquaintance with the muddy roadway.

The robber laughed, as indeed most anyone might, and courteously allowed Bo time to regain his feet. This time he rose dripping brown goo from his red curls, as well as his nose and nearly every other part of his anatomy.

"Timing off," Bo admitted ruefully.

"My poor darling," Anne sighed.

"Coo, wot a sad sorry sight ye be, covey," the thug remarked shaking his head. "Pity. Like ya. Like the skirt too, real plucky. I almost wish I could let yez go, but now that Clem's gone and I don't have to split the ready, cain't see as 'ow I can. Must thankee fer scarin' 'im off. Won't stop til 'e reaches Tothill I wagers.

"Now, if yez would just go to join up wit the lady we can get this done all right and tight and old Bob will be on 'is way. Looks like it's comin' on ta rain, and I don't like ta get wet."

"Don't know. We both could stand a bath," Bo spluttered, wiping mud and grit from his eyes and stumbling blindly back to Anne to place one grimy arm protectively about her shoulders. "Shoot us, did you say?" he questioned blankly—as if the truth of the matter had just hit him. "Funny. Don't remember any enemies. But spare the lady. Never harmed anyone. An angel, I say, a regular angel."

"Not yet, guv," the bad man corrected Bo. "But soon. Step clear, or do I shut yer lights first and 'ave the gel face the grim reaper alone?"

"You bastard!" Bo shouted, dropping his drunken pose. His rage was so all-consuming that he could form no other plan but yet another frontal assault. Thus he charged bull-like into the line of fire while desperately praying for a miracle.

Two shots rang out, their reports so nearly simultaneous as to be heard as a single blast, and moments later two bluish clouds of smoke wreathed the three still figures lying in the roadway.

First to move as the haze cleared, his ears ringing from the assault of two pistols fired so close by, was Bo. He shook his buzzing head and the resulting burst of pain assured him he was still alive. Presently he became aware of a dull ache in his shoulder, and he reached inside his coat only to have his fingers come away sticky and wet. Obviously he had been shot. This surprised him, for he had thought it would hurt more than it did. He gawked stupidly at his fingers for some moments before more pressing concerns could crawl into his rattled brains by way of an earthy curse reaching his ears.

"Lawks, almighty," bellowed the footpad who had called himself Bob. "Her's damn near blowed m'leg clean off." More exclamations followed, interspersed with a multitude of dire oaths and thieves' cant, as Bob hauled himself up by pulling on his mount's stirrup and hoisted himself painfully into the saddle. Bo watched dumbfounded as Bob used his good leg to kick some life into his broken-down steed and disappeared in the same direction his mate Clem had chosen minutes earlier.

Bo took a minute to congratulate himself on the successful routing of the hapless hired killer before the realization that he had had little to do with that success riveted all his attention—and all his fears—in the direction of the coach.

Anne! Where was Anne? He crawled on his hands and knees toward the coach until he saw the gleam of her white dress in the pale moonlight. Quickly he checked her slim form for injuries, and when he saw that there were none, he deduced that she had merely fainted. A still-smoking pistol lay beside her and he gawked at it in amazement.

Anne soon roused and threw herself into Bo's arms, earning herself a fierce one-armed hug and an admonition to moderate the enthusiasm which was well on its way to squeezing the rest of his life's blood out through the hole in his shoulder.

"Wh-where is the robber?" Anne questioned timidly while applying a ripped-off portion of her petticoat to her beloved's wound with an economy of movement and lack of squeamishness that would have totally astounded her fastidious mother.

"When I saw you throwing yourself at his pistol so bravely I was so enraged that I just shut my eyes and fired. I didn't *kill* him, did I, Bo? Please say I didn't kill him!"

"Only winged him, more's the pity," Bo answered, with that lack of sensibility only a man could show. "Leg wound, not too bad for a woman, I guess," he added by way of compensation.

Anne looked puzzled. "I hit him in the leg? How can that be? I distinctly remember aiming at his heart. I am just glad I didn't kill him, no matter what, for then I should be," she shivered convulsively, "a *murderess!*"

"Never so, my sweet. A heroine. Yes, a regular heroine," he concluded, and then placed a resounding kiss on her startled, half-open mouth. Their interlude, however, was short-lived, as they could no longer ignore the banging and muffled oaths that came from atop the carriage.

Once freed, Harrow quickly bundled the triumphant pair into the coach and turned the horses back the way they had come. "Bedlam-bait, the pair of them," he consoled himself. "Those coves could come back any time, with fifty more like them, and they're billing and cooing like doves in the park." He flicked his whip out over the horses, which were already moving at a spanking pace. "Hie! Git moving, you worthless plugs."

As soon as the lights from the Squire's house were visible through the trees, Harrow shot off his blunderbuss. By the time the carriage plunged to a rocking halt before the main steps the entire party was stationed on the portico.

"We was set upon by murderers, my lord," Harrow shouted down to Jared. "Hired killers, they were, out to stop this carriage and do away with anyone inside." Harrow was just finishing his tale as Jared flung open the carriage door. The first thing he saw was a muddy male hand gripping the inside latch. Attached to that hand was a chubby brown bear who was, once again, catapulted unceremoniously to the ground—this time before an audience that either shrieked, fainted from fright, shouted in surprise, or exploded into laughter, depending on their individual spleens.

As Anne climbed decorously down from the carriage she once again had to sigh, "Oh, Bo!" before the events of the evening proved to be too much for her; whereupon she daintily swooned into Jared's available arms, her father's being already burdened with her mother's more than ample form.

It was left to Lady Chezwick to bring some order to the scene, which she did with the speed and precision of a field marshal organizing his troops. Carriages were called for and the guests bustled on their way before—as one pert young housemaid remarked—the cat could lick its ear.

Lady Chezwick's enthusiastic waving of burnt feathers revived Anne and her mother in time to hear Bo's garbled description of the near-tragedy, and his blush-riddled account of his "lucky shot," which had resulted in the ignominious dispatch of one of the would-be murderers.

To be completely fair to Bo, it was due to Anne's urging that he took credit for the deed. As she had explained to him, she did not relish the thought of being touted a heroine—or, much worse, eyed askance by the neighborhood biddies who would object to the "blood on her hands." Even more, although she was too wise to say so, she disliked the thought of the ribbings Bo would take if anyone were to know that, not only had he failed to protect his fiancée, but that his fiancée had saved him!

The unraveling of the night's events, embellished by the editorial additions of colorful adjectives like "blackhearted murderers" and "bloodthirsty butchers"—as related in Amanda's line-by-line translations of Bo's clipped speech—was enough to send the Squire's good wife into a shrieking bout of hysterics before she could be ushered away to her room.

Once there, a maid dosed her mistress with a liberal two fingers of laudanum in a tooth glass, placed a hot brick at her toes, and left her to moan, "My baby, my poor baby," until she realized she had lost her audience—whereupon she promptly fell asleep.

Across the hall from this chamber the local doctor, who fortunately had been in attendance at the party, had already surveyed Bo's wound and—announcing it was a mere scratch—promptly bled his patient, neatly patched over the wound, mollified Bo by rigging up a rather natty sling, and repaired downstairs. There he helped himself to a heavy snifter of the Squire's best smuggled French brandy.

By now Amanda had recovered from her first flush of excitement (an elation that was justified, since Bo and Anne were quite safe, and since the mere thought of cutthroats in the vicinity provided the first bit of interesting news since the prize sow on Jared's home farm gave birth to a two-headed piglet) and was puzzling over a few of the evening's revelations.

"Jared, dearest," she ventured as the Delaney carriage, its

muddy squabs heavily padded with rugs so as not to ruin their fine clothes, once more headed toward Storm Haven, "do not one or two things about this assault seem a bit, er, *puzzling?*"

"In what way, pet?" he answered, having already made up his mind about the incident and decided to keep his opinions secret from the females in his family.

"Well, for one thing, Bo said the highwaymen were hired by someone. For another thing, they were planning to murder Bo and Anne instead of just robbing them—an unnecessarily violent way of disposing of witnesses to their chicanery when masks would have been just as effective. And for a third thing," once her mind was set rolling it seemed to gather momentum with each turn of the carriage wheels, "I think they were waiting for our particular coach, with its crest so prominently marked. Jared!" she exclaimed, as she twisted in her seat and grabbed his arm with both her gloved hands, "I think they meant to stop *us*. To kill *us*, Jared!" she shouted as she shook his arm. "It was *murder meant for us!*"

Jared groaned. So much for protecting his simple little wife. He should have know she was about as dimwitted as his old school dean. "Yes, pet," he informed her while disengaging her fingers from about his arm—which was fast becoming numb from her convulsive grip. "I have deduced as much myself."

A snort came from the darkness on the far side of the carriage. "Easy enough to figure that part out. The question is, Nephew, of the many persons you have offended in your misspent youth, *who* could have been so insulted as to wish to put a period to your existence?"

"That may be 'whom', Aunt," Amanda interjected pointlessly.

"Not a who or a whom, my dear, loving wife and not-so-loyal or devoted aunt, but a *what*—some inhuman monster, a particularly base and slimy thing at that. Do not credit the beast by calling it a man. Besides, there is none, even among my enemies, who would be so low as to employ such base tactics. Indeed not. They would call me out, as gentlemen are honorbound to do."

"*Gentlemen!* Hah! If slapping a fellow silly about the head and face with a glove before putting a hole in him makes one a gentleman, I am glad I was born a female. Such a bunch of vain, pompous prigs, too stiff-necked to back away from the slightest tussle! Oh, no, far better be it to sully up a fine meadow with

their wine-soaked blood than to talk things out man-to-man."
Lady Chezwick pointed a lace-enclosed finger at her nephew,
who had opened his mouth to debate this statement and
succeeded in shutting it with her next words.

"Be that as it may, there is a grain of truth in what you said,
Nephew, if one but looks deeply enough. The scoundrel who
hired those dregs of society to do his dirty-work can certainly be
called a thing. And that *thing*," she intoned in a fair imitation of
London's foremost barrister, "can be none other than that
simpering ninny, Freddy Crosswaithe."

Once delivered of her indictment, she crossed her hands
firmly across her bosom and retreated into the darkest corner of
the carriage, from which could shortly be heard a gentle snore.

It was the only sound to break the silence of the remainder of
the journey—a passage of miles Amanda spent shivering
nervously in her husband's firm embrace.

Chapter Nine

"I WAS not best pleased by your note, Jared, garbled as it was, but—as it served as an excuse to delay my arrival at that damp cave laughingly called my country estate—I am indebted to you." Kevin Rawlings, the new Earl of Lockport, looked deceivingly at his ease, buckskin-clad legs elegantly crossed as he leaned back in his chair. Sipping from a tall glass of spirits, he was outwardly the picture of unconcern, as his shrewd eyes searched the drawn face of his host. If the truth be known, he had traveled from London to Storm Haven in record time, having ridden his horse almost to the ground after receiving Jared's message relating the near-disastrous attack on Bo and Anne.

After downing three fingers of port he asked, "How stand things now? Is Bo up and about?"

Jared drained his own glass, then headed for the sideboard and the decanter that stood there. "Bo is on the mend, thank God, and the hero of the entire county. Anne never strays from his side and, indeed, I believe him to be the happiest of men," he said with a rueful grin.

Kevin rose restlessly from his chair, for four hours in the saddle had not served to make prolonged sitting advisable just yet. He crossed the room to look out over the gardens that had been in full bloom before he left but were now showing signs of the changing season. "Perhaps you'd better start from the beginning, old friend. Your letter mentioned a plot of some sort."

"If I'm right, Kevin, it's not a very pretty tale."

"I didn't imagine it would be, with bloody wounds and nasty men woven through the plot. But I want to hear all of it."

"Very well, sit down and I'll see we aren't disturbed." After locking the library doors Jared poured them both another stiff drink, then told Kevin all he knew about the nightmare that was now six days long and showed no signs of abating. "It was supposed to be robbery—at least that was what they intended us to think. Bo decided not to put up a fight, because Anne was with him and Harrow had already been put out of the fray. Poor Bo soon learned the error of his thinking when the highwaymen were overheard discussing the merits of robbery before or *after* doing away with their victims."

"Good Lord, that's crude," Kevin drawled. "Obviously ghoulish fellows. I'd as lief kiss a great hoary bear as touch a body not yet cold."

Jared raised his eyes to the ceiling before asking Kevin if he had anything else to say before he—the mere teller of the tale—proceeded. Kevin relinquished the speaking floor with a regal inclination of his blond head.

"They were riding toward Storm Haven in my carriage. *Mine*, Kevin. It was Amanda and me they were after. It was only by the grace of God that Bo's battle yell frightened off the one hoodlum and his single shot somehow found its home in the second one's leg, putting him to the rightabout as well."

"Grace of God, my sainted Aunt Sarah. Dumb luck's more like it, knowing Bo."

Jared angrily waved the comment aside, unable to see any humor in the situation. "Don't you see, Kevin? My own curst folly almost caused the death of two dear friends. Bo always said Freddie was no good and so did Amanda; they both tried to warn me. But, no, I was the smart one, I laughed at the two of them."

Jared's voice took on a tone of desperation as the real source of his agitation was disclosed. "Look what it has brought me: two good people whose lives were nearly snuffed out just as they are barely started, and my wife upstairs in our bedroom with her mind locked in a dark box to which I cannot find the key. She doesn't speak, Kevin. She barely eats. She just sits there all the day long, and at night she lies beside me like a stick of wood, refusing my arms.

"She is sure it is her marriage to me that has put us all in danger, and she is possessed with fears for the baby and me. If she hadn't insisted on a child, she tells me, none of this would be happening now. I know women get strange ideas when they're in her condition, but she's convinced she is a jinx and even Aggie can't get through to her." Jared dropped into a nearby chair and covered his face with his hands. "She can't go on like this or I'm going to lose her, Kevin, and I'll die without her."

Kevin was sympathetic to Jared's problem, but his thoughts were uppermost on the first part of the story. "Tell me why you are so sure it was Freddie—and why do you say 'they' instead of 'him'?"

With great effort, Jared took hold of himself and rose to his feet. He was so tired: He hadn't slept more than a few hours at any one time since the night of the party. Squire Bosley was too involved with his upset household to act officially, so Jared had taken charge of the investigation. He spent every moment he could spare with his wife, but she barely knew he was there. Immersed in her depression, she had retreated into a space Jared was not allowed to enter.

"How can I answer you?" he said at last. "Bo told me what he heard and it confirms the thugs were hired by someone, a 'gentry mort.' My only enemies—at least the only ones of which I am aware—are Blanche and Freddie. Blanche knew about the party, and she also knows Amanda is increasing. We know she obligingly made Freddie aware of that fact, because you wrote to me about it. Denton wouldn't raise a hand against me—that would be rather like killing off the golden goose—but Blanche and Freddie could have hatched this little plot.

"Freddie must have been livid when he found out he will soon be second in line for the title, possibly even farther removed if Amanda proves fruitful in the coming years. What better way to assure himself of the title than to remove both me and Amanda by faking a robbery in which both of us die!"

"All right, you have my vote for Freddie, but I still don't understand how you figure the dear Blanche in all this. A woman scorned? Surely that is a bit much," said Kevin.

"Blanche and I had rather a bad falling out while I was in London, and Amanda further fanned the flames when Blanche was visiting here by saying I had told her all about it. I didn't, of course, but it was not a meeting Blanche would wish made public. It would not surprise me a bit to learn she and Freddie were working together in this. After all, would you have suspected Blanche of coming to Storm Haven in the first place?

"I only wish I had some real proof—but unless Bow Street tracks down either of the robbers, I can see no way. I would have gone to London immediately myself and wrung the truth out of Freddie, but I cannot leave Amanda, even for a day. That is why I wrote to you. If you were to see Freddie, perhaps you could find some answers."

"I'll find them, all right," Kevin assured him, not knowing if his deep concern lay more with the sad young girl upstairs or the desperate man before him. "I'll find them if I have to pull Freddie's forked tongue out by its roots!"

Kevin rose slowly and patted his friend on the shoulder. "Stay with your wife, Jared. She needs you. If I hurry I can be back in town in time to take my mutton at Freddie's club. I'll contact you as soon as I know something." There was nothing to be seen of the fop he so loved to portray when Kevin strode purposefully toward the door.

As Kevin passed through the door to leave the house, a small plump body brushed past him as if he weren't important enough to acknowledge. This rotund little woman was followed more slowly by Harrow—a large plaster still on the back of his head—and carrying a well-worn cloth bag that served as the only luggage the woman possessed.

The new arrival planted herself firmly in the entrance hall and gave a very unladylike bellow. "Where is my baby? Take me to her at once! I do not have time to shilly-shally all day down here."

While her announcement still echoed in the foyer, three maids, two footmen, and an irate Lady Chezwick appeared on the scene. The woman quickly picked out Lady Chezwick, and as that lady made her way down the staircase, the new arrival advanced on her with a purpose of mind that made the slighter woman back up a step or two involuntarily. "Where are you keeping my baby, madam?"

"Y-your b-baby, you ask? We have no baby here. We will, I mean, we shall someday, but as yet . . . Oh, fiddle! How dare you barge into my nephew's home, appearing to all the world no more civilized than a chimney sweep!"

Harrow put down his bundle and cleared his throat. "Beggin' your pardon, my lady, but I believe she means Miss Mandy. This here is her old nurse. Lord Storm sent me off for her a few days ago."

"Yes, and a fine crawling pace you set getting me here, Harrow. You never were fleet of foot, even as a lad." With a curt nod the woman dismissed the old man and he gratefully quit the hall.

She turned back to Lady Chezwick and grimaced. "Dirty old man, Harrow. Always was. Always smelling of horses and the like. But tolerable all the same—if you remember to stay upwind that is."

If the woman was not overly impressed with Harrow, the same could be said for Lady Chezwick's feelings toward Amanda's old nurse. She tried to stop the woman from approaching the staircase, but to no avail, for the heavier woman just elbowed her aside and began mounting the stairs two at a time, her skirts hiked up to show her plump calves.

Lady Chezwick called after her. "What is your name?"

"Beulah Farthingale."

"And shall we call you Beulah?" Lady Chezwick screeched.

Beulah turned at the head of the stairs and leaned over the banister. "You do and be ready to suffer for it. I answer only to Nanny." And with a flip of her straggly grey hair she was gone from sight.

Nanny turned instinctively toward the main bedchamber and threw open the paneled door with a bang. Sally, who had been trying to coax Amanda into swallowing a few spoonfuls of beef broth, jumped back, startled out of her wits. She was given short shrift, and was sent sniffling from the room with a flea in her ear about mollycoddling those able to do for themselves.

As Sally went looking for Lady Chezwick, Nanny closed and locked the door and took stock of the sad-eyed girl who looked at her rather blankly.

"Why is it dark in here in the middle of the day, may I ask?" she bellowed to no one in particular as she went to the windows and threw back the curtains. "There, that is more the thing. Now," she announced, "isn't that much cheerier? It looked like a funeral in here."

"There could have been a funeral, Nanny. Two of them, in fact, both of them my fault." Amanda's voice was low and emotionless as she added, "Please leave me."

Nanny sniffed loudly. "Leave you! Leave you, is it? After I was dragged across half of England on the most bumpy roads Harrow could find? I left a nice cozy room at my sister's, too, I'll have you know, and all because you are acting the idiot. Don't just sit there like a dashed waxwork, pick up that spoon and start to eat. Later I'll get you some real food, but that slop will have to do for now."

Amanda continued to sit with her hands folded in her lap, so

Nanny came over and grated into her ear, "Eat it, my fine young miss, or I shall hold your nose and force it down your throat. Lord rest your sainted mother, I've done it before."

Amanda ate. Amanda also bathed. She allowed Nanny to tie back her hair in a pink ribbon. How the old woman accomplished these miracles while being constantly besieged by furious poundings on the door from Lady Chezwick and Jared she didn't really know, but after a time everyone went away and left her alone with her charge.

Finally satisfied that all of her baby's creature needs had been taken care of, Nanny decided to have a little talk with Amanda. Slowly she drew out of the girl the story of that fateful night—and Amanda's deep sense of guilt.

"So now it is your fault, eh? And I thought you were all grown up. Child, you were no more to blame for those poor children's ordeal than I was. Who are you, that you should be singled out for such power over the fate of anyone save yourself? I suppose that, if Harrow had succeeded in killing me in his attempt to hit every hole in the post road, that would *also* be your fault. My, I never thought I'd live to hear of such conceit.

"I will say that what you are doing now is a downright sin. Harrow tells me your poor husband is beside himself worrying about you, and so is everyone else. By all that knocking and yelling I'd say you're pretty important to a lot of people, sweetings. Surely they don't regret your entrance into their lives! If you've brought love to them I'm sure they're more than willing to take any pain that goes with it, just as you would willingly share their pain.

"And what about your child? It seems to me you're just helping that Freddie person along, instead of putting your faith in that fine husband of yours. But if you keep on this way it will hurt the wee one and that *would* be your fault. Well, my fine young know-it-all, what do you have to say to that?"

Amanda broke down, then threw herself into her old nurse's arms to cry for the first time since she had tried and found herself guilty of leading her loved ones into danger. Nanny cradled her against her ample bosom, rocking her gently back and forth as she had done so many times in the past, wiping away a tear or two of her own every little bit. After a time she pushed Amanda away slightly and admonished, "That will be enough of that, young lady, or you shall give the babe the hiccups."

Amanda wiped her streaming eyes with the skirt of her gown.

"Oh, Nanny, I am so glad you are here. I promise to be good now."

Nanny crossed to the bell-pull and called for a maid, but was not surprised when—instead of a servant—a very large man came barreling through the door with concern written all over his face.

"She'll be all right now, my lord," Nanny announced, and stepped back as Amanda gave a little cry and hurled herself into her husband's arms. "You can stay only an hour, my lord. My baby needs her rest," she warned loudly before she closed the door behind her and nearly knocked over the hovering Lady Chezwick as she entered the hall.

Nanny looked the noble lady up and down and calmly said, "I would like to be shown to my room now, madam, unless you had something else to mind."

Lady Chezwick's mouth opened and closed a few times before she wordlessly beckoned for the woman to follow her. But little did Nanny know that only her success with Amanda had saved her from having her ears soundly boxed!

The two spent the rest of the day circling each other like game-cocks, pecking one minute, retreating the next, until at last an uneasy peace was settled between them. But it was a peace that would erupt into open warfare at scattered times for the rest of their days.

Lady Wade, clothed in a filmy dressing gown, was deciding between a gown of blue satin and one of pink brocade, uncertain which would do more to enhance her beauty that night at the theatre, when her maid burst into the bedroom. She was obviously upset about something.

"Curse you for a fool, Mary! How many times have I told you to knock before entering my bedroom? What if I had been entertaining? You had better mind your step or I shall take my hairbrush to you again."

Mary bobbed up and down in a series of small curtseys as she tried to catch her breath and explain her presence to Lady Wade. "B-but, milady, there is a *man* downstairs."

Blanche was not impressed. "What of it? Have him hand in his card and push him out. I am not receiving today."

"He is most insistent, milady."

"Naturally. All my suitors are of the impatient sort. It will do him well to cool his heels for a while." She shrugged her shoulders. "Very well, I will see him now. I confess a slight interest. Tell him I shall be down in an hour or so, if he cares to wait."

There was a shuffling at the door and Mary cried out in fright as an ebony cane maneuvered her backwards out of the room. Blanche turned away from her mirror at the sound, and was shocked to see the new Earl of Lockport leaning negligently against the door-frame—his beaver hat still cocked rakishly over one eye.

"As you may observe, slut, I did not deign to wait. Kindly put something more substantial over your udders, as I wish to speak with you and your appearance could put me off milk for a sen'night," Kevin drawled, his handsome face wearing a dangerous look.

It took a lot to frighten Blanche Wade, but she was frightened now. Her eyes raked over Kevin's lanky frame, deceiving in its modish rigout, and she could read the animosity in his very posture. It would seem she had erred in dismissing Jared's friends as insignificant. But where was Chevington? Where there was one there was invariably the other, yet Kevin was alone. She would rather have faced the bumbling Bo, for Kevin was looking decidedly nasty.

Blanche opted for a show of bravado. "I will ignore your insults, noting their origin, and agree to forget this little incident if you leave at once. If not, I have no choice but to have the servants remove you by force."

Kevin allowed a slight smile to crease one side of his face. "That would be most amusing, Blanche. If you are referring to the two lackeys I met downstairs, I think they are occupied at the moment, endeavoring to replace their teeth." The smile left his face and his voice turned cold. "No, bitch, you and I are going to chat undisturbed." He strolled over to a pink satin chair and inclined his head toward her. "Do join me in resting your bones as we speak, for I have a feeling that what I have to say may take some time."

Blanche sidled toward her dressing table and reached slowly behind her to open a small drawer. But before she could pull out the jeweled pistol that lay there, Kevin reached down and tugged at the small rug near his feet. At his firm yank, Blanche was sent reeling to the floor as the pistol skidded across the room and into a corner. "Naughty, naughty, madam! Those little toys are dangerous, you know."

As Blanche picked herself up heavily, she rattled off a string of curses that succeeded only in sending Kevin into a shout of wry laughter. Utter frustration brought tears to her eyes and she threw herself at Kevin's feet, sobbing out pleas for mercy. "What have I ever done to you, my lord? Why are you punishing me so?"

Kevin looked down on her with distaste. "Very well performed, Blanche. You should have done well trodding the boards, although I doubt Mrs. Siddons would be much afraid that you would steal her glory." He nudged her roughly with his highly-polished boot. "Get up, hag, or you'll ruin the finish and my valet will be after my head. You bore me with your hysterics, so let us get on with the reason for my visit. Where is Freddie?"

Blanche sat back on her heels and feigned surprise. "Freddie? Freddie who? I must know a hundred Freddies."

"Lord Storm's cousin Freddie, of course. I have a message for him from his cousin." Any doubts Kevin may have had as to Blanche's involvement in the murder plot were dismissed as he watched the color drain from her face, leaving her looking ugly and old.

"J-Jared?" she questioned softly. Jared was dead! Freddie told her his men could not fail. What was this madman talking about?

"Yes, madam, Jared Delaney—the man I left at Storm Haven yesterday, ministering to his wife who has been thrown into a deep fit of depression by a dastardly plot that unfolded a week ago against Jared and herself. It nearly resulted in the deaths of our mutual friends, Bo Chevington and his intended bride. I speak to you of victims, slut, victims of a plot hatched in sick and evil minds. But then, you wouldn't know anything about that, would you?"

Blanche's sharp green eyes narrowed as she tried frantically to get the facts straight in her mind. Damn Freddie! Could he do nothing right? How did his men make such a stupid mistake? "I-I don't know what you are talking about, Kevin. Have Bo and that dear child suffered some sad accident? They were both fine when I saw them not a month ago at Storm Haven."

"Please, do not insult me with your lies, Blanche. Your game is up and Freddie has flown and left you to shoulder all the blame. Now," he offered conversationally, "before I squeeze the breath out of you, perhaps you wish to try to save your neck with some home truths."

"You are mad! I know nothing of what you imply. I am the affianced wife of Peregrine Denton, and I . . ." She let out a piercing scream as Kevin reached down and grabbed one dangling gold earring between his gloved fingers, giving it a vicious twist.

"I have other little tricks I would enjoy trying out on you if you persist in your lies," he told her, still in that same mild tone.

Blanche tried to push away his hand, but he knocked her fingers away with his cane and gave her earlobe another painful pinch. "Do not push me, cow. I could learn to enjoy this."

She talked then, loud and long. She told Kevin how she had informed Freddie of Amanda's coming child and the date of the engagement party. She had sought revenge on Jared—who had promised her marriage and then reneged—but she swore she knew nothing about any murder attempt. Freddie had left the city for his new hunting box in Scotland last week and she had no idea when he would return.

"That is all I know, Kevin, I swear it!" she sobbed. "How was I to know Freddie would try to kill Jared? I don't want that, I love Jared!"

"You have a strange way of loving, you miserable creature. I never could see Jared's taste in women until the fair Amanda." He rose from the chair, a large portion of Blanche's long hair held tight in his fist so that she was forced to her feet with him. He twisted her head around and leaned close to her face as she cried out in pain that mingled with fright. "I would advise you to say nothing to Freddie of our little visit. I want him to enjoy his victory while he is in Scotland, but on his return I shall be calling on him."

"You can prove nothing!" Blanche shrieked. "You have only your word against his. He was out of the country when this attack you speak of took place."

"I do not wish Freddie to stand before the bench and have his neck stretched. Oh, no. I want him to squirm like the slimy eel he is—right on the hook he shall see dangling in front of his face until such time as I decide to reel him in. Deny me that pleasure, Blanche, and I will be back to visit you again." Kevin put his finger under her chin and lifted her face roughly to his. "And you will not like it, madam. You will not like it at all."

"*What is going on here?*" came a voice from the doorway. "Unhand my intended, you scoundrel!"

Kevin turned to see Peregrine Denton charging at him like an aging bull. He sidestepped neatly and Denton went crashing to the floor by reason of Kevin's strategically outstretched cane. Kevin then tipped his hat at the two, congenially bid them good-day, and took his leave.

"What was all that about, dearest?" questioned Denton from the floor.

"Quiet, you dolt!" Blanche shouted. "Sit down and shut up. I need time to think." She stepped over the confused man and began muttering to herself, "So the Delaney bitch still lives, does she? Well, not for long!"

Denton was dense, but not so much so that he didn't know Blanche was talking about killing his stepdaughter. He bore Amanda no great love, but killing her would bring a swift end to the allowance he had quickly learned to appreciate. Besides, why would Blanche want Amanda dead?

Not heeding her command to stay put, he gathered up his hat and cane and slunk out of the room. Why had Blanche been so nasty to him? What was Rawlings doing in her bedchamber? He would have to return to his lodgings and think on it.

As he was expendable to Blanche's plans and knew too much now to be left wandering the countryside, he would have been wiser to remove himself from London with all speed. But Denton was in love, and a man in love does not always think clearly. A stupid man in love does not think at all.

Kevin stayed a week in London, making discreet inquiries about Freddie and visiting Blanche one more time to be assured she did not know the location of Freddie's hunting box. Denton proved an equally uninformative source who only asked of Kevin many questions regarding the recent upheaval at Storm Haven. The man was so distraught by Blanche's rude treatment of him, however, that Kevin felt honor-bound to take him under his wing—so to speak—out of courtesy to Amanda. Doing so would also satisfy his mind as to the extent of Peregrine's involvement in any plot against his two friends.

At the end of the week Kevin knew he must take his leave of the city and report to Jared. Since he had not seen Peregrine in two days, he forced himself to make one last call in order to enlist the man's aid in alerting Jared as soon as Freddie showed his face in town. It was still early when he called at Denton's lodgings, and a rather slovenly woman dressed in her night-clothes barely opened the door a crack before informing him Mr. Denton was still abed and not receiving.

Kevin turned to leave and then a whim of caprice tickled his brain. He whirled to insert the tip of his cane between the door and the frame and commanded the woman take him to Denton. The crone stepped back sprightly enough at the color of Kevin's coin, and she pointed out Denton's bedroom before testing the money with her teeth.

Don't know where Denton spends his money, Kevin thought, but it surely ain't on his servants or his lodgings. What a mess! He knocked sharply on Denton's door with the head of his cane, but when there was no answer he let himself into the darkened room. It took several moments for his eyes to adjust to the gloom—and then what he saw made him turn his head away in disgust.

Peregrine Denton's enormous body was sprawled at the foot of his bed, his nightcap still on his head even as he hung over the edge of the mattress, his mouth agape and spewing forth great raucous snores. Kevin manfully approached the bed, scented handkerchief to his nostrils, and prodded Peregrine's bare belly with the tip of his cane. "Rouse yourself, you drunken sot!" he bellowed.

At long last Denton spluttered, groaned, and woke sufficiently to attempt to brush away the object that was in danger of impaling him. "What the devil is going on here?" he roared as he struggled to an upright position and surveyed the nattily-dressed dandy who had the temerity to invade his bedchamber.

Rawlings returned the look, his handsome face a study in genteel disgust. "Dipped a bit deep last night, friend?" he observed sarcastically. "What's the matter? Woman trouble, I wager."

As his memory came pouring back, Denton moaned self-pityingly and cradled his head in his hands. "She threw me over, Rawlings. Sent a note round crying off our engagement with some nonsense about a 'disparity in our ages.'" At Kevin's shout of amusement Denton realized he was entirely alone in his misery and, blubbering like a babe deprived of his sugar plums, he wiped at his eyes with the tassel of his nightcap.

"Ah, you poor man," Kevin clucked in mock sympathy. "All your dreams of wedded bliss shattered by a heartless hussy."

Denton noisily blew his nose into a crumpled kerchief. "Yes. Oh, yes, indeed. I have been sorely, sorely used." He made a last swipe at his tear-reddened eyes and Kevin watched as a dim light suddenly went on in Denton's equally dim brain—causing the jilted man to screw up his face in confusion. "Yes!" he shouted, tossing his nightcap to the floor. "I have been used. But to what purpose? To what end?"

Rawlings quietly supplied an answer. "I believe your step-daughter figures in here somehow, don't you agree?"

It all came clear to him then—the verbal slip Blanche had made concerning Amanda, and Denton's resulting perplexity. Kevin was almost softened to Denton's sincere heartache but his emotion stopped short of extending the man any pity. Instead he rudely advised the man to hare himself off for unknown parts, before Blanche recalled her indiscreet ravings and decided Peregrine's presence on this earthly coil was no longer necessary to her schemes.

"Are you inferring, sirrah," Denton blustered angrily, "that dear angel would seek my *death* because of some grudge she nurses against my stepdaughter?"

"Oh," Kevin replied with a wicked grin, "and Amanda said you were dim. I must tell her she was mistaken." With that he donned his new curly-brimmed beaver, awarded Denton the sight of a perfectly executed leg, and turned for the door. "A prudent man would be packing by now, I believe," he supplied in passing, and even before the front door could close behind him he heard Denton calling loudly for his housekeeper.

"Poor dumb fool," he muttered half to himself as he tooled his curricle through Mayfair. The knocker, he saw, was gone from Blanche's door—the accepted method of informing callers that a person was away from home. There was nothing for it but to return to Storm Haven and put the facts before Jared.

It confounded him that there was no proof to tie Freddie or Blanche to the attack on Jared's coach, even though he was prepared to deal with them outside the law. That would, of course, necessitate flight to America afterwards, and in truth the loss of his newly acquired lands and fortune did not appeal. But Jared's dilemma was much worse, for he had a family to consider. He had thought of hiring ruffians, as Freddie had done, but dismissed the idea. He wanted Freddie to *know* who killed him, wanted him to sweat and quiver with fear as the pistol was pointed. There could be no substitute for the chance to watch him plead on his knees for his life as he, Kevin Rawlings, avenger of the innocent, calmly took aim.

During the journey to Storm Haven he considered and rejected plans to bring Freddie and Blanche out into the open. He arrived at his destination with only one thought firm in his mind: Freddie was not done. He would try again, and they would have to be ready for him. For now all four of them would be targets—Bo, himself, Jared, and the increasingly pregnant Amanda.

After Kevin's return to Storm Haven he, Bo, and Jared spent many long hours closeted in Jared's study planning their next moves—only to realize the next move must come from Freddie. There was no way of knowing where in Scotland the man was. But if Blanche had been lying and *did* know, she was sure to have contacted him. He would know of the error his henchmen had made, even if he were out of touch with the London dailies.

Yet, as the weeks passed without incident, the three men began to believe Freddie must have fled the country for good, knowing full well what would be waiting for him if he dared show his face in England again. In any event, an item in the columns saying Blanche had set sail for Italy went a long way toward relieving their minds.

Then one day a letter arrived from Denton, the return address rousing Amanda to wonder what her city-loving stepfather could possibly find to amuse himself in the wilds of Cornwall. "Rusticating for his health," Jared suggested, with tongue firmly in cheek. And, though Amanda was confused by this answer, she was not interested enough in Denton to pursue the subject.

Amanda was subdued these days, but with Nanny's scoldings and Lady Chezwick's pleadings she began to take up the threads of her life and look forward to the birth of her child. Because of her depressed state, and then because of her increasing bulk, there were no social events at Storm Haven. The weeks passed quietly and swiftly until the first snowfall of the season made them realize that Christmas would soon be upon them.

One snowfall followed another and the freezing temperatures kept any of the white blanket from melting, so that by Christmas Eve, Storm Haven was effectively cut off from the outside world. No one was able to leave, but more importantly, no one was able to approach. With the thought of any trouble from Freddie at least temporarily removed, Jared and Kevin relaxed their surveillance and concentrated on making this a Christmas the ladies would never forget. Bo had continued on at the Squire's, pending his marriage to Anne early in the Spring.

On Christmas Eve, Amanda sat in the blue salon contemplating the small feet stretched out before her on a small footstool. "You know, Aunt, if it were not for Sally's good judgement I could be wearing green slippers with a blue gown. I cannot remember when last I saw my toes. I believe I must be the most ungainly creature alive."

Lady Chezwick harbored some reservations on the—to be polite—rather enormous size of Amanda's stomach, but as she had never borne a child herself perhaps she was just being overprotective. "Nonsense," she said now, "Jared tells me daily how beautiful you are."

Amanda made a face. "Perhaps he has been drinking too deep. He must be castaway if he finds his swollen wife appealing. Even Sally giggles as I struggle in and out of the tub; it is really quite embarrassing."

Her aunt laughed and shook her head as she applied herself again to the tiny sweater she was knitting—blue, of course, for the child had to be a boy—when the doors of the salon burst open and two sets of legs surrounded by a huge, snow-dripping evergreen came crashing into the room. "Good heavens! A Christmas tree! By all that's wonderful, I haven't had a tree since I was a child." Lady Chezwick clapped her tiny hands in glee and rose to help Kevin move aside a sofa to make room for their enormous burden.

Jared poked his head out from behind the branches, his handsome face red with cold and his blue eyes dancing like a child's to ask, "Do you like it, infant? It will be my very first Christmas tree, ever, and the first of many that we will share." Amanda, in the way of women in a delicate condition, promptly burst into tears whereupon Jared dropped the tree on Kevin's booted foot and dashed to her side.

"Dear heart, what have I done to upset you?" he asked on bended knee. Amanda shook her head in the negative and kept on weeping. Jared sat back on his heels and turned his eyes to his aunt in mute appeal.

"The child is overcome with happiness, nephew. Any fool could see that," Lady Chezwick informed him while wiping away a tear of her own.

Jared slapped the palm of his hand against his forehead. "I give up! Amanda, darling, dry your eyes before you flood us all out of the room. I only meant to make you happy."

Amanda lifted her head from her hands and smiled moistly at her concerned husband. "I know, Jared. Forgive me for being such a noodle. I don't know what could be the matter with me, for I was not so poor-spirited before. I never cry, you know that."

Lady Chezwick stepped in and explained, "It's the baby. Women do some dashed queer things when they're breeding. Your mother, Jared, as I recall, developed a terrible craving for pigs' feet. Made me positively ill, it did."

A muffled voice came from the depths of the tree. "Now that we have all that settled, would you mind terribly lending me a hand with this, old friend? It is not a small twig I am holding up, remember? Ah, that is better, I was beginning to feel like a pin cushion."

The next half hour was spent dragging the tree from room to room, and then from corner to corner, as Amanda and Lady Chezwick tried to decide where it would show to best advantage. It finally found a resting place in the music room when Jared and Kevin became balky and refused to move "the damned thing" another inch.

Nanny and Sally and the rest of the staff busied themselves in decorating the tree and Cook supplied some freshly-made popcorn to string around it. By the time the last presents were put underneath and everyone had had a late supper it was more than time to retire, but Jared asked Amanda to stay behind a moment while he fetched something from his study.

When he came back Amanda was snuggled up cosily in the corner of the sofa, her hair shining in the firelight that was the only illumination in the room.

Jared stepped up behind her and placed a kiss on her hair. "Happy, pet?"

To answer him she reached up her hand and drew him down to her for a kiss. She then motioned for him to join her on the sofa and they sat, her head on his shoulder and his arm about what was left of her waist, gazing into the fire.

After a time Amanda felt her eyelids starting to droop and suggested they retire to their bed. "It will be a long day tomorrow, love, with you wishing to exchange presents in the morning instead of tonight. I believe Aunt Agatha will be up with the chickens to shake boxes and peek under all the wrappings. Did you see her tonight? She was as happy as a child."

"Yes, my sweet, and think of her joy next Christmas when our son will be the center of attention. This house has not known the joy of a child's laughter in many a long year, and it will be a welcome sound." He pressed his lips to her hair and murmured, "Have I told you lately what a wonderful job you have made of our home? Even Kevin has remarked on it, and begs your help in restoring his late uncle's residence."

Amanda frowned slightly. "I have been meaning to discuss Kevin with you, but do not wish to appear to be wanting to see him gone. You know how much I enjoy his company, but isn't it time he took up his duties as earl? He has been in the country with us since Bo and—since late September. That is an extremely long fit of rustication, is it not?"

"Perhaps he cannot tear himself away from my wife. Do you think I should ask him his intentions?"

"Now you are bamming me, Jared. I know Kevin stayed so you would both be on hand if Freddie were to make another attempt on our lives. No, don't shake your head as if I were rambling. We have never really discussed what happened to Bo and Anne, for you insisted it was robbery and no more. But I knew differently. All my suffering wasn't simply because we did not travel with them that night.

"They weren't attacked because they happened to be abroad that last evening. It was because they were in our coach. Please do not treat me like a child, Jared. I wish to know the whole truth."

So the uneasy peace was over, Jared thought sadly. While he had been busy trying to protect Amanda from the whole truth, she had only been allowing him to think she believed his version of the story. "What has your little mind ferreted out, imp?"

Amanda faced forward and stared into the flames. "I know that Lady Wade is involved in some way. I feel sure of it, only I cannot quite understand why. Poor stepfather, he was just a pawn in her ugly game, wasn't he?" She turned her face back toward her husband. "That was her purpose in coming here, wasn't it? To hurt us?"

Jared found himself telling Amanda everything he knew about the plot, and after Amanda indulged herself in some quiet tears she pleaded with him, "Is there nothing we can do? I am gratified to hear that Lady Wade has left the country, but I feel certain Freddie will return to try again."

Even in the semi-darkness of the quiet room, Amanda could see the forbidding expression on her husband's face, as he cursed himself yet again for being a thousand times foolish for not recognizing the monster in Freddie before things had a chance to go this far. At last he sighed and told her, "There is nothing we can do to prove what we think, pet. Blanche fled London for Italy after Kevin paid her a little visit, and I am sure we have seen the last of her, as I said. But as you fear, we think Freddie is another matter. We know he was in Scotland at the time of the murder attempt, but we have lost all trace of him since. He must have gotten word of the failure of his hirelings and may never return." He paused a moment and then stated coldly, "He must know that if he ever shows his face in London again I will kill him."

Amanda felt herself going cold and gave a little shiver. Immediately Jared was all concern as he hastily tried to reassure her that he, Bo, and Kevin were more than able to deal with any of Freddie's schemes now that they were aware and on their guard. "But after the New Year, Kevin must be on about his business if he is to enjoy the coming Season in London. I hate to think of all the enterprising mamas he will have to face, now he has the title." He got up from the sofa and knelt in front of Amanda as the music room clock struck twelve.

"It is Christmas, my love. I have a small present that I wish you to open now."

Jared reached into his coat pocket, drew out a thick cream-colored envelope, and laid it gently in her hands. "I vowed this to you before we were wed, though you had no idea of my intentions. I only hope it pleases you, dear heart."

Amanda looked puzzled as she opened the envelope and pulled out a sheaf of very official-looking documents. She had Jared bring a candle so she could read them, and after a few moments uttered a faint cry and hugged her husband closely to her breast.

The deed to Fox Chase fell unheeded to the floor.

Chapter Ten

THERE was a break in the weather a few days after Christmas, and Kevin and Jared rode out to Squire Bosley's so that Kevin could pay his respects to the family once more before taking his leave of Storm Haven. Amanda was nearing her last month of pregnancy and naturally declined the carriage ride, even though she was bored with her confinement to the house.

The two had been gone nearly an hour when a man came galloping into the courtyard, calling loudly for Lady Storm. Amanda gladly stopped unraveling yet another mistake in her knitting, and plunked down the product of a once-pristine white bundle of wool. Her unenthusiastic fingers had made it into a light grey length of vague shape that could have resembled a tiny sweater—if the observer tactfully overlooked one slight imperfection in a garment that had inexplicably grown one tiny sleeve too many.

She rose to meet her urgent-sounding caller.

He was brought to her in short order and gasped that Lord Storm had been thrown from his horse on the road to the Squire's, and was even now lying at death's door at the man's cottage beside the mill.

Lady Chezwick grabbed hold of the swaying Amanda and quickly asked the whereabouts of Lord Rawlings. "If you be meanin' the dandy wit the guinea gold hair, he said how's he darsent leave hiz lordship, that hurt he be." The man turned to Amanda and said, "He's askin' fer yer, milady."

"I must go to him at once! Aunt Agatha, call Sally and have her get some blankets loaded into the carriage. And, oh, yes, some brandy, too. Send a footman for Jennings and tell him I need the carriage brought around immediately. He is to drive me, for Harrow is still abed with his cold." She was halfway from the room as she called out, "And have Tom ride for the doctor. Hurry! There is no time to be lost."

During the ensuing confusion no one noticed the man as he slipped into the blue room, or observed his actions as he studiously positioned a sealed envelope atop Jared's desk.

Within minutes Amanda was descending the steps of Storm Haven, wrapped in a voluminous cloak, and Jennings helped her into the carriage. Once inside she was amazed to see Lady Chezwick already installed and tried to make her go back into the house.

"Nonsense, child. Nanny is taking care of all preparations there and you cannot set out alone. I do have some small experience in nursing, you know." She tapped on the carriage roof with the stick Jared had given her for Christmas, and at her signal Jennings set the carriage in motion, following the man's lead.

Amanda was nearly frantic with worry, and to her the carriage seemed to crawl along the road, but she knew Jennings was right to set this pace because of her condition. When at last they pulled off the main road and into a muddy track, Amanda was almost beside herself with anxiety. She had alighted almost before the carriage came to a complete halt, with Lady Chezwick directly on her heels.

The two women were too distraught to notice that Jared's Devil and Kevin's mount were nowhere to be seen. It wasn't until Amanda pulled open the door of the cottage, however, and stepped inside, that she heard Jennings' quick "Milady, somethin's queer here!" before he was swiftly silenced by a blow to the head from their guide.

Amanda froze on the doorsill in confusion as a silky voice from the large kitchen sent a shiver of pure terror down her spine. "So we meet again, Cousin. How kind of you to answer my summons so promptly."

"Sweet Mother of God," Lady Chezwick cried as she pushed past Amanda into the room. "Frederick Crosswaithe, you deranged monster, what is the meaning of this?" She marched directly up to where he stood, and would have dealt him a resounding slap but for the quick averting of his head.

"Peter! Get this old harridan off me!" he screeched.

"Harridan, is it? I never did care a rap for you, you odious boy." She raised her walking stick and advanced again toward her nephew, intent on clubbing him heavily about the head and shoulders. "I'll rattle your brains for you, you vacant-faced nitwit!"

Freddie was saved from a sound beating by the intervention of his valet, who approached Lady Chezwick from behind and grabbed her in a bear hug, lifting the slight woman clean off the floor and depositing her in a decrepit chair in a nearby corner. Her attack thwarted, she remembered she was a gently-bred lady and promptly swooned.

All this took place in only a few moments—moments in which Amanda experienced profound relief that Jared was not injured, followed by the realization that she and Lady Chezwick were good and truly caught in the unholy clutches of a man who wanted nothing more than the deaths of everyone she held dear.

Her mind moved swiftly on, figuring that Jared would soon be returning to Storm Haven to discover her disappearance. It dawned on her then that this trap Freddie had set up was not only for her, but for her husband too—with herself as the lure. In the melting snow the carriage tracks would not be easily followed, but still she was afraid Jared would race unthinkingly into an ambush and certain death. She must warn him—but how?

Freddie broke into her musings by taking her arm roughly and drawing her further into the room. "Unhand me, you villain, or it will go badly with you," she warned, rather theatrically.

"I doubt that, dear coz," Freddie replied. "There is an old acquaintance of yours here who has some very unpretty plans for you. Our plans have been delayed already by this dratted weather, and we wish to be rid of you before you whelp." He chuckled at his private joke and bowed for her to proceed him to a chair.

Amanda heard a noise and turned in time to see the real miller and his family being herded out a back room and through the door leading toward the mill. Bo's attacker, Clem, his love of money overcoming his fears, marched at the end of the line. It was some time before Clem returned to the cottage to tell his master he had done what he had been told to do.

"You have not harmed them?" Amanda gasped. "I saw six children in that group."

"No, we have not—although do not think I would hesitate to

order it if you do not cooperate with me. For the moment this good man here has merely drugged them with some concoction that blowsy witch Blanche cooked up in her cauldron."

"Jared will have your liver and lights for this, you bastard!" Amanda shot at him.

"I doubt that very seriously," Freddie drawled back at her, very much in his element in the role of bully.

Amanda changed her tactics. "You do realize you will never get away with this madness. We already know of your first attempt on us, which nearly killed our good friends. You should have stayed out of the country. Now you will all hang."

"You can prove nothing if you have not had a warrant put out for my arrest. I know there is none, you see. As for dear Blanche, she will have to look out for her own neck once this is over as it is revenge alone that she is seeking—or so she says." He examined a small smudge on his lemon-yellow breeches. "I do believe the woman is of rather a nasty nature, perhaps even a bit mad. A pity you are to be placed at her tender mercies. But enough of her, for I have more important things to concern myself with than that tramp. As for myself, I will emerge from this whole affair completely blameless, and the picture of the bereaved relative. My mourning at the graveside will be most convincing."

Lady Chezwick gave a loud sniff at these words, and turned her head toward the window in dismissal. She did not for a minute underestimate Freddie—or overestimate him either—and was confident Jared would soon arrive and set all to rights. Amanda was more inclined to draw Freddie out, as it was obvious he was gloating over his own cleverness. To her mind he was more than a little unhinged himself; perhaps if she knew his plans she could find a way to thwart them. Freddie drew up a chair near the fire and gladly expounded on his scheme at great length.

It was a complicated bit of deception, she had to admit. The women would all be nice and cozy until Jared and Kevin arrived. That they would eventually come was certain, for Clem's note— left in clear view—told of the kidnapping of poor Lady Storm by desperate men who had a grievance against her husband. The note, which demanded money to flee the country, was a bait he could not resist. The mill was set for the rendezvous, where Jared was to hand over a large sum for the safe return of his wife.

"And if I know my dear cousin Jared, he will act in his usual egotistical manner, damning the thought of any ransom and charging at once to the mill in hopes of finding—if not you, chit, then at least a clue to your whereabouts. No finesse, our Jared. None at all," Freddie clucked in mock sympathy.

Once inside the mill, Jared and any companions would quickly be subdued and the remainder of the plan put into action. It would all come out as a love triangle that ended in tragedy.

"You have thought long and hard, Cousin," Amanda spat, "but you seem to forget the mill family. They can attest to our abduction at your hands."

Freddie smiled as he answered her, "That is where Blanche's genius comes to the forefront. Peter," he said to the young valet who had been standing in the shadows, looking more uncomfortable by the minute, "tell the ladies my name, if you please."

Peter had the decency to blush as he muttered, "As I referred to you so many times in the days we had to stay here until Lord Storm rode out, you are the Earl of Lockport, my lord."

"Exactly. The family has been in that back room ever since our arrival. They have never seen me, only Peter, Simon, and Clem. But even so, those country bumpkins could not know the difference, one of the gentry being much like the other to them. Peter took great pains to put the miller in his confidence, telling him how you despised your husband and planned to run off with Rawlings. Today's abduction was carefully planned by you both to look like a kidnapping, so that suspicion would be taken from Rawlings and the two of you could slip away unnoticed once any search proved fruitless. Your plans to do away with Jared by luring him to certain death at the mill will appear to have backfired, and Jared will slay his friend in an insane rage before turning the gun on his faithless wife."

He ended his little recital by saying, "With you and your lover both dead, Jared will have nothing to live for save the rope, and in despair, he will take his own life, leaving a note to that effect. It is that simple."

There were flaws in his plan, the most glaring being the unexpected presence of Lady Chezwick, as Amanda was quick to point out.

"I am not unduly concerned with the old crone, I am sure Blanche has something in her bag of tricks that will react in much the way as a seizure—one to which an elderly lady confronted with three tragic deaths might easily succumb."

Amanda forcibly restrained her raging aunt and tried again.

"But the servants at Storm Haven were told Jared was injured. Do you really believe anyone will swallow the story whole about Kevin, Jared's dearest friend, being behind the entire affair? That seems preposterous."

Freddie shook his head as if he were trying to explain sums to an ignorant child. "A mere ruse, easily believed as a bit of the hoaxed abduction. As to Jared's great love of Rawlings, you forget you were seen in the company of both Rawlings and my cousin unescorted last Spring. Your reputation would lead anyone to believe you capable of playing your husband against his best friend, especially now that Rawlings has come into the title. Jared will end up the figure of pity—that really amuses me—when it is found that you carried Rawlings' seed, not his.

"Among Blanche's more valuable talents is an uncanny ability to copy handwriting. You see, with samples of your fine copperplate obtained from that poor fool Denton and various letters taken from Rawlings' lodgings in his absence, it was a simple matter to invent some very incriminating love letters from the both of you. Blanche seems to have a real hatred for Rawlings, for some strange reason. But be that as it may, once several of Rawlings' notes describing the so-called kidnap plot are found in your reticule, and a particularly torrid missive from you agreeing to the idea is taken from Rawlings' waistcoat after his untimely end, there should be a swift end to any speculation."

Amanda felt her spirits dropping rapidly. "That, I imagine, is also the manner in which you will produce Jared's suicide note?"

"Oh, but that is already written. Would you like to hear it? It is a particularly moving piece."

"Kevin and Jared both have many friends in London. None of them will believe this havey-cavey plot. You are sure to be unmasked in the end, for there are just too many unbelieveable twists to your story."

"It is entirely possible, but that will not happen until some weeks have passed. I have no real love for Storm Haven or the title, if the truth be known. I shall simply withdraw all my inheritance from the Exchange immediately, and Peter and I will depart for sunnier climes. Alas, I am weary of ducking my creditors and see no need to spoil them by finally paying up. Ah, yes, I do believe between the money and the jewelry I shall be tolerably comfortable."

"And Blanche?" Amanda deliberately watched Peter as she

asked this question; he had seemed disturbed when Freddie had spoken poorly of her earlier.

"Not being able to become Lady Storm, she will no doubt wish to settle for some of the Delaney money. She is badly dipped, you know, Wade's money being long gone. Yes, Blanche believes she will share in the booty—an idea I must confess I fostered." Freddie crossed his legs and leaned back against the seat. "There are storms on the seas between here and Italy, I hear. Many persons have slipped overboard during such violent upheavals. Need I say more?"

The valet's eyes darkened and he quickly averted his head, but not before Amanda had taken in his expression. So the handsome young Peter was not totally devoid of finer feelings. Perhaps this information could be of some help. The way matters stood at the moment, Amanda was ready to grasp at any straw or seek escape at even the slightest opportunity.

But when Freddie, his confidence overwhelming his judgement, turned his back on Amanda just long enough for her to make a bolt for the door, much hampered by her skirts and her swollen middle, the fleet Clem had no difficulty in forcing her back into her seat beside the fire with a breath-taking shove. As her body made contact with the sturdy, unpadded chair, a searing pain ripped down her side and she cried out.

Lady Chezwick was beside her in a moment, asking her where she felt the pain, but as quickly as it had come it was gone. A second pain, more centrally-located in her abdomen, came some minutes later. It was not mentioned to her aunt, nor were any of the ones that followed it at regular fifteen-minute intervals.

Would her baby be born before Freddie killed her? And if it were—how long would it survive? Right now Lady Wade was in the next room, telling Freddie that there was no need to keep the women alive until Jared appeared. Oh, my dear God, Amanda prayed silently, let him arrive in time.

Jared and Kevin had spent some three hours at the Squire's house, discussing the various precautions Jared had taken to both protect Amanda and keep informed of Freddie's possible return to the city. The Squire had been taken into their confidence from the beginning, Jared believing the man was owed an explanation for the attack on his youngest daughter.

189

The thin, wintry sun was fast fading when young Tom came riding at them at a gallop, waving his hat and screaming at the top of his lungs. "My God, something's happened to Mandy!" Jared exclaimed, and spurred his horse forward to meet the oncoming rider.

"H-harrow sent me," Tom gasped as they came together. "Yer ta come home fast! Miss Mandy's gone."

Jared didn't wait for any further explanation, but yelled at Kevin to return to the Squire's and fetch Bo before leaving Kevin to curse Freddie Crosswaithe in terms so colorful and original young Tom could only stare at him in open-mouthed awe.

Within minutes Jared's Devil pelted into the courtyard at Storm Haven, where Jared jumped from his mount and bounded up the stairs into his home.

Harrow met him in the foyer and explained he had been abed when Amanda ordered the carriage brought around. "She were told you had a fall, my lord. A man came to lead them to some cottage where you were supposed to be laying close to death."

"How long ago?" Jared shouted while racing to the gun room, where he took down three pair of his best pistols.

"Lady Chezwick and Miss Mandy are gone near three hours, sir. As soon as Tom told me I smelled something queer. Jennings drove them, and you know he's a good man. He'd have had word back by now if he could."

"My aunt is with her? Thank God for that, at least." Jared steeled himself to be calm while he carefully loaded all of the pistols and strapped an evil-looking sword about his waist.

"What's forward?" Kevin questioned as he and Bo burst through the doorway some minutes later to run at once to pick up the remaining pistols from the table. Before Jared could answer, he was interrupted by an outraged Nanny who insisted on being taken at once to her baby. "She's near to breeding, you know."

Jared stamped into the blue room, Nanny and the rest close on his heels, and accepted the stiff drink Kevin poured for him. "I know that, Nanny, but we have no idea where she's been taken. I don't even know if they are alive, though I feel almost certain they will be kept safe until I reach them if I read mine enemies' twisted minds correctly. I sincerely hope my aunt is being as disagreeable as she is capable."

"So you don't know where Miss Mandy is? And I suppose

sittin' here swillin' brandy is goin' to find her?" Nanny shrieked.

Jared's eyes narrowed in anger as he gritted, "Get her the hell out of here, Kevin, we've got to think." Nanny left—as far as the other side of the closed door, that is—so that when the note Jared soon found was read aloud she knew what she had to do.

"Harrow!" she screeched at the concerned old man. "Bring Lady Chezwick's traveling coach around. It's slow, but well sprung, as her ladyship does like her comforts. We must be ready to set out at once."

"Where to, you daft woman?" Harrow asked. His head ached badly with his cold, but he would have driven head-first into hell if he could but find Miss Mandy.

"I heard his lordship mention a mill not ten miles from here. We'll station our coach nearby and out of the way. Once the dear child is safe she will need me to take care of her; the old lady will have fallen to pieces by now and be no help at all."

Harrow brightened perceptively. "Yer got a good head on yer shoulders, Beulah. I'll just step in and tell hiz lordship what we're about so he can set his mind to ease." Jared was more than happy to give Amanda's two old servants something to do, and readily agreed to the plan after Harrow promised to keep well out of sight.

The rotund woman moved with amazing speed up the staircase, dragging a weeping Sally in her wake, and within half an hour the heavily-loaded coach was on its way. Inside were Tom, who had somehow smuggled his slight body aboard, and Nanny. Both were shoved into a tiny space that was all that was available, for the rest of the coach was taken up with bundles of warm clothing for Amanda and Lady Chezwick, as well as medicine, blankets, and food. There was even a small layette packed for the baby. "You never know, Tom, when the wee one might come after the jostling my poor baby will get on this godforsaken road."

Kevin and Bo were still locked in the library with Jared. Kevin was pacing the room in his anxiety to be off. "Would you be so kind as to tell me what we are doing here? We should be riding."

Jared shook his head and continued to stare into the flames. "That's just what we shouldn't be doing. Bo here was right when he said I underestimated Freddie, and now I may be tending to give my cousin more credit than he is due. But I think he *expects* us to come pelting after Amanda—and right into a trap. My God, man, do you think I don't want to go charging out after my wife? But I want to save her, not be the cause of her death." He looked up at his agitated friend and asked him to summon a footman.

He then dashed off a note to the Squire, informing him of the kidnap plot and asking him to present the note to the authorities in the event of any tragedy. "That should put a spoke in Freddie's wheel if he's out to make himself blameless in this episode," he commented as the footman left the room with the note.

Bo—who had until this moment been keeping his own counsel—decided it was time he kept his end up, so to speak, in the proceedings. "Own score to settle, old man. Like a whack or two at Freddie meself. Coming on to dark, though. Better shove off, what?"

"Not yet, Bo. First we must have a plan. This mill is well known to me, and I wager the thaw has made a right pretty mess of the lane leading to it from the main road. Considering Freddie and his abhorrence of night travel in general, I am more than half certain Amanda will not be moved until morning."

"Unless the mill is truly just a spot Freddie picked for his so-called *exchange,* and Amanda is either hidden away elsewhere or—even worse—on her way to London or some such place," Kevin interposed with a sigh.

"Vote the mill," Bo stated, rising rapidly to his feet. "Tally-ho, gents. To the hunt!" He was halfway to the door before he realized no one was following and so he retraced his steps to his chair, where he sat impatiently staring at his friends as if willing them to action. Soon his eyes, like Kevin's, focused solely on Jared. The worried husband continued to lean back in his chair behind the desk, tapping the top of a long wooden letter opener on the cut-glass inkwell in front of him.

"Deuced wearing on the nerves," Bo commented to no one in particular after a time.

Kevin shot him a fierce look. "Quiet, you numbskull. Can't you see Jared's conjuring up a plan of attack?"

At long last Jared's fine black eyebrows arched skywards and a particularly nasty smile curled up one side of his mouth. "Gentlemen, I have decided on our course of action." Ignoring Bo's aside to Kevin that suggested this plan had not popped into Jared's head any too soon, he continued. "As it is full dark with no little moon to act as guide, I am almost completely sure Freddie, and Amanda, will remain as guests of the miller for the night. As he will surely set out to some pre-planned untraceable location at first light, it is imperative we act swiftly."

"Said so. Don't listen, none of you," Bo interrupted as he turned to Kevin. "You said he was thinking. Not such a deep one if *I* said it first."

"Stow it, you lunkhead," Kevin hissed, and then prodded Jared to go on. "If our resident wise man dares speak again I'll just pop him one in his brain-box. You know," he winked broadly to ease the tension, "that so ample portion of Bo's anatomy, most mercifully shielded from our sight as long as he remains seated."

"I say," the offended gentleman began, before hastily clapping a pudgy hand over his mouth as evidence of his return to a nearly-mute state, as Kevin made a threatening gesture in his direction.

"Call a halt, gentlemen, please," Jared intervened as he rose to walk around to lean on the front of the desk. "As I was saying, Freddie is, for the moment, within our grasp. The only problem will be in capturing him and any hired men he may have with him—no more than two if I am any judge of Freddie's thin pockets and cheeseparing ways—without causing harm to the ladies. To that end I propose we ride out ourselves, as too many men crashing through the trees would be more an encumbrance than a help. Now listen carefully, old friends. Here is my plan."

Kevin and Bo were still arguing as to who was in charge of their end of the campaign while Jared was striding for the door. Without breaking stride he called over his shoulder, "Kevin, you take Devil, he's sure-footed and fast. And Bo, you're to ride that new bay mare I acquired last month. That plug of yours wouldn't last a mile at the pace I wish to set. If I know Harrow, he ordered her saddled before he left."

As they loped toward the stable area Kevin inquired as to Jared's mount. "I shall ride Tempest," he told him. "There isn't another horse in England will take me faster to Amanda's side."

Kevin stopped dead in his tracks. "Are you mad, man? That beast won't let you on his back."

Bo agreed. "Feed him. House him. Don't mean he loves you."

Jared ignored them as a groom approached with the black stallion and, as he had guessed, the bay mare.

Kevin smiled at Jared's romantic gesture and saluted him briskly. "Don't knock me down with the breeze as you fly by. That is, if you can get that beast to carry you." Then the smile left his face and the three men solemnly shook hands. "Good luck, old friend," he intoned gravely. Then he and Bo were astride their horses and gone.

Jared continued on into the stables, where Tempest was standing quietly in his stall. The great red stallion eyed the now-familiar figure warily as Jared opened the stall door and drew the horse out. Slowly he fastened a bridle and saddle on the horse, then stepped back and looked Tempest square in the eye. "Mandy needs us, boy, and you're the fastest way to her side. I've lost much time deciding on the right course of action, and I'm counting on your swiftness to help recapture some of those precious minutes." He turned away, then and cursed himself under his breath. "The tension has unhinged me, by God. Perhaps Kevin was right. This idea was a romantic gesture at best; now I'm left without a decent mount. Listen to me, reasoning with the brute!"

As he stood there with his back to the horse he felt a nudging in the small of his spine, a nudging that nearly sent him sprawling. He whirled to face the horse and hope flared in his chest. Without waiting to figure out exactly why he thought it would work, he swung up onto Tempest's back and urged him forward.

They rode like the wind, the tall man and the giant horse, moving forward as one toward the main road. "*To Mandy!*" Jared shouted in Tempest's ear, feeling half-giddy with elation and not a small bit ridiculous at the same time. Within minutes they passed his friends and their bracing cheers brought a grin to Jared's face. As he flew past Harrow a few miles further down the road he shouted, "Don't go too close. And if you value your ancient skin, keep that nosey old harridan inside quiet."

Harrow shouted back, "Yes, sir, milord. Ride him, milord, ride him hard!"

Jared let out a whoop before man and horse disappeared from sight over the next hill, kicking up a spray of ice and slush as they went.

Inside the coach, Nanny—who fortunately for her master had not heard the latest adjectives he had applied to her—was trying desperately to keep her Sunday-best hat on her head as she bounced higgledy-piggledy all over the coach. "If I live through this night I shall murder Harrow on the morrow. All men are just little boys, Tom, and I do believe they enjoy this mad chase."

"Yes, ma'am," Tom replied dutifully. What was the old

woman so het up about? Harrow said no one would hurt Miss Mandy until his lordship showed up, and *he* certainly wouldn't let anything happen to her. By jiminey, when he wasn't thinking too hard about Miss Mandy he could be pretty excited by this adventure himself! He pushed Nanny's ample form back into the corner as she bounced over onto him. *Women,* he sneered to himself. Lily-livered creatures they were, all of them!

Freddie Crosswaithe was becoming a bit disenchanted with the night's events as they had so far unfolded. The meal Clem's cohort had prepared was almost entirely inedible, the cottage was cold and offered only a mediocre fire in the cavernous fireplace to warm him. Jared should have ridden up at least two hours since, and, curse the luck, it was snowing again. Where could his unreliable cousin be? Didn't the dolt realize he was upsetting their well-laid plans?

Freddie chewed on his bottom lip as he stood in the darkness, watching the approach to the mill through a gap in the homespun curtains. As his confidence in Blanche's genius waned, his appreciation of the quarterly allowance Jared had paid him seemed less and less a hardship.

And where was Peter? He would have to be spoon-feeding the miller and his family to be taking this long. He should come relieve his master, for this standing about in his high-heeled slippers was hard on his tender insteps. Freddie called for Clem to come away from his obvious—while unbelievable—enjoyment of his dinner to take up a position near the windows so he could go and seek out his valet. The man on guard, Simon or Simeon or whatever, reported he had not seen Peter since that man had taken a tray to the ladies in the loft of the cottage.

Freddie's eyes narrowed and he climbed swiftly to the bedroom, where Amanda and Lady Chezwick impatiently awaited their rescuers.

Amanda was lying atop the miller's feather bed fully clothed, her bloated belly looking even more distended now than it had when she was upright. Lady Chezwick had been dozing fitfully in a chair but roused as her niece spoke.

"So, Freddie," Amanda teased, "your plan seems not to be working out as you had hoped. Did you really think my husband would come rushing in here willy-nilly without giving a thought to your treachery?" At his outraged expression she gave a weak laugh and said, "You rely heavily on my husband's love for me; perhaps I should tell you that ours was a marriage of convenience. Right now Jared and his friends are probably all warm and cozy at Storm Haven, celebrating his happy release from an unwanted union by indulging in a game of slap and tickle with two or more of the housemaids."

Lady Chezwick was quick to confirm Amanda's lies. "That is true, you poor, misguided moron. This chit purposely compromised Jared into marriage, a fact you must be aware of if you saw them together at that awful inn, and he was constrained to wed her. She may have been penniless, but she was still a Boynton, you know. You don't know how near you were to the truth when you named Rawlings as father to her spawn. To be absolutely correct, however, you must realize the girl could only be guessing if she were to single out any one man for that dubious honor."

Amanda turned her head away to hide her smile. Aunt Agatha was certainly heart and soul into her role, but doing it a bit too brown, to Amanda's mind.

Lady Chezwick, willing to run any rig in the hope it would discommode her obnoxious relative, decided to push her point home further. After all, she knew Freddie from long ago and knew just where to aim her barbs. "Jared *will* arrive, though. I believe he has a score to settle with you on quite another matter. But it is apparent to me that he delays until you rid him of his unwanted wife. So once again, Jared wins. He will have shed this common baggage—a blessing, I assure you—and your neck shall stretch in his stead. Ah, Freddie, you were always so adept at playing the fool."

Freddie was breathing heavily now, his thin face screwed up in an expression of confusion mixed with disbelief. "Enough! You are both lying. I saw your concern for each other earlier, and the chit's fear for her precious Jared. You are just trying to confuse me."

"A task I have always felt lamentably simple, I might add," pointed out Lady Chezwick with an exaggerated sigh. "Always did take after his father; I cannot imagine what Hortense ever saw in him. No doubt she's spinning in her grave with shame right this minute."

Amanda chuckled at the first bit of humor to strike her since this entire nightmare began. Then she sobered and asked, "Ah, Freddie, forgive us for bamming you. It's just my relief at realizing all my fears of the past months were unnecessary. Strange as it may seem as we are indeed your prisoners, I am no longer the least bit afraid. Bo was wrong and my so-very-astute husband was correct, you are a harmless looby—all bluster and no bite. I am astonished you are let out alone. But I am keeping you from something, I am certain. What errand brought you to our gaol, Cousin? Have you misplaced our keeper?"

Freddie scanned the room and saw the two grease-filmed plates of barely-eaten stew on a side table. "Then Peter *was* here with your food. Why haven't you eaten? Are your stomachs a bit queasy as you contemplate your fates?"

"Indeed not," Amanda rejoined, assuming an air of great calm. "I would not feed such swill to the hogs on the home farm. When Jared comes it will be time enough to eat." Amanda could see a fine layer of sweat on Freddie's upper lip, a strange phenomenon in such a chilly room. He did not look so sure of himself anymore, and if the sounds she had been hearing this half hour or more from the next room were any indication, he was soon to be unsettled further.

"Your man Peter was in to us about an hour ago, but deserted us to follow Lady Wade to that little bedroom under the eaves and we have been alone ever since. Perhaps he is helping her chew that sad excuse for meat in the stew. Do you play chess, Freddie?" she continued without a pause. "If you can unearth the traveling set from the pocket of my carriage I would dearly appreciate the diversion. My aunt has been sleeping all this while, she is that confident of her nephew's ability to rescue us." Her voice dripped innocence as she inquired, "Why Freddie, wherever are you off to now? You do not have to feel ashamed if you have never mastered the game; perhaps a rousing round of snakes-and-ladder would better suit your talents—although I myself haven't indulged since I left the schoolroom!" The door closed heavily, and Freddie locked the door on the feminine laughter that tore away at his already shredding nerves.

"I do not know what we are finding so amusing, pet," Lady Chezwick said at last. "He means our death."

Her niece shrugged her shoulders and commented, "I was more in awe of him before, when I was in the first flush of panic. But Jared and Kevin will be here soon and I believe I have more faith in my husband's intelligence than I do in Freddie's schemes. The only person I fear now is Lady Wade. In that I agree with

Freddie, for the woman is quite mad—and dangerous." Amanda grimaced as another pain began in her lower back and wrapped around to grip hard at her stomach. "I only hope Jared arrives before his son," she gasped. "*O-o-o-h*, this one is quite strong, I fear."

"This one? *This one!* Good heavens, girl, do not tell me you are planning to give birth in the middle of all this fracas—and in a miller's loft, no less? Really, you'd think you could have timed it far better than that." Clearly Lady Chezwick was quite incensed.

As the pain eased, Amanda smiled weakly at her harassed aunt and apologized. "I am afraid I have little to say in the matter. The imp has taken it quite out of my hands. Do you by chance know anything to the point concerning our responsibilities if birth becomes imminent?"

From the blank expression on the old lady's face it was apparent she did not. "This should prove educational then," Amanda quipped half-heartedly. "Jared has been so worried about this day, you know. Wouldn't it be wonderful if all the commotion were over by the time he arrived? Please do help me out of this gown and under the covers, for I believe I should then be more comfortable. Is there a nightgown of some sort in one of the drawers of that chest? I doubt it to be all the crack but at least I should feel less like an overstuffed pigeon. Oh, dear lady, I am rambling and I know it. Please forgive me."

Lady Chezwick gathered the frightened girl into her arms and rocked her for a few moments. "We will contrive, my dear child. We will contrive. As you say, it could even prove to be *wonderful*."

Suddenly they were shaken by voices raised in anger in the next room, and they clung tighter together as they strained to hear what was being said. "Perhaps Freddie has found his valet," Amanda whispered with a gleam in her golden eyes. "And if he has, was Peter alone?"

Amanda had thought all along that Peter showed an inordinate amount of interest in Lady Wade, and—if her opinion of the woman was correct— Blanche would lose no opportunity to amuse herself by passing the time with such a handsome, virile-looking specimen.

In this she was very right. Blanche considered it a challenge to lure away the loyalty of Freddie's prized valet, for she detested the man necessity had forced her to deal with and jumped at the chance to upset him. Luring his valet into her bed (and sympathy) would be quite an accomplishment, and such a superb physical specimen should make easy work of ridding her of Freddie. Once her passion for the brawny boy had waned, he too would be easily disposed of. Most importantly, if there were any chance for it to be otherwise, why should she settle for just a portion of Freddie's inheritance—when with a little luck she could have it all?

She had been playing up to Peter behind his master's back ever since they had first met in Scotland at Freddie's ramshackle hideaway. Rawlings had frightened her badly, and she let it be known that she was going on a repairing lease before setting out for the border. The boy had been very difficult, swearing his allegiance to Freddie, but over the weeks she had steadily wormed away at his resolve with her enticing smiles and the occasional brush of her hand as he held her chair or fetched her fan.

His capitulation was inevitable, but why did he have to choose tonight? It was damned risky, bedding the lad with Freddie downstairs, but Peter had been insistent. She didn't know that he feared the dawning of a new day might well bring his death, or that he was determined to at least know a woman the way a man should before facing hell's everlasting fires.

After a few half-hearted disclaimers pointing out the danger involved in such a daring act, that same threat of discovery sent delicious shivers of excitement down Blanche's spine. "Oh, all right, my fine young buck. But I warn you, don't dawdle!"

He didn't. It wasn't too many minutes later that he bent his tall frame to negotiate the small doorway back to the hall, and it was a simple matter for Freddie to secure a good grip on the valet's ear as he roughly piloted him the few steps to the ladies' prison. "Stay in here and guard these two, you miserable traitor," Freddie warned, "and don't believe a word either one of them says. Is everyone to desert me in my time of need?" he ended with a small sob. Then he stormed out, locking the door from the outside.

That done, he pushed open the door to Blanche's room and advanced purposefully inside. The prisoners and their gaoler were afforded the dubious pleasure of listening to Blanche's ear-splitting and highly unladylike protests as Freddie's somewhat feminine attack of slaps and shoves made short work of the astonished peeress. After binding her hands to the bedposts with the sash from her own robe, he gagged her with a strip of rough blanket and—looking at least partially vindicated—he quit the room.

Peter was one frightened young man. He shook his head sadly and cast his worried eyes over his, it now seemed, cellmates. He hadn't liked any of this from the beginning, but loyalty to the man who had rescued him from the workhouse prevented him from backing away from the situation. Until now. Now he would gladly stay locked in this room with Lady Storm and wait for her husband to come for her. Perhaps then they would not send him to Newgate.

Peter was only seventeen years old and had no wish to die. Blanche had given him his first taste of what he had felt missing in the unwelcomed sly pettings of his employer. Maybe it wasn't a very worthy reason to want to live, but he longed to enjoy such pleasures again.

In despair he turned his woebegone face toward the women. His look was met by two pairs of wary eyes and a barrage of quick questions. He tried to tell them he would protect them from Freddie, but that promise ended in a sob as he sank to his knees on the floor. Lady Chezwick relieved him of the pistol Freddie had somehow overlooked and patted him gently on the head. "We'll protect you, lad, never fret," she promised the boy.

Once Peter was calm Lady Chezwick took time to examine the weapon for a moment, then struck a determined pose. "This is not a time for faint hearts, Peter, my boy," she said with some spirit. "That being the case, I would consider it a kindness if you would show me how to work this blasted thing."

Chapter Eleven

EVEN in the bitter cold of the January evening, Tempest was heavily lathered by the time Jared turned into the slush-clogged lane that led to the mill and Jared's breeches were foam-flecked and stiff with perspiration. He walked Tempest to a spot not five hundred yards from the cottage, dismounted, and left the great beast tied to a nearby tree, promising to provide him with better shelter as soon as he might. If left standing too long he knew the horse could become mortally ill, and even if he escaped Freddie's plans for him surely Mandy would murder him.

The cottage was in near darkness, as he had suspected, but as he circled around to the rear he could see a faint sliver of light coming from an upstairs dormer window. Mandy! It had to be; why else would a candle be burning in a room too far from the view of the road to be of use to the kidnappers? Quietly he crept to a small ground-level window and looked through the murky glass. He could make out the figure of a short, ugly-looking man sitting at table, the half-eaten joint of some sort of game clenched in his filthy fist and a bottle of cheap gin at his elbow.

Jared wondered what Freddie had done with the miller and his family, and hoped they had not come to any harm. There was more to this fairly large main room, but the poor quality of the glass and the wavering light cast by the fire furnished the remainder with only a flickering pattern of strange shapes that he could not make out. He stepped carefully away from his vantage point and, in a near crouch, half ran back to the shelter of the trees.

Again he approached the cottage, this time angling toward the front of the building. He arrived in time to see a most unhandsome fellow, with two long pistols shoved into his belt and an evil looking club in his hand, slipping outside the front door and taking up a position that would afford him a clear view of the approach to the cottage.

So there were at least the two he had been sure of, thought Jared. Add to that dear Cousin Freddie and his shadow, the so-handsome valet, and the odds were not nearly as bad as they might have been.

He still had some time for reconnoitering before Kevin and Bo arrived, so he decided to see if there was a ladder he could use to gain entry to the upstairs room where he was sure his Amanda was confined. This was to be his end of the plan he had gathered together so quickly at Storm Haven. He was to somehow gain entry to the cottage—even if it meant allowing himself to be captured—so that one of the small rescue party would be close to Amanda if the evening's events turned ugly. As he did not relish the thought of handing himself over to his cousin quite so easily, his option of climbing in through an upstairs window was most appealing.

The door to the mill proved to be unlatched, and once inside Jared not only found a ladder, but the miller and his brood as well, all snoring soundly in one corner of the room, a pile of half-empty plates by their sides. A quick sniff at the food remaining in the large iron pot that had obviously been the source of their meal confirmed Jared's fears that the unfortunate family had been drugged. Further investigation found them all to be breathing easily, even the youngest.

Jared hefted the rough ladder onto his shoulder and was about to leave when he heard a muffled sound coming from one of the covered bins in the rear of the building. With pistol at the ready he crossed to the bin and threw back the lid, exposing the tightly bound-and-gagged figure of his coachman, Jennings. The man was swiftly released and he immediately snatched up an evil-looking pitchfork to be used, as he told his Lordship, "with a willin' and happy hand" should anyone try to harm the defenseless mill family as they slumbered.

Once Jared had positioned the ladder in line with the window where he had seen the light, he re-checked his pistols, tucked them more firmly into his breeches, shed his greatcoat, and climbed stealthily toward the faint light that guided his way.

The window opened easily under his hand, and he made a mental note to double check all the locks at Storm Haven so that his security would never be so easily breeched. He slid the sash all the way up and placed his booted foot inside, where it found purchase on a homemade chest that creaked dangerously under his weight. When he had hauled the rest of his big frame inside he choked back an exclamation as his eyes became accustomed to the faint light and he could see none other than Lady Blanche Wade—bound and gagged as thoroughly as had been Jennings, and twice as angry.

Blanche first implored Jared with her eyes, then tried vainly to verbalize her pleas before realizing the man before her was not only unsympathetic to her plight but actually seemed to be deriving pleasure from it. Her entreaties turned to unintelligible curses and she struggled fruitlessly against her bonds.

"One down," Jared murmured tonelessly, and his eyes quickly darted around the rest of the room to make sure he was alone before he went to the door. Turning at the last moment, he executed a flawless bow in the direction of the livid Blanche before making his exit.

He tiptoed the few steps of the hallway to listen with his ear at another, larger door, and was rewarded by the sound of his wife's voice as she made a rather odd statement: "Here comes another one, Aunt Agatha. They are much more frequent now."

What the devil was going on? He tried the door unsuccessfully, but the homemade lock was not made to withstand the strength at the command of a man possessed with fear for his wife. As the lock gave with only a faint click, Jared leapt cat like into the room—only to come up short at the sight that greeted him.

Amanda was propped up in an enormous feather bed with an outlandish pink nightgown all but drowning her; its neatly embroidered neckline was gaping badly, and the sleeves had been rolled up at least six times. Pacing the uneven plank floor with her grey hair sadly disarranged and a look of harassed impatience on her face was his Aunt Agatha, still in her cape because the room was very cold.

That problem was being remedied, however, by a hulking brute who was fanning the flames of a small fire on the hearth. It was this person who claimed Jared's immediate attention, and he quietly shut the door and pointed both pistols at the stooping man as he quietly advised him to raise his hands.

"Whatever for, Nephew?' Lady Chezwick barked in exasperation. "Dear Peter here was only trying to make us more comfortable, unless of course you have any long-suppressed urge to rid yourself of your only aunt by allowing her to freeze to death. Oh, do put those horrible things away and let us get on with our business. I am glad to see you, by the by, but you took your own sweet time in getting here, didn't you?"

Jared let his pistols drop limply to his sides at this cavalier treatment of his derring-do. He was speedily brought to his senses by the sound of Amanda's unavoidably delayed greeting, given just as soon as her latest pain passed. He ran swiftly to her side and gathered her clumsy figure into his arms.

"Are you all right, my brave darling? I have been out of my mind with worry." This question came from Amanda, who was rather miffed when Jared laughed softly and commented that he was not being held hostage by anyone, and that the concern voiced would have sounded better had it come first from him.

"But what are you doing in this bed, imp? You look lost in that tent of a gown, and surely it would have been warmer to have remained dressed."

Lady Chezwick tried to inform her nephew that the birth of his heir seemed imminent, but Jared had really spoken randomly to cover his great relief at having found Amanda safe. He interrupted his aunt's jumbled explanation to begin the second phase of his mission—that of seeking out his despicable cousin and separating his stringy body into a dozen or more unequal parts.

Peter spoke then, explaining that Freddie had taken leave of his senses and tied up Lady Wade, who had formerly been one of the leaders in the plot. He was now downstairs, the valet continued, waiting for Lord Storm and the Earl of Lockport to arrive. "There be two men with him, my lord, two very nasty men. But if you would please not hurt the master, my lord. He really don't mean no harm," the servant explained haltingly. " 'Tis that terrible Lady Wade what talked him round to the thing. Scarey, that's wot that lady be, right scarey. But it is a game to the master, sorta like playacting, you see. Not overfull in the brain-box neither, begging your lordship's pardon, him being your kin and all."

Jared looked to his wife, who confirmed this with a nod of her head. "I have had ample time to observe Freddie for myself, dearest, and what the boy says is true. The ninny weaves a fine drama, but I just can't see him in any of the leading parts. In truth, I'd be willing to wager he wishes he'd never started this whole thing."

Lady Chezwick was not to be overlooked in any cataloguing of Freddie's character, the lack of it, or his degree of guilt in the attempted murder or her own kidnapping. "That spindley jackanapes below hasn't the brains to find his way out of a room, even if the only doorway were decorated in foot-high red letters spelling 'Out: This way, you vacant-faced twit!'"

Jared dismissed his aunt's humor and, unaware of any problem other than the most obvious ones, jibed, "You are destined always to pick up strays, aren't you, my love? All right, if you believe the boy is to be trusted I will bow to your judgement. We'll discuss Freddie another time. Kevin is on his way with Bo, if they have not already taken up their places outside. With all this idle chatter we have dawdled away more than enough time for their part of the plan to have been put into action. Freddie has been very accommodating in eliminating Lady Wade and isolating the both of you out of sight and sound. Indeed, we might have spared time for a hand of whist, were we so inclined."

As his aunt made a rude face at him, Jared went to the draperies and pulled them back before putting a lighted candle at the window. In a few moments came the sound of pebbles pinging lightly against the panes. "Ah, that would mean Kevin is in place." He kissed his wife on the forehead and told her to stay where she was.

"Hummph!" muttered Lady Chezwick, who had been feeling quite neglected anyway. "Where do you think she would be going at a time like this, to tea with the King?"

"Aunt!" Amanda warned, and the lady reluctantly held her tongue. Jared had enough on his plate without worrying about Amanda and the child.

After signaling to Kevin that he was in position and ready to make his move, Jared left the bedroom and listened outside the door until he heard Peter bar it with a chair. He then tiptoed carefully to the head of the stairs and waited in the shadows, mentally picturing the events taking place in the darkness outside the cottage.

. Jared had instructed Bo and Kevin to eliminate any guards, but he had left the method of removal to their discretion. If those two stalwart protectors of helpless females approached the problem in their usual hey-go-mad way, it was no more than could be expected of the same gentlemen who had once dared a midnight invasion of the second floor bedchamber of one of their Cambridge deans in order to gain an audience with that man. That mad start was later explained to be in the way of pointing out to the old prunepuss the humor to be derived from the monkey sporting a top hat and cutaway coat that had attended evening prayers.

The dean was not to be deflected from his set course, alas, which had included the dismissal of the miscreants for the remainder of the term. Indeed, those poor innocent lambs, whose intentions were of the most noble, found themselves (and one rather rank-smelling monkey) firmly banished from the scene of their disgrace for the space of *two* terms.

Some dozen years of exposure to polite society had perhaps helped discourage such lapses, but their unusual solution to the problem of the lookout and his mate proved that once-rampant flair for the bizarre to have been only shallowly concealed beneath a thin veneer of sophistication.

As the farce began to unfold Clem had just finished the physically comforting chore of relieving himself against the cottage wall. His cudgel shoved beneath his arm, he was busy rebuttoning his breeches when a slightly bored voice coming from the blackness off to the right of him drawled softly, "I must say, my good fellow, that's a deuced shabby way to treat good English soil. *Tch, tch.* Just see what you've done, man: There won't be sprout nor flower in that whole patch come spring if you persist in these wanton showers of destruction."

"Wot do I cares for yer blinkin' posies?" Clem was nonplussed enough to reply as he whirled, still groping with his buttons, to search out the disembodied voice of his taunter. Before his slow wits could more than begin to alert him to danger, he felt a discreet tap on his shoulder and whirled around yet again. This time he was presented with a clear view of his unexpected company before a beefy fist solved all his problems of how to deal with this turn of events—by effectively dropping him into a deep and dreamless sleep.

Kevin had advanced in time to receive the unconscious form of the now-harmless lookout, and Bo quickly shared the burden by taking firm hold of Clem's ankles. They carried him off to the mill and the ungentle arms of Jennings, who took great delight in stuffing the unprotesting thug into his own recently-vacated hideyhole.

The pair then returned to the cottage and Kevin, first placing a finger over his lips to warn Bo to silence, banged on the heavy door and called out, "Me bloody arse is 'alf froze. I wants a spell inside, I does. Git yer carcass out 'ere mate, afore me dabblers snap off."

Shortly sounds of shuffling footsteps and half-hearted curses reached their ears, and they took up positions flat against the wall on either side of the door.

The light from the fireplace cut a pie-shaped wedge in the cobbles outside before the shadow of a man appeared, closely followed by the fellow himself. "Yer ain't bin out 'ere no more 'en 'alf a blinkin' minute, ya bawlin' babe. Git o'er ta where me peepers can spy ya out, ya bloodless ninny, and it's warmin' yer arse real good I'll be." The man waited for an answer, and when there was none he stepped further out into the path to call, "Clem, where the bloody 'ell are ya, ya thievin' 'ound?"

"Why, if I may be so bold as to put a word in here, sir, I might be able to give you the whereabouts of the worthy Clem," informed a silken voice, just before the cottage door was silently nudged closed.

"Wot the . . ." the kidnapper breathed as two London dandies moved toward him. He took a tentative step backwards before the chubby one sighed and commiserated, "Too bad. Nowhere to go, you know." Freddie's hired man turned to face the second gentleman, but found his demeanor no less encouraging as that man simply lifted one beautifully-manicured finger and crooked it in a gesture that beckoned the frantic man closer.

"No, I don't," the man croaked, for his throat seemed strangely tight. But the ensuing near-silent struggle was painfully predictable in its outcome, and soon a second storage bin was put to good use by the highly-delighted Jennings.

"Beggin' yer leave, sirs, but I can't but puzzle why you went to such trouble over these two no-goods. Tappin' em so gentle-like on their noggins when a knife betwixt the ribs 'ed be just as quiet—and a heap less work than heftin' em inta me so as ta keep em mum," Jennings put in, as he lowered the lid on the second neatly hemp-wrapped body.

"Lud, no! Messy. Can't stomach the sight of claret," Bo responded, horrified.

Kevin interpreted. "What Mr. Chevington means is that we, as law-abiding subjects, abhor unnecessary violence. Right, Bo?

Besides," he continued, with a grin that made him resemble a slightly raffish choirboy, "it was much more fun this way."

Inside the cottage Freddie was fast becoming hysterical with fear. That his two hirelings had disappeared boded no good, but had they merely run off—or had they fallen afoul of Jared? Why does everything happen to me, Freddie wailed in his heart of hearts. Even Peter had fallen victim to the Delaney charm and deserted him. He should be standing with his master, protecting him from Jared.

Freddie's thin hold on his nerves finally slipped away and he ran to the bottom of the stairs and screamed out his valet's name. "Peter. *Peter!* Come here at once. Everything is going wrong. I wish to return to London."

When Freddie received no answer to his yells he was forced to consider the last of his options—Blanche. But before he could begin to climb the staircase the menacing form of his cousin appeared at the head of the flight like some horrid ogre from a particularly violent nightmare.

"I think it is appropriate at this time to say something profound, such as: The play is over, Freddie. The actors have no more lines, and the audience has all gone home. All that is left is the moral to this twisted tale, one most assuredly denouncing the evils of jealousy and greed." As he spoke Jared descended the steep flight, his eyes never leaving the thoroughly-cowed form of his cousin.

"It wasn't my idea, Jared, none of it. I swear. It was all Blanche's scheme," Freddie babbled in a thin, wailing voice. "It was her snickering and suggesting that drove me to it. Forgive me, dear cousin, for I meant no harm. Your wife and the old biddy have suffered no injury, surely you see that."

"Dear me, yes," came Kevin's amused voice from the doorway. "There's a grain of truth in there somewhere, Jared, if we can but find it. For you did do this poor lad dirty, proclaiming loud and long how you'd never wed. And then you tugged his little rug of security from beneath him by not only bracketing yourself but by showing all the signs of begetting a bloody legion of little Delaneys to push your cousin out of his place in line." Obviously Kevin's first flush of anger had faded, and rather than putting Freddie to the tortures of the rack—as he had promised himself he would do—he was now finding himself feeling almost sorry for the man.

Bo seemed to be of the same forgiving nature. "Shabby, that's what it is. For shame, Jared."

Jared listened to his friends' judgement of his inhumanities toward his cousin without bothering to inform them of his already-formulated plan to ship Freddie off to America, where he would receive an allowance of one thousand pounds a year as long as he agreed to keep his high-heeled feet firmly planted in the soil of that country. To do otherwise would only bring a dirty mantle of scandal down around his wife's shoulders, and that he would avoid at any cost.

The Lady Wade was a different bag of worms altogether, for her hatred and desire for revenge seemed to know no bounds. Yes, her disposition could prove to be a bother.

Just then Kevin, who had disappeared upstairs, reappeared with the disheveled Blanche bumping and tripping down the stairs at his heels. Her strangled mouthings prompted Kevin to remove her gag, and she immediately launched into a scathing denunciation of Freddie—and an equally earnest declaration of her own innocence.

"Lawks, Kevin, put that rag back! Can't abide hysterical females," Bo pleaded, his hands clapped over his ears. Kevin laughed and did just that, but then made the fatal mistake of pitying the lady over the bluish tinge to her bound hands and loosened her bonds a trifle.

When Freddie decided to mount another attack on Jared's family loyalties, Blanche—her sweat-slick hands slipping from her bonds with almost laughable ease—saw her chance and took it. She was at the door before anyone noticed her movements, and through it and running for all she was worth into the black night before a chase could be mounted.

She ran like she had never run before, her skirts hiked up around her knees as she plunged headlong into a concealing stand of trees. Just for a moment, to catch her breath and search out the most direct path for her flight, she leaned against a snow-damp trunk, willing her heart to stop pounding so in her breast. And then she saw it. A horse. Saddled and bridled and ready to ride!

Blanche had ever been an indifferent rider, but never before had she encountered the particular trouble this horse began to dish out the moment she was settled in the saddle. Mindless of her rough sawing on his reins, the big red stallion refused to budge an inch. And then something most extraordinary happened: The horse knelt down on all fours and rolled to one side, dumping the incensed Blanche into a slushy, cold puddle.

"Stupid beast!" Blanche screeched, and dealt the horse a vicious kick in his rump, a move that caused the steed merely to utter a horsey laugh.

Thoroughly incensed and dripping with muddy water, Blanche wished fervently for the luxury of enough time to find a big stick and beat the ignorant brute senseless. But as every moment was of the essence, she settled for another kick and then, raising her sodden skirts, loped off toward the main road on foot.

By the time Jared and the others reached Tempest, the stallion had regained his feet and was shaking himself free of the twigs and bits of bramble that still clung to his coat.

"It would seem Lady Wade passed this way," Jared observed, tongue in cheek.

"Ah, well," Kevin observed, slightly out of breath, "either the lady will freeze her over-stuffed arse off or she'll bamboozle some poor sot into giving her a lift into town. Either way, I grow fatigued by it all, old chums, and suggest we adjourn to the mill for refreshments."

"Toddy, most like," Bo said, shivering.

So that was that. Jared turned reluctantly and walked toward the cottage. Bo led Tempest to the shed beside the mill, where he would rub him down and feed him some oats if there were any to be had. In any event, Harrow and Tom should be arriving soon now that Jared had fired the two agreed-upon warning shots, signaling all clear.

Jared felt oddly numb, as if he couldn't believe the nightmare was finally over. He did not feel any elation or sense of victory, just relief that the danger had at long last passed.

When he got to the house he met Peter on the stairs. "Where are you going, lad? I thought you were to stay with the ladies."

"They tossed me out, my lord. I'm to heat some water over the fire. Is the doctor on his way?"

"Peter, it is very late and I am exceedingly tired," Jared replied testily. "What the devil are you talking about?"

Peter grinned and said, "Why, sir, Lady Storm is giving birth. She . . ."

Jared was gone, up the stairs three at a time, to dash into Amanda's room and shout, "Plague take you, woman, why didn't you tell me you were going to have the child now?"

Amanda struggled to a half-sitting position and asked, "Where have you been? It's been an age since we've heard anything. Is everything all right?"

"Thanks to you and my somewhat mercurial friends, I have decided to deal lightly with dear Freddie. He's off for America on the next possible ship. He, er, feels an urge to travel. Blanche escaped us for the moment, but—since she has neither the connections nor the resources to launch another attack on us—I think I may safely say we have heard the last of Lady Wade. But never mind that. Peter says you are going to have the baby. Is he correct?"

"Jared, I have been going to have this baby for some months now, you must have become used to the idea by this time. Do not fly so to the alts if it just happens to be tonight. Though I *would* appreciate it if you could find a doctor, for Aunt Agatha is a bit overcome."

The old lady sniffed. "Overcome? That is certainly a mild way of putting it. Jared, for the love of heaven get us a doctor or a midwife or anyone else who comes to mind. Having instructed Peter to boil water, I have completely depleted my store of knowledge on the subject. I will not even know what to do with the dratted water when he brings it ," she ended, plopping down into a chair and fanning herself wildly with her handkerchief.

Amanda took that moment to have another contraction—a very strong one—and she reached out her hand for Jared, who raced to her side. The spasm passed after a bit, no more than a minute, but to Jared it seemed like an hour. He let go of Amanda's hand and sped to the top of the stairs. "Kevin! Kevin for God's sake, where are you, man?"

"No need to shout, friend. I am coming up to pay my respects to the ladies. The men the Squire so thoughtfully sent along have taken away the nasty felons; Bo is escorting Freddie to London in your coach with Jennings at the reins; and Peter is heating some water on the fire. Good man, he. Freddie trained him well. However do you suppose he knew I wished a refreshing wash?"

Jared raced down the steps and grabbed his friend by the shoulders. "Curse your primping, posturing soul, Kevin Rawlings! Amanda is having the baby. Take Devil, ride for Sir Stanley. And fetch him here at once."

Kevin's smile abruptly drooped and he set off to find Sir Stanley, an exceedingly fine physician who just happened to have his winter residence in the district. Little did Jared know, thank goodness, that Sir Stanley was away from home, spending the Christmas holidays celebrating his son Rupert's engagement to a pale little child with a yearly income of over twenty thousand pounds.

Rather than return empty-handed, Kevin pelted to Storm Haven and rounded up the elderly local doctor Amanda had summoned to treat Jared. All this took time, time in which the arrival of Harrow with Nanny in his wake was looked upon by both Jared and Lady Chezwick as being on a par with manna from Heaven.

"Where is my baby?" Nanny queried as she headed unerringly to her mistress' side. "Harrow, brew me some tea, and plenty of it."

Jared was confused. "What does tea have to do with delivering a baby?"

"Absolutely nothing I can think of, my lord, but I am frozen to the bone after spending a small lifetime in that drafty carriage, and I want some tea," Nanny answered calmly.

"But Amanda is in pain. There is no time for sipping tea!"

"Harrow," she called, ignoring Jared. "Send Tom upstairs with the baskets from the carriage. I had a feeling they'd be needed. Oh, and, my lord, I have not yet seen Miss Mandy but I am sure there is time and enough for tea. First babies are not in as much of a rush as their parents are."

Jared yelled after the woman as she neared the top of the stairs, "Well this one is. It shouldn't even be here for another month, you daft woman! I'm coming with you."

Nanny would have blocked the door, but Jared picked her up bodily and set her to one side before taking up his position next to his wife's bed. "I have sent Kevin for Sir Stanley, love. Do you think you can hold on until he arrives?"

"I'll do my utmost," Amanda replied, trying to hide her distress, "but I am not sure your son wishes to wait upon the gentleman."

Nanny was more direct. "Bring a man in to take care of my baby? I never heard of such a muddle. What can a man know about these things? You men get us all into this state, and not one of you is a pennyworth of good at getting us out of it. I dare any man to try to come in this room once Miss Mandy and I get down to serious business."

Lady Chezwick had recovered a bit at the sight of Nanny so masterfully taking charge. For once she found herself in complete charity with the feisty old nurse. "Here, here!" she added, gaining herself a rare look of approval from Nanny.

Jared would have taken umbrage with the women but for Amanda's detaining hand on his sleeve. "I trust Nanny implicitly, dearest."

Jared wanted to continue the debate but Nanny insisted he leave the room. "We don't need any swooning fathers in here."

Jared's jaw set stubbornly. "I'm staying!"

"If you insist, my lord, but you may be called upon to help. Can you do that?" Nanny jibed, irrespectful of both his exalted rank and thundercloud expression.

He could. He would! His father stayed and helped comfort his wife, didn't he? He was no less a man than his father. Amanda's hand tightened on his again as she gave herself up to another pain. Jared wiped her brow with the cool cloth Nanny handed him and the fight was on—Jared praying his father had been wrong and Amanda out to prove that she was right.

Lady Chezwick roused herself from her pacing and hand-wringing long enough to gulp down two cups of tea and only four or five small cakes brought from Storm Haven before announcing she was too overset to eat a bite. Meanwhile Nanny busied herself arranging blankets under Amanda and setting out the small layette she had brought along in anticipation of tonight's event.

Finally all the preparations were done and they settled back to wait for the birth. After an hour of this Amanda finally got angry. "You are all staring at me as if I were going to burst at any moment. Jared," she said with as much composure as her tired body could command, "I would appreciate it very much if you would take yourself and your hangdog look down to the kitchen. We will call you when we need you."

Jared protested loud and long but finally gave in when Amanda appeared to be on the verge of tears.

"Good," she commented as the door closed behind him and Nanny firmly locked it. "Perhaps now we can get on with it. I never knew a man could be so useless, much as I adore him."

Before long a subtly different sort of pain began wrapping

itself around her middle, giving her an uncontrollable urge to bear down. This time Nanny came to her side and stripped off her covers, placing one pudgy hand on Amanda's swollen stomach. "All right now, Miss Mandy, when I say so I want you to push. Come on. Now. Push!" She hauled herself heavily onto the bed and spread Amanda's bent legs. "We'll soon be done, love. Rest a moment now. When the pain comes again I want you to push for all you're worth. Do you hear me?"

Amanda heard her. She called Lady Chezwick to her side and grabbed onto her with both hands. When the next pain came she pulled on her aunt's arms until the slighter woman almost fell into the bed with her. "Good heavens, Amanda, I had no idea you were that strong. Perhaps I should call Jared back in here."

"You do," her niece gasped, "and I shall . . . do you an injury. Can you really believe . . . I want my husband to see me like this . . . with Nanny popping up from be-between my legs like a . . . a jack-in-the-box? I would never forgive you."

The two older women smiled slightly and went back to their work. There was a banging on the door and Jared called out, "Kevin found a doctor, Aunt. Unlock this door and let us in."

Amanda bit her bottom lip and shook her head vigorously in the negative, her confidence in Nanny complete. "Go away, you stupid men," Nanny screeched. "This here is women's work!"

"The devil it is! Nanny, you let us in or I will break down this door. Amanda! Make her open the door."

Lady Chezwick went over to the doorway and raised her voice in a most unladylike way. "Now you listen here, Nephew. You are becoming a bore. Your wife does not need you or the doctor. We are progressing quite famously with Nanny. Go downstairs and find the poor doctor a drink now that he has been brought here. He can examine the baby when we are ready."

Amanda bit her hand to hold back a cry of pain as another contraction gripped her. It would not do to have Jared hear her cry out, for then he surely would break down the door and see her in this ignominious position. When the contraction eased she called to her husband, "Jared, listen to your aunt. Please, Jared, as you love me— *go away!*"

He went.

Kevin was waiting with some homemade mead he had searched out when the banished men entered the kitchen. He soon had a glass pressed into the doctor's hand and returned to a vantage point beside the fireplace to watch his friend—and to stay out of his way.

Doctor Grimsley was complaining loud and long about being dragged all over the countryside on a fool's errand, but Kevin soon sent him to check on the still-slumbering miller and his family. When he returned to yet another mug of warm mead he decided to make the best of the situation, at least for as long as the mead held out.

Harrow and Tom looked in for a minute, then wisely took themselves off to the small back room to tuck into the food Peter had unearthed from one of Nanny's well-packed baskets. Freddie's former valet had obviously found a home at Storm Haven. All three sat and discussed the oddities of the gentry while listening for sounds from the kitchen.

"For God's sake, Jared, I would appreciate it if you would stop this incessant pacing," Kevin drawled, "I am getting a crick in my neck watching you. Go sit down and get a grip on yourself. You're falling apart. It's a good thing Bo's not here to see this. Fair unman the fellow to see a friend go all to pieces like this. Ah," he purred as Jared made for a chair, "there's a good fellow."

Jared stared at the rough-hewn chair for a moment before sitting down, his bright blue eyes gazing blankly into the middle distance. Kevin's lip curled. "Stap me if that ain't worse. You look like a damn unpretty statue—God of War, most likely. I'd as lief you paced."

Jared shot him a look which would make most men head for the nearest door, then jumped up to resume his pacing. "What the devil are they doing up there? It must be hours since they threw us out."

Kevin pulled out his watch and checked the time. "Oh, yes, indeed, hours and hours. As a matter of fact, dear boy, it has been precisely twenty minutes. You know, it's a jolly good thing I went for the good doctor here, for I think *you* need him. I say, worthy sawbones, do you have something in your little bag for my friend here? He's acting dashed queer."

"You'd be the same if it were your wife up there," Jared shot back at him.

"Doubt that highly, friend, since I don't have the foggiest wish to put my head in a noose if it means ending like you. You ain't no fun anymore, dash it all. And once you have your heir you'll probably be staying at Storm Haven and building up the estate for the squalling brat. Bloody bore if you ask me."

"Nobody did. Shut up, Kevin, would you? Just shut up."

The sound of Jared's measured pacing was the only one in the room for some time—until a cry was heard from above them. "Amanda!" Jared ejaculated, and took off up the stairs before Kevin could stop him.

"*Let me in!* Amanda? Are you all right?" He pounded on the door like a man demented until he heard another cry and realized it must have been the child that he heard. By this time Kevin, Harrow, Tom, Peter, and even Grimsley had joined him, making a small crowd on the narrow landing. It wasn't too many minutes before a broadly-smiling Lady Chezwick opened the door a crack to stick her head out at the waiting men.

"Aggie, how is my wife?" Jared managed to get out.

"The little dear is just fine, Nephew. Slightly fatigued of course, but what a fine—no, better than that, *splendid*—job she did. Simply first-rate. I don't know when I have enjoyed anything more. A real experience it was."

"I am gratified we could all entertain you, Aunt. Now let me pass through to see Amanda." His relief had made him magnanimous, but not that much. He wanted to see Amanda for himself.

Lady Chezwick blocked the door. "Nanny says we are not receiving yet. We must have all nice and pretty, and then only the doctor may come in."

Shortly Nanny could be heard to call for Grimsley, who smiled the smile of the extraordinarily privileged before sliding in through the slight opening Lady Chezwick made for him. Both Jared and Kevin craned their necks for a look inside but Lady Chezwick closed the door heavily in their faces.

"Stubborn old dragon, your aunt," Kevin remarked. "By the way, Jared, what is it?"

Jared ran his hand through his hair. "What is what?"

"The *child*, you nitwit, the child. What is it?"

Jared's face went blank. "I forgot to ask," he said dumbly. "A boy, I suppose."

Kevin shook his head in disgust. "Well if that don't beat everything. You get the gel into all this trouble and then don't even bother to find out if you picked a winner. And they call Bo a slow top. Ha!"

Tom giggled aloud, then howled as Harrow boxed his ears. The three servants withdrew to the landing, where they all congratulated each other—as if personally responsible for the successful conclusion of the night's events—before turning as one man at a sound from the bedchamber.

The door opened slightly again and Lady Chezwick poked her head out to say, "Be quiet out here, you fools! The doctor can barely hear himself think!" She tried to close the door again but Jared stuck his foot in the opening and demanded to be told the sex of his child.

A smile of unholy glee lit Lady Chezwick's tired face. "Which one?" she quipped, and quickly shut the door on Jared's slack-jawed face.

A half-hour and two mugs of mead later the new father was finally allowed in to see his family. He tiptoed into the room rather sheepishly and saw Amanda sitting against a great heap of pillows, dressed now in a pretty yellow nightgown and with a wide lemon-colored ribbon holding her black tresses away from her face. If she had been lovely before she was radiant now, and Jared felt near to bursting with love for her.

Belatedly he noticed each of her arms was cradled around a small white bundle from which slight sounds emitted. Jared swallowed heavily and approached the bed with awe in his eyes. "Mandy?" he whispered.

She smiled warmly up at her husband. "How tired you look, dearest. I am sorry we couldn't be quicker, but with two it takes a bit longer. Do you wish to see your children?"

Jared nodded, not trusting his voice as Amanda uncovered first one and then the other white bundle. Two small heads covered in coal-black fuzz greeted his astonished gaze. He saw two sets of eyes, one set closed and the other open, so he could observe that they were startling blue in color.

He saw two sets of little hands, closed into tight fists and looking no bigger than walnuts. "Aren't they both beautiful?" Amanda demanded.

He looked again at the two beet-red faces that reminded him greatly of the aged Archbishop of Canterbury and tried to show his delight. "Beautiful."

Amanda indicated the child on her left and said, "This one is your son. I think I would like to call him Beau, but we shall spell it like Mr. Brummel does because no one ever calls Bo 'Buford', and I really think Buford a horrid name anyway."

Jared nodded his agreement. So he had a son! It was the first he knew of it. He looked again into the deep blue eyes and decided that, once the redness was gone, the child might just be handsome. "Beau? Yes, I would like that, and Bo will be most flattered. I wonder if George Brummel will demand to be a godfather or give us the cut direct for pirating his coveted title. Beau Delaney, Eighth Lord Storm. Very good."

"And this," Amanda was openly preening now, "this is your daughter."

Jared peered down at the sleeping child, but then jumped back as the almond-shaped eyes suddenly opened. As they did so he saw two slate-grey orbs looking up at him—well, almost up at him—as one eye was aimed straight ahead while the other looked off in quite another direction. "She's cross-eyed!" he exclaimed.

Amanda laughed and explained that all babies did that particular trick. "Watch for a moment and they'll straighten again." They did, and Jared breathed a deep sigh of relief. "Nanny says my eyes were grey when I was born. She thinks Anne will be a lot like me."

"Anne?" Jared felt a warmth spreading deep inside him and his voice was thick as he whispered, "A fitting tribute to two dear and beloved friends, and at last a way to make amends for the terrible fright they suffered in our names. Very good, infant. You have tied up all our loose ends quite nicely." He smiled then and held out his hand to stroke his wife's cheek.

"That will be enough of that, young man," came a voice from the doorway. Lady Chezwick bustled into the room with Nanny fairly nipping at her heels, and they each swooped up a tiny bundle and headed for the padded bench under the dormer.

"I've made up some sugar treats for the little ones, Miss Mandy, until you can help us out yourself. Lady Chezwick here and I have been talking, and we figured out that between the two of us we should be able to handle these two young darlings until we can return to Storm Haven."

Lady Chezwick beamed as she pressed a kiss on Beau's—or was it Anne's?—forehead. "Nanny, I do believe they should have extra blankets. It is a bit chilly in this corner."

"Nonsense, my *dear* Lady Chezwick, it is perfectly fine in

218

here. I have taken care of more babies than you've had hot dinners, and if I may say so . . ."

Amanda and Jared were no longer listening. Jared had taken the opportunity of having his wife at least partially alone, and had gathered her into his arms for a gentle embrace. For several minutes they were in their own secret world, all cares forgotten, exchanging words of love and other silliness that had nothing to do with the unexceptional behavior expected of conventional parents. Tomorrow was time enough to think of such mundane things as transporting his new family back home, or explaining Amanda's rather bizarre choice of a miller's cottage for her lying-in.

As the heat of the battle now going on over the proper method of swaddling a baby drifted to their ears, Jared whispered to his wife, "You are the cleverest of women, imp. If you hadn't the sense to produce *two* Delaney's, we would have needed the wisdom of Solomon to keep peace in the house."

Amanda just smiled sleepily and kissed her husband on the tip of his aristocratic nose. "I believe you may have had some little bit to do with it, my lord, if my memory serves."

"Impudent puss," Jared roared, "will you never learn to hold your tongue?"

"Never," Amanda replied, as she curled up like a contented kitten for a well-deserved nap.

Epilogue

THE SPRING SEASON of 1812 was about to begin officially with the first Wednesday evening gathering of the *haut ton* at Almack's.

Lady Sally Jersey hid a shiver of unladylike glee as she recalled the scandal Lord Storm and his outrageous bride created in this very room only one short year ago. Thank goodness, she admonished herself guiltily, gathering about herself the cloak of respectability for which a Patroness of the Assembly should be known, there is no possibility of a repetition of any such flagrant impropriety tonight!

Still, her more daring second self wickedly reminded her, it certainly would serve to liven things up just a tad. In truth, she was beginning to think the Marchioness of Gurney had silently passed on to her Maker, she had been sitting still as a waxwork for so long; and only the slight undulating movements of the purple three-foot-high ostrich plume stuck in the good woman's turban persuaded the Patroness that the lady still breathed.

There were some absences less lamented by the peeress—the most notable of these being that of the so-encroaching Lady Blanche Wade. That lady had caused a momentary flutter by eloping with a long-time admirer, followed by that duo's precipitant departure for India and the bridegroom's post with the East India Company.

Blanche's new mate—charmed by his bride but more besotted by the thought of the late Lord Wade's fortune (now sadly depleted, as was known to anyone with even a ha'p'orth of brains, which the groom evidently had not)—had refrained from divulging to her that he had just days earlier been disinherited by a family who had several times over been forced to pay off an irate father, and had not two farthings to rub together.

It was a marriage, so said Society, of equally-deserving parties, and not a few persons voiced the desire to be a fly on the wall when the lovebirds got around to discussing their mutual finances. It only served to prove, Lady Jersey pontificated, that there was someone for everyone in this world.

Meanwhile, the perpetrators of Lady Jersey's fondly-remembered *faux-pas*, completely unaware of the auspiciousness or perhaps infamy of this anniversary date, were at that same moment busily engaged in bidding their two tiny offspring a fond good night before turning in early themselves—a practice that was fast becoming a most enjoyable habit.

And so it happened that just as Lord Storm and his Lady were entering the huge master apartments at Storm Haven, to indulge in a comfortable coze—and perhaps one or two other less wordy, but still highly pleasant diversions—Almack's musicians were striking up a lively tune that, if nothing more laudatory could be said concerning it, at least served to startle the napping Marchioness from her near-comatose state.

Lady Jersey seized upon this moment to sweep into one of the side card-rooms to ferret out any malingering bachelors whom she would bully into standing up with one of the plethora of wallflowers that seemed even thicker on the ground this year than last.

Alas for the enterprising Lady Jersey, this badly-timed exit from the main rooms lost her the opportunity of witnessing Kevin Rawlings, newly-named Earl of Lockport, in the act of allowing a footman to relieve him of his high-crowned ebony silk hat, midnight-blue velvet evening cape (lined with sable, of course), pristine white kid dress gloves, and decorative malacca cane.

Stepping to a nearby enormous gilt mirror to assure himself of the perfection of his appearance, the Earl then sauntered lazily to the fringe of the dance floor, a room he had scorned for the past decade. Ignoring the startled gasps and high-pitched whispers that greeted his unexpected presence—and not bothering to hide the expression of pained boredom that marred his otherwise handsome face—he shifted his pale eyes about the room with the air of someone in search of something already out of reach.

Kevin reminded himself yet again that the chances of

discovering another jewel as precious as Amanda in the whole of England, let alone within the so-insipid ranks of the *ton*, were less than heartening. Suppressing a self-pitying sigh, he straightened his satin-encased shoulders and prepared to set his so-recently titled, wealthy, and therefore highly-eligible and sought-after self up as fair game for all the husband-hunting ladies present tonight.

Life had a strange way of forcing a man down paths he had sworn never to trod, and the title of earl brought—along with its varied benefits—the responsibility of setting up his nursery with the minimum of delay.

If only it were possible to find a woman so lovely, so intelligent, so thoroughly unique as Amanda, perhaps the sacrifice of his freedom would not be so sorely felt. Drat Jared and Bo anyway, deserting their friend in his hour of need!

As Lady Jersey, her eyes alight with unconcealed glee, descended upon the near-to-cringing earl with this Season's dough-faced Chatsworth debutante in tow, Kevin wondered wildly if the eventual prize, no matter how suitable, could possibly be worth the struggle.

But, alas, that is another story.